An Emotional Roller Coaster

A Book by Gaurav Bhide

New Delhi • London

BLUEROSE PUBLISHERS
U.K.

Copyright © Gaurav Bhide 2025

All rights reserved by author. No part of this publication may be reproduced, stored in a retrieval system or transmitted in any form or by any means, electronic, mechanical, photocopying, recording or otherwise, without the prior permission of the author. Although every precaution has been taken to verify the accuracy of the information contained herein, the publisher assumes no responsibility for any errors or omissions. No liability is assumed for damages that may result from the use of information contained within.

BlueRose Publishers takes no responsibility for any damages, losses, or liabilities that may arise from the use or misuse of the information, products, or services provided in this publication.

For permissions requests or inquiries regarding this publication, please contact:

BLUEROSE PUBLISHERS
www.BlueRoseONE.com
info@bluerosepublishers.com
+4407342408967

ISBN: 978-93-7018-095-6

Cover design: Daksh
Typesetting: Tanya Raj Upadhyay

First Edition: April 2025

!! Shri Chatushrungi Devi!!

!! Harr Harr Mahadev!!

!! Shri Swami Samarth!!

This book is dedicated to my beloved family—my mother, Amruta Bhide, my sister, Mayuri Bhide Gujar, my brother Shardul Bhide. They resurrected me from the shallows of hell. I am grateful and thankful for my Family. My Ajji, I miss you a lot, your absence leaves a void in my life and heart. I am grateful for the precious moments we shared and created. As I pen these words, I wish you were here to see them, Dad. This book is a piece of my heart, and I wish I could share it with you, Daddy.

AN EMOTIONAL ROLLER COASTER.

This is a work of fiction. Names, characters, places and incidents are either the product of the author's imagination or are used fictitiously, and any resemblance to any actual persons, living or dead, events, and locales is entirely coincidental.

AUTHOR'S INTRODUCTION

Gaurav Bhide is a passionate storyteller, entrepreneur, and creative enthusiast. With over a decade of experience in multinational companies, Gaurav has traversed the corporate world, cultivating valuable insights and life lessons.

However, it's his love for writing that has always been his true north. Gaurav's passion for crafting fictional romantic novels stems from his innate desire to explore the complexities of the human heart.

Beyond writing, Gaurav's interests are as diverse as his personality. An avid sports enthusiast, dancer, and fitness aficionado, he lives for the rush of adrenaline that comes with pushing boundaries. Travel and adventure are his oxygen, fuelling his creativity and inspiring new stories.

The core of Gaurav's being is his love for family. He cherishes the bond he shares with his loved ones, and they remain his greatest source of motivation and strength.

Through his writing, Gaurav hopes to touch hearts, spark imagination, and leave a lasting impact on his readers. " An Emotional Roller Coaster" is his debut novel, and he looks forward to sharing many more stories that celebrate the beauty of love, life, and relationships.

TABLE OF CONTENTS

Chapter 1. "Nava's Nocturne." 1

Chapter 2: "Rajveer: The Unyielding Heart" 6

Chapter 3: "When Cupid Takes Flight" 9

Chapter 4: "Love Knows No Distance" 40

Chapter 5: "Bhuvaneshwar Bound" 47

Chapter 6: Emotional Turmoil 99

Chapter: 7: "Rajveer's Reckoning" 115

Chapter 8: "Fractured Bonds". 124

Chapter 9: A Cage of Silence 136

Chapter 10: The end of agonizing uncertainty. 139

Chapter 11: "The Pursuit of Approval" 144

Chapter 12: A Month of Blossoming Bonds. 154

Chapter 13: The beginning of the end 156

Chapter 14: The last nail in the coffin 163

Chapter 15: Cheers To the new beginnings!! 178

Chapter 16: "Whispers in the Moonlight." 184

Chapter 17: Dolphins, Friends and a boat 195

Chapter 18: Rajveer's conflicted heart and his damaged soul. 213

Chapter 19: The Hidden Cascade 221

Chapter 20: Ripples of the heart. 226

Chapter 21: A Month of Atonement. 239

Chapter 22: "Nehal's leap of Faith" 245

Chapter 23: "Love's New Address" 250

Chapter 24: "Sunkissed Serenity" 295

Chapter 25: "Margarita nights and Villa delights" 301

Chapter 26: "Unravelling the Past" 307

Chapter 27: "Turbulent Emotions" 315

Chapter 28: "Infinite Love" 322

CHAPTER 1.
"NAVA'S NOCTURNE."

The rain hammered against the attic windowpane, mimicking the frantic beat of Navas heart. Each drop a tiny drumbeat, a relentless rhythm that mirrored the pounding of her own anxieties. Below, the wind howled like a banshee, tearing at the ancient oak tree that stood sentinel over the crumbling house in Manali.

Nava shivered, pulling the worn woollen shawl tighter around her shoulders. The attic has been a sanctuary, a refuge from the suffocating expectations of her society. But tonight, even its dusty charm could not shield her from the storm brewing within.

A low growl rumbled through the eaves, followed by a raucous squawk. A raven, its feathers slicked with rain, perched on the windowsill. Its obsidian eyes gleamed with uncanny Intelligence. Nava, usually captivated by the wild creatures that frequented the old house, felt a shiver crawled down her spine. The raven seemed to scrutinize her; its gaze unwavering, almost judgmental.

Suddenly, a flash of lightning illuminated the room, revealing a figure standing in the doorway. A man, tall and imposing, his features obscured by the shadows. He held a lantern, its flickering light casting long, dancing shapes on the wall, shadows that seemed to writhe and twist like tormented souls of forgotten dreams.

Nava's breath caught in her throat. Rajveer. Her heart skipped a beat, and butterflies erupted in her stomach. She was well aware that this might be the last time she would lay her eyes upon him, hear him, feel him, and touch him. The last time she felt goosebumps on her body is when she embraced him in a hug. After four long years together, they were soulmates, loved each other immensely, they never even thought of being apart from each other. They were completely and madly in love but God had other plans for them.

From the shadows appeared Rajveer.

Rajveer Rana was built like a warrior. Broad chest, neatly curved shoulders, huge forearms, good biceps, and well-defined four pack abs. He has a shock of unruly black hair that perpetually defied gravity, and his eyes, the colour of a stormy sea, held a mischievous glint.

Nava was born and raised in Iran until she was ten years old. Her family, including father, mother and her elder sister, moved to Bhubaneshwar, Odisha, India, where her father established a secondary school. The transition for Nava wasn't easy, the new culture, new language, and new everything. She always felt out of place, never truly belonged in this foreign land, until Rajveer. It took her eight years to find him, when she did, it was as if the missing piece of her existence finally snapped into place. He became her home.

And now, she was about to lose him.

(I have edited the chapter upto now. The details about the character doesn't resonate with the rest of the book and it might be too much of information for the readers. I ended the chapter with mystery which will enhance the curiosity.)

A girl with bright, sparkling eyes that seemed to hold a perpetual twinkle.

Her hair, a vibrant shade of auburn, often falling into playful waves around her face.

She has a small, upturned nose and a smile that could melt glaciers.

Her clothes reflected her cheerful personality—bright colours, floral patterns, and a touch of whimsy.

Nava was the epitome of kindness. She has a gentle spirit and a

genuine concern for others' feelings. She always offered a helping hand, a listening ear, and a comforting hug.

Even when faced with challenges, Nava maintains a positive outlook. She believes in the goodness of people and the power of hope.

She has an insatiable curiosity about the world. She loved exploring new places, trying new things, and learning about different cultures.

She has a vivid imagination and a knack for finding beauty in everyday things. Painting and nature were her escape.

Nava is a bit of a klutz, often tripping over her own feet or bumping into things. Her clumsiness, however, only adds to her charm.

Nava talks to her plants, believing they

understood her.

She collects quirky souvenirs from her travels and secretly collects brightly coloured socks.

She could never resist a good pun.

Nava sometimes gets so caught up in helping others that she neglects her own needs.

She can be overly sensitive to criticism, overthinking smallest things, and carrying unnecessary worries.

Nava dreams of traveling the world and becoming a physiologist.

Nava has a close-knit family who adores her. Though she was born and raised in Iran, when Nava was ten, her father had to move to India. Her father had opened a secondary school, in Bhubaneshwar, Odisha. She stayed with her parents and her younger sister Tabassum. Born and raised in a happy-go-lucky foodie family, they use to have lots of fun. Education was of upmost importance to her parents, as they always told her: Money comes and goes, but if you are well-educated, then you can come back from any phase of life in flying colours.

She carried their words with her.

CHAPTER 2:
"RAJVEER: THE UNYIELDING HEART"

A prominent tattoo of Nava's name adorned his left bicep. He had got that tattoo on their second anniversary. He stands tall, beaming with confidence.

He faces his fears head-on, even when it's terrifying.

He shows kindness to underdog, even when it's unpopular.

He finds unique solutions to problems and sees the world in a different light.

He doesn't give up easily and pursues his goals with unwavering focus.

He struggles with patience and often acts before thinking.

He can be quick to anger and struggles to control his emotions.

He prefers solitude and finds social situations draining. He's still struggling to find his place in the world and figure out who he truly is.

Rajveer Rana had never been one for large friends circle. Instead, he has his bro gang— close-knit brothers who would do anything for each other, and go to any such lengths. He values their years of friendship and loyalty, because of his raw, true nature he doesn't have many friends.

He does not give or take any bullshit, a no-nonsense, straight forward guy, and does not talk behind anyone's back. If he likes you or not, he will convey it to your face. Rajveer has a clean and a soft heart and has an amazing sense of humour. He is just 23 years old.

Rajveer loves Cricket like a billion others in India, but for Rajveer, he loves watching, and playing cricket. He does not miss any matches. When he played, he played to win. Deafeat was never an option. Apart from cricket, he likes playing chess, and he is very good at it, a skilled passed down by his father. He has many moves and plans up his sleeve, he modifies his approach to suit his opponent and most of the time he ends up in the winning side.

The Rana Family.

The Rana family is an upper-middle-class family residing in a posh neighbourhood in the Pune city.

Shubhangi Rana, the matriarch of the family is a beautiful and elegant woman in her late forties. A devoted mother. With her warm smile, gentle demeanour, and caring nature, Shubhangi is the glue that holds the family together.

Anya Rana, the younger sister of Rajveer is a bright and vivacious teenager. She is a finance student. With her bubbly personality, infectious laughter, Anya brings joy and enthusiasm to the family.

Reyansh Rana, the youngest member of the family, is a mischievous and playful young boy. He is a bundle of energy, with his curious nature, adventurous spirit, and loving heart, Reyansh is the darling of the family.

Together, the Rana family is a loving and supportive unit that values tradition, education, and personal growth. They believe in living life to the fullest and making the most of every moment.

Three years back

CHAPTER 3:
"WHEN CUPID TAKES FLIGHT"

A night in Pune, HardRock Cafe, 31st December 2009

The night was electric. The café was alive with music, laughter filled through the air, and the aroma of food and drinks weaved through the crowd. On the new year's eve , Rajveer and Parag were having the best times of their lives, dancing, partying, and drinking honey-blended Tennessee whiskey on the rocks. This was their third round, they were totally in the vibe, moments later, the beats of YMCA started playing. Hard Rock cafe staff started performing on the BAR with their skates on, moments later, a fire show ignited the bar. The atmosphere was ecstatic, the crowd was totally in the vibe, and at the stroke of midnight everyone wished happy new year to their loved ones. There was a fireworks show ignited exactly at 12 am, the lights which came out vibrated the place in bright colours. Rajveer thought that he was at the right place at the right moment to enjoy this serenity. Rajveer and Parag ordered tequila shots, and gulped them down within seconds. They were quite high by then, then they both decided to go out for some air and nicotine. As they were seated on the smoking zone of the pub, they saw people sitting on their respective tables.

The pub buzzed with low hum of conversation and clinking of glasses. Smoke curled lazily to the ceiling, mingling with the dim light filtering through the stained-glass windows.

Rajveer was nursing a glass of whiskey, lost in his thought, his eyes suddenly locked onto a vision of loveliness. She walked into the café with the confidence of a supermodel, her long, raven-black hair cascading down her back like a waterfall of night. Her full, rosy lips curved into a gentle smile as she scanned the room. But it was her kindness that truly caught Rajveer's attention. As she made her way through the crowd, she noticed a women struggling to pick up a few items that had fallen from her purse. Without hesitation, the beautiful girl rushes over to help, kneeling beside her with a warm smile.

As Rajveer watched, feeling mesmerized, the girl gently gathered the scattered items and handed them back to the grateful women. Her eyes crinkled at the corners as she smiled, and Rajveer felt his heart skip a beat. There was something that made him feel like he was drowning in the depths of her eyes.

As the girl stood up and continued her way, Rajveer could not help but follow her with his gaze. He was captivated by her beauty, her kindness, and her radiant energy. Who was this mysterious girl, and what was she doing here, on New Year's Eve, in this crowded place? Rajveer was determined to find out.

Rajveer and Parag went back to the bar, She made her way towards the bartender, her every move a captivating performance. He watched as she ordered a drink, her voice a soft husk that sent shivers down his spine.

He knew, with a certainty that this was the beginning of something.

After a long silence between friends,

Rajveer notices the mystery girl from across the room. He is immediately drawn to her smile and the way she interacts with her friends.

Parag overhears the mystery girl's laughter and is instantly intrigued. He finds himself drawn to her infectious personality.

Rajveer and Parag looked at each other, they didn't say anything as on how the other person was feeling. They noticed that she was with her group of friends—all stunning, they didn't look like they were from India. There was a special magnetic pull towards them, Rajveer and Parag decided to challenge them for a game of pool. The challenge was gleefully accepted by the mystery girls' group. First, they introduced themself to each other. The mystery girl, Nava, introduced her friends Nisha and Anahita.

Rajveer, while playing pool, accidentally knocked over a drink near the pool table. He profusely apologizes, and Nava, with a warm laugh, assures him it is of no issue. The friends, through their initial interactions, find themselves drawn back to Nava's group for further conversation.

Unconsciously, both Rajveer and Parag tried to engage with Nava more, perhaps by making her laugh or offering to buy her a drink. As the night progressed, both friends start to realize they're developing deeper feelings for Nava. The pool game ended with narrow victory for the boys. They cheered and headed back to the bar to order some food for the group. Seated around the table, the group indulged in foods. The pizzas, fries and nachos were yummy after a night of dancing, playing, and partying. They all were hungry, it was refreshing. Then after the dinner, Rajveer in front of the group asked Nava for her number, there was an awkward silence; after blushing for some time, Nava gave her number to Rajveer. Parag was shocked and stared at Rajveer, but Nisha and Anahita were giggling most of the times, clearly enjoying Nava's discomfort. Rajveer felt happy of how things turned out for him tonight, then the group called it a night.

Rajveer and Parag were driving back from the party, late at night. The atmosphere was a mix of exhaustion and lingering excitement.

Rajveer: (Yawned) Man, that party was a blast!

Parag: (Smiled) Yeah, it was. Though, I think I'm officially old. All that loud music felt like torture.

Rajveer: (Chuckled) You're getting soft, Parag. But seriously, did you see Nava? She looked incredible tonight.

Parag: (His smile faltered slightly) Yeah, she was.

Rajveer: I finally got her number. We had a great chat. She's really cool.

Parag: (Forced a laugh) That's awesome, man. Good for you.

Rajveer: (noticed the swift) You seem a bit... off. Everything alright?

Parag: Yeah, fine. Just tired.

Rajveer: You sure? You seemed really interested in her earlier.

Parag: (Stammered) Oh, uh, yeah. I was just... curious. You know, getting to know people at the party.

Rajveer: (Narrowed his eyes) Come on, Parag. Don't beat around the bush. You were checking her out.

Parag: (Sighed) Alright, fine. I was. But it's no big deal. I wasn't going to do anything about it.

Rajveer: (Slightly confused) Why not? She seems like a nice girl.

Parag: (Looked out the window) It's complicated. Besides, you got her number.

Rajveer: (Placed a hand on Parag's shoulder) Hey, look, I didn't know you were serious. I'm really sorry, man. I didn't mean to step on your toes.

Parag: (Smiled weakly) It's cool. No worries.

Rajveer: You sure?

Parag: Yeah, I am. Let's just enjoy the ride.

Rajveer: (Smiled) Alright, my friend.

(Silence settled between them for a while. Rajveer glanced at Parag, who is staring intently at the road. He knows his friend is still a bit down but decides to let him process things in his own pace.)

Rajveer: (Changed the subject) So, what are your plans for the weekend?

Parag: (A small smile returned to his face) I don't know yet. Maybe we could grab some coffee tomorrow?

Rajveer: Sounds good.

(The conversation continued on a lighter note, but the unspoken tension still lingers in the air. Parag tried to put on a brave face, but Rajveer knows his friend is still a little hurt. He resolves to be more mindful of Parag's feelings in the future.)

The next morning, Rajveer got up feeling excited and happy. Today, I will call Nava. Just the thought of hearing her melodious voice sent a soothing sensation to his ears. Then he remembered, Parag was not completely OK with it. He quickly called Parag, they had a meaningfull conversation, in the end, Parag gave Rajveer his blessings to pursue Nava and was happy for him.

With a clear conscience, Rajveer called Nava next.

Rajveer: (Nervously) Hey Nava, it's Rajveer.

Nava: (Surprised and a little flustered) Oh! HI, Rajveer!

Rajveer: Hi. I, uh, I was just thinking about you and... well, I wanted to see how you were doing.

Nava: I'm good, thanks. How are you?

Rajveer: I'm... I'm good too.

(Short pause)

Rajveer: So, uh, did you enjoy yesterday's party? And Happy New Year, by the way.

Nava: (laughed softly) Happy New Year. I just loved yesterday's party it was awesome, the Hard Rock Cafe, the vibe, and the energy everything was just surreal.

Rajveer: Same. It was just the place you liked or the company?

(Another pause)

Nava: (Smiled) You sound a little nervous.

Rajveer: (Laughed nervously) Yeah, maybe a little. It's not every day I call someone out of the blue.

Nava: Well, I appreciate it. Obviously, I liked you and your friend, do you think I randomly give my phone number to strangers? (giggled) It was nice to hear from you.

Rajveer: Yeah, me too. Maybe we could... maybe we could grab coffee sometime?

Nava: (Smiled) I'd like that.

Rajveer: Great! How about... how about tomorrow?

Nava: Tomorrow works for me.

Rajveer: Okay, cool. I'll text you the details.

Nava: Sounds good.

Rajveer: Okay, bye Nava.

Nava: Bye Rajveer.

(They both hung up, smiling)

On second of January, 2010, they met in the cafe, named "Cozy Cuppa". It was a hidden gem nestled in the heart of the city. Its exterior was unassuming, with a simple wooden sign bearing its name. But the moment they stepped inside, they got enveloped in a warm and inviting atmosphere. The walls were painted in a soothing shade of golden brown, and the floors were made of dark hardwood, polished to a soft sheen. The air was thick with freshly brewed coffee aroma, and the soft hum of indie music played in the background, adding to the cozy ambiance.

Rajveer arrived first, dressed in a crisp white shirt and dark jeans, looked every bit of handsome and charming young man he was. Nava, on the other hand, looked stunning in a bright yellow sundress, her long black hair cascading down her back like a waterfall.

As they spotted each other, their eyes locked, and they exchanged shy smiles. Rajveer, ever the gentleman, quickly got up from his seat and walked over to Nava, holding out his hand in greeting. Nava, feeling a little flutter in her chest, took his hand, and they exchanged a warm handshake.

"Hi," Rajveer said, his deep voice sending a shiver down Nava's spine. "You look beautiful."

Nava blushed, feeling a little self-conscious, but also thrilled by the compliment. "Thanks," she replied, her voice barely above a whisper. "You don't look so bad yourself."

Rajveer chuckled, his eyes crinkling at the corners, and Nava's heart skipped a beat. She was already smitten, and they had only just met!

As they sat down at a cozy little table by the window, Rajveer and Nava both felt a sense of nervous excitement. They had spent time together at the New Year's Eve party with friends around. This was the first time they were meeting alone and they both were eager to see if their chemistry would translate to real life.

As they sipped their coffee and chatted, they both could not help but steal glances at each other. Rajveer was mesmerized by Nava's bright smile and sparkling eyes, while Nava was captivated by Rajveer's chiselled features and charming personality.

Their conversation flowed easily, as if they had known each other for years. Rajveer was impressed by Nava's intelligence and wit, while Nava was charmed by Rajveer's sense of humour and kindness.

As the afternoon wore on, they both eased into the conversation.

Nava: (Smiled warmly) Rajveer! You made it. I was starting to worry you haven't recovered from hangover.

Rajveer: (Chuckled) Wouldn't dream of missing our... coffee date. Though, after that whirlwind of a night at

Hard Rock, I think I'm still recovering. You know, the noise, the crowd... and you.

Nava: (Blushed slightly) Oh, you mean the... energy? It was... electric, wasn't it?

Rajveer: (Eyes twinkled) Electric is an understatement. I haven't felt that spark since... well, I don't even remember.

Nava: (Took a sip of her latte) Me neither. It was... unexpected. But definitely not unwelcome.

Rajveer: (Leaned forward slightly) So, tell me, Nava. What makes you tick? What are you passionate about besides making my heart race?

Nava: (Smiled) Well, I'm a bit of a nerd. I'm Studying Physiology. And I am learning Bharatanatyam.

Rajveer: (Intrigued) Bharatanatyam? Wow!! So that's the secret behind your beauty and fitness.

Nava: (Eyes sparkling and blushing) Well!! I give my best. I love dancing.

Rajveer: (Impressed) That's amazing! I would love to see you perform one day. You must be incredible on stage.

(Nava blushes, looking down at her hands.)

Nava: (Nervously) Th-thank you, Rajveer. That means a lot coming from you.

Rajveer: (Teasingly) I'm serious! I can already imagine you in a beautiful saree, dancing to the rhythm of the music. You must be a vision to behold."

(Nava's blush deepened, and she looked up at Rajveer with shining eyes)

Nava: (Laughed nervously) You're making me nervous, Rajveer. But I'll take that as a compliment.

Rajveer: (Smiled) It's a genuine compliment, Nava. I'm really looking forward to seeing you dance someday.

(Nava smiled back at Rajveer, feeling a spark of attraction between them)

Rajveer: So, what did you think of HardRock Café?

Nava: (Laughed) Honestly? A bit too loud for my taste. But you know, it wouldn't have been the same without you there.

Rajveer: (Smiled softly) You think so?

Nava: (Nodded) I do. You... you brought life to the music.

Rajveer: (Reached across the table, his fingers brushing hers) I think you might have done the same for me, Nava.

Nava: (Breath caught) I... I think you might be right.

Rajveer: (Suddenly serious) You remember my friend Parag from Hard Rock Cafe? He had taken a shine towards you, I wasn't aware at the time, when I asked for your number.

Nava: Ooh, I wasn't aware. (giggled) Is everything okay between you two?

Rajveer: Absolutely, I have his blessings, no confusion there.

Rajveer and Nava both knew they had found something special. Their connection ran deep, and their chemistry was undeniable. A long silence stretched between them, both were gazing into each other's eyes, the outside world didn't matter to them. They were lost in each other, admiring, where words felt unnecessary. They both knew in their hearts that they were attracted, it was just a matter of time who approaches first.

Rajveer knew in his heart that it was just a formality. Then, Nava broke the silence.

Nava : (After clearing her throat) Raj, I wanted to tell you something. Actually I don't live in Pune, I am here on a vacation. I stay in Bhubaneshwar with my family, here I am staying with my cousins. I will be leaving Pune in three days.

Rajveer: (Blood drained from his face and his heart pounding with anxiety. He just have three days with Nava before she goes to her city?)

I wasn't aware of that. Wow, that's some news. I never asked you about your whereabouts, we were just caught up in our world. Can we meet again before you go back? Maybe we can go for a ride outside Pune?

Nava: Sure, I was going to ask you the same thing, I am glad it happened on its own. Tomorrow, I have some plans with my cousins, but the day after, we can spend the day together.

Rajveer: (Gleefully smiled) Perfect! I will show you around Pune and few places in the outskirts. We will travel, have some good food, and then after dinner, I can drop you home.

Nava: Sounds great! I have to go now. My cousin might be worndering where I am.

They stood up and moved across the table to hug each other. They lost track of time, and the place there were in. When they pulled away, they kissed each other's cheeks, the actual magnetic pull was to kiss on the lips, somehow they managed to avoid it. Rajveer offered to drop her home, but Nava shook her head. Rajveer stopped an auto for her, bargained the price where Nava wanted to go, and watched as Nava rode away.

Rajveer went back to his place, was resting on his sofa, thinking about all the wonderful things happened to him in the last two days, how lucky he was. Then his heart sank, thinking this relationship will end up in a long-distance, assuming Nava accepts his love tomorrow, which in his heart, he was sure.

He called Parag and gave him the updates, Parag was happy for him, and wished him luck. Then Rajveer called his boss and requested leave for the day after tomorrow, which his boss hesitantly granted.

Next day, Rajveer was physically present in the office, his heart was somewhere else. His thoughts kept wandering back to Nava— her smile, the way her eyes lit up when she spoke. The feeling was overwhelming. He had fallen for her. Whenever he got free time, he texted Nava, smiling whenever she replied. But he tried hard to focus on his work, setting his phone aside. At the end of the day, he was happy as their time to meet was nearing. He went to gym, worked on biceps and chest a few more sets, because of the adrenaline rush, he ran on the treadmill. After gym, he called Nava. They spoke for two minutes or so before hanging up. He had this whole itinerary planned for tomorrow. At home, he wanted to tell his mother about Nava. But then he thought, "Let me propose first. If she says yes, I will have ample of time to tell my mother.

Rajveer could hardly sleep, somehow he managed five hours. He got up in the morning, dressing with care, he wore his best clothes— blue jeans, black t-shirt and a trendy bike jacket. He took his bike and left to pick up

Nava, who was running a little late. Reaching on time, he called her. Nava said she will be down in a jiffy.

Nava came after 20 minutes, they smiled at each other. Then he gave Nava a helmet to wear, which was she hesitant to, she said she trusted Rajveer to keep her safe. Rajveer said, "Obviously I will do whatever it takes to keep you safe dear, but roads, traffic, people are unpredictable, accidents happen all the time. It's safe to wear a helmet because once you are on the road everything is not really under riders control." Nava said, "It took half an hour for her to set my hair at home, helmet will ruin it." Rajveer laughed and said, "At least, your make up will be intact dear it is for your own safety." Nava wore the helmet, and they took off on his Duke 390 which is meant for power, speed, and longer rides.

After an hour's ride with traffic, they reached Pune Okayama Friendship Garden.

Tucked away from the bustling city, lies a surreal place in Pune that looks refreshingly green everywhere around as far as you can see! Spread across 10 acres of land, this garden is inspired by a 300-year-old Japanese Korean garden developed by Ikeda Royal family in Okayama, Japan.

This is the biggest Japanese garden in the world outside Japan and had been featured in many Bollywood movies. The garden has become a key attraction in Pune, and is also referred as Pu. La Deshpande Garden, in fond memory of Pu. la Deshpande a renowned Marathi writer.

The verdant lawns and the soothing ambience revitalize one's senses and kindles their spiritual call. One can experience unexplained happiness and contentment just as they step into the garden.

The attractions within the garden include a waterfall, a pond, lanterns, artificial hillocks, and a forest. The landscape of the garden is so diverse, as one walks through the serene pathways listening to the rumbling sound of the stream and the chirping of the birds, one can witness the change in the garden landscape. The type of plants ranges from Plums, Pines, and willows to Japanese camellias, specifically Tsubaki and Sazanka.

As they strolled through the garden, hand in hand, absorbed the " vatavaran" of the beautiful garden. Rajveer felt nervous and anxious inside. The plan was simple—he would propose today. Just yesterday, he felt pretty confident, certain she would say yes. When the time came, his throat went dry, and all of a sudden he was short of words. He let go of her hand as soon as he started sweating. He started overthinking— what if she doesn't fel the same way? If he didn't confess now, he might never get a chance.

Nava felt that Rajveer was restless, not mentally present. She had a feeling or hoped of what was coming next, she broke the silence,

Nava: You look handsome today, Raj. The glow on your face— is it from working out or something else new?

(Rajveer was taken by surprise as her words pulled him back from the daze. He blushed)

Rajveer: Thank you. Am I really glowing outside? He didn't dare speak about the turmoil he was experiencing inside.

Nava: Yes, Raj. Looks like you don't want to share the secret behind your glowing face, I guess.

Rajveer: There is no secret dear. It's just an after effect of a beautiful girl standing and walking besides me, the happiness from within is just reflecting outside.

Nava: Aww!! Now you are just being modest. Thank you for the compliment.

Rajveer: (After gathering some courage he needed)

Nava, from the moment I saw you until now, I have been experiencing feelings which I never have before. You are the most beautiful girl I have laid my eyes ever upon, yet you are so humble, soft, grounded. So well-mannered and not one shred of arrogance, tell me, girls like you really do exist in the real world? Or am I just dreaming the whole time?

Nava: (Blushed from ear to ear, from the corner of her eye, she noticed Rajveer was not looking at her. Which meant she doesn't need to keep her happiness inside. She smiled widely) Wow! That's an interesting way to compliment a person, But thank you, the secret is I have been bought up like this by my parents. And I guess the beauty which you are talking about is hereditary, because honestly I hog like anything, I am a big-time foodie, not particularily health-conscious. But as you know, beauty lies in the eyes of the beholder.

Rajveer: (Smitten and impressed by her)

There are so much things I can learn from you; I was wondering if you could be my girlfriend?

Nava: I am a girl, you just need a friend. I am confused here, Rajveer.(teased him)

Rajveer: (Chuckled) After a long pause, he removes a beautiful bunch of red roses from his sack. Standing close to Nava, long enough to gaze into her eyes, he said the words he had been dying to say—I LOVE YOU, I love being with you, love talking to you. Whenever you are around, there is this energy. A kind of bliss I never experienced before.

Nava: (Blushed, her cheeks turning red. Her hands slightly trembled as she looked into his eyes.)

I love you too, Rajveer. I feel the same about you. She hugged him before tears could escape her eyes. They held each other tightly, experiencing the ecstasy as their hearts had just become one. They could feel each other's heartbeats, sinking in each other's arms, without much effort. Naturally they faced each other and started kissing passionately, unaware of their surroundings. As Rajveer felt her soft, sensitive lips, he pulled her closer, his strong hands tighly wrapped around her waist. In that moment, Nava felt secure, complete, madly in love with him.

The moment he had been dreaming of for so long had finally arrived, and it was even more perfect than he had imagined. As Nava's lips curled into a radiant smile, Rajveer's entire being was flooded with joy, relief, and elation. He felt like he was walking on air, his feet barely touching the ground.

She felt like she was floating in a dream, with Rajveer's loving arms wrapped around her, holding her close. The word "yes" had barely escaped her lips before Rajveer swept her into a passionate kiss, sealing their love forever. As they stood there, lost in each other's eyes, Nava felt a deep sense of belonging, knowing that she had found her soulmate in Rajveer.

As they hugged, the world around them melted away, leaving only the two of them, suspended in a bubble of pure bliss. Rajveer's heart beat in perfect harmony with Nava's, their love pulsing through every cell of their bodies. In this moment, they knew that their love would last a lifetime, and that they would cherish every moment they spend together.

Time stood still as they basked in the glow of their engagement, their love shining brighter than any star in the sky. Rajveer and Nava were lost in their own little world, where nothing else mattered except the love they shared.

After the magical moment, Rajveer took Nava for lunch at a restaurant near by the lake. The restaurant, named "Lakeview Bliss," was nestled among the tall trees and lush greenery that surrounded the serene lake. The exterior of the restaurant was designed to blend seamlessly into the natural surroundings, with wooden accents and large windows that offered breathtaking views of the lake.

As they stepped inside, they were greeted by the warm and inviting atmosphere of the restaurant. The interior was tastefully decorated with a mix of modern and rustic elements, featuring comfortable seating areas, wooden tables, and cozy fireplaces. The aroma of delicious food wafted through the air, teasing their taste buds and building anticipation.

The real magic of the restaurant was its expansive outdoor seating area, which offered stunning views of the lake. The patio was adorned with comfortable couches, colourful throw pillows, and stylish lanterns that added a touch of warmth and magic to the ambiance. On a clear day, you could see the sunlight dancing across the ripples of the lake, creating a mesmerizing display of light and water.

Nava: (Smiled softly, eyes sparkling) I... I can't believe this is actually happening.

Rajveer: (Took her hand, his voice husky) Me neither. I've been waiting for this moment for what feels like forever.

Nava: (Leaned closer) You know, I've been waiting too.

Rajveer: (His gaze intense) I've never felt this way about anyone before. You're... you're incredible, Nava.

Nava: (Blushed) You're not so bad yourself, Rajveer.

Rajveer: (Chuckled) Bad? I think I'm the luckiest guy in the world.

Nava: (Smiled) I think I might be luckier.

Rajveer: (Leaned in to kiss her) Don't think about it. Just feel it.

(They share d long, tender kiss. The soft music and the gentle lapping of the water against the shore surrounded around them, adding to the romantic atmosphere.)

Nava: (Pulled back, breathless) Wow.

Rajveer: (Smiled) Wow is right.

Nava: (Looked into his eyes) I can't wait to see where this goes.

Rajveer: (Took her hand again) Me neither. Let's make some incredible memories together.

As their food arrived, Rajveer took a bite.

Rajveer: (Smiled, his eyes still sparkling from their earlier kiss) Nava, this paneer butter masala is... amazing. But not as amazing as... well, you.

Nava: (Blushed, twirling a strand of hair around her finger) Rajveer, you're going to make me spill my cold drink. But yes, It's good, though, isn't it? I always crave it after... after a big moment.

Rajveer: (Chuckled softly) A big moment? Is that what we're calling it now? My heart nearly jumped out of my chest.

Nava: (Looked down at her plate, a small smile playing on her lips) Me too, Rajveer. It felt... right. Like coming home. Even the butter roti seems happier today.

Rajveer: (Reached across the table and gently took her hand) Speaking of happy, I've never been happier. This view, this food, and... you. It's perfect.

Nava: (Squeezed his hand back) It is perfect. I never thought... I never thought I'd find someone like you. Someone who... who sees me, you know?

Rajveer: (lifted his glass) I see you, Nava. Every part of you. And I... I'm falling for you, more and more every second.

Nava: (Eyes met his, a soft glow in them) Rajveer... I think... I think I'm falling too. Hard. This paneer butter masala is going to have some serious competition for my favourite thing now.

Rajveer: (Laughed, a genuine, joyful sound) Oh, it's on! We'll have to have a paneer butter masala taste-off every week. Loser buys dessert.

Nava: (Giggled) Deal. But you're going down. My mom makes the best paneer butter masala.

Rajveer: (Winked) We'll see about that. But even if your mom's is better, I'll still be the luckiest guy in the world, because I'll be eating it with you.

Nava: (Leaned slightly closer) You always know what to say, Rajveer.

Rajveer: (Whispered) Only when I'm with you, Nava. You bring out the best in me. And the hungriest. (He gestured towards the nearly empty dishes) Shall we order dessert?

Nava: (Laughed) Only if you promise to share.

Rajveer: (Grinned) Sharing is my specialty. Especially when it comes to you.

Rajveer (While savouring Choco lava cake with Vanilla ice cream)

(Casually)Baby, I want to take you to Taljai post dessert, Are you up for it?

Nava: I have never heard of such a place. What is it actually?

Rajveer: It is located in the heart of Pune. A nature trail surrounded by trees all around, and beautiful flowers, it is peaceful there. We both can walk hand-in-hand for hours, trust me you will enjoy it. If we are lucky, we may be up for a surprise there!

Nava: I trust you with my heart, the place sounds tempting, how much do we have to walk? What is the surprise, Raj?

Rajveer: (Laughed) As much as you want, my classical dancer. You shall see when we get there.

Nava:(Finished the dessert) Sounds exciting, lets go.

Taljai Hills, located in the heart of Pune, is a lush green oasis that offers a serene escape from the hustle and bustle of city life. This scenic hill is a popular spot for nature lovers, fitness enthusiasts, and those seeking a peaceful retreat.

As they ascended the hill, they were greeted by a tapestry of lush green forests, dotted with tall trees, shrubs, and an array of vibrant wildflowers. The air was crisp and clean, filled with the sweet scent of blooming flowers and the songs of birds.

The hill offers several walking trails, ranging from easy to challenging, that cater to different fitness levels. As you walk, you can enjoy breathtaking views of the surrounding landscape, including the sparkling waters of the nearby Katraj Lake.

Taljai Hills is also home to a stunning array of flora and fauna. The hill is a haven for birdwatchers, with over 100 species of birds documented in the area. You might even catch a glimpse of the majestic Indian peafowl, the national bird of India.

As the sun begins to set, Taljai Hills transforms into a magical realm, with the sky painted in hues of pink, orange, and purple. It's the perfect spot to watch the sunset, and enjoy a picnic with loved ones, or simply sit in silence soaking in the natural beauty of the surroundings.

Rajveer and Nava walked hand in hand on Taljai hills. Smiling, giggling, feeling like they are the happiest people on earth right now. After walking for a few kilometres, on their left, Rajveer spots a beautiful peacock and pointed it to Nava.

Nava held her breath, her eyes wide with wonder. Before her, the magnificent creature preened, slowly swaying from side to side. The vibrant green and turquoise feathers shimmered like jewels. Then, as if by magic, he began to unfurl.

One by one, the iridescent plumes unfurled, a breathtaking explosion of colour. Emerald greens, sapphire blues, and ruby reds danced before Nava's eyes, creating a mesmerizing kaleidoscope. The peacock seemed to sway in a silent, majestic dance, and his long, elegant neck arching gracefully.

Nava felt a shiver of awe course through her. The air around them seemed to thrum with a vibrant energy, a symphony of colour and motion. It was as if the peacock had captured the essence of the rainbow and woven it into his magnificent display.

Lost in the spectacle, Nava forgot to breathe. The world around her faded away, replaced by the mesmerizing dance of the peacock. It was a moment of pure enchantment; a memory she knew she would cherish forever.

Nava: (Catching her breath) Raj, was this the surprise you mentioned in the restaurant? I have seen peacocks before, but not like this, in action, how did you know the peacock was going to open its feathers?

Rajveer: Yes, Baby. Honestly, I had no idea, it was a stroke of good luck, looks like the nature wants us to have a great time, and is helping me to impress you more.

Nava: I'm impressed; how much more do we have to walk?

Rajveer: (Laughed) After having a filling lunch, I thought a few kilometres walk would be helpful for us. We can turn back whenever you want, just say the word.

Nava: Yes please, if you don't mind. There is hardly any network here, if my sister calls, my phone would be out of coverage that will make her worry.

Rajveer: Okay, let's start walking towards the exit. I have booked a table at a romantic restaurant, I know you like hukkah, how about we head there?

Nava: I really wish, Raj. But it's already evening, I don't know if my sister has called me or not. Let's go outside first. I'll check with her and let you know.

Rajveer: Okay cool.

Once they near the exit of Taljai hills, Nava immediately received a call from her mother, she steps aside to receive it. Rajveer waits for her, keeping some distance between them, thinking she is just 18, she must have a lot of restrictions and her sister's responsibility here. I don't think dinner is a good idea after all.

Nava: Raj, I need you to drop me home as soon as possible. My sister was calling me while we were inside the hills, but since she couldn't get through, she got worried and called my mom. She just gave me an earful.

Rajveer: (Felt guilty for bringing her here) Sure, dear. Please calm down. Let's head towards your place straight away, I don't want you to be in any kind of trouble because of me.

Nava: I convinced my mother that I am far but safe. I told her it would take a couple of hours to reach, so let's sit and talk somewhere else for an hour or so, then you can drop me back.

Rajveer: Sure, I know a place nearby, let's go.

Rajveer and Nava settled into the booth at Cafe Coffee Day. Nava ordered a latte and Rajveer goes for the devil's own, cold coffee with ice-cream.

Cafe Coffee Day, corner booth. Rajveer sips his coffee; Nava stirs her latte.

Rajveer: (Smiled) So, last hour Huh! Feels surreal.

Nava: Yeah, it does. Time flies when you're having fun, they say.

Rajveer: (Teasingly) You're trying to make me feel guilty?

Nava: (Chuckled) Maybe a little. But seriously, these past few days have been amazing.

Rajveer: (Reached across the table to hold her hand) I know, right? I'm going to miss you terribly.

Nava: (Squeezed his hand) Me too. But hey, technology exists. We can video call, message, and...

Rajveer: (Interrupted) And visit each other. You'll come back to Pune, right?

Nava: (Smiled) Of course, I will. I have to see you again. And show you Bhubaneswar.

Rajveer: Deal. I'll come visit you. But you have to come back soon.

Nava: (Sipped her latte) Promise. Now, tell me, what are you going to miss most about me?

Rajveer: (Pretends to think) Your laugh. It's contagious. And your presence. The aura we share, it's pure and magical.

Nava: (Blushed) Oh, come on.

Rajveer: It's true!

Rajveer: What is your routine like? Once you reach home.

Nava: Well, in the morning, I go to my college. Once I get back, I help my mother in the kitchen and then I go to my father's school to help him out. In the evening, we have our prayers, then dinner.

Rajveer: Can I call you in the evening every day?

Nava: Text me first, then we can coordinate, Please don't get me wrong, but I am young, can't tell my parents about us yet. Whenever it is possible for both of us, we will talk. We can definitely video call on Sundays.

Rajveer: Sounds good.

(A comfortable silence falls between them. They hold hands, enjoying the last few precious moments.)

Nava: (Looked at her watch) Oh dear, look at the time! We should probably head

home soon.

Rajveer: (Stood up) Let me drop you.

Nava: (Smiled) You don't have to.

Rajveer: I want to. Besides, I need to make sure you get home safely.

Nava: (Leaned in to kiss him) You're the best.

Rajveer: (Smiled) You're the best. Now come on, let's go.

(They leave the cafe, hand in hand, ready to Savor the last few moments together before Nava's departure.)

CHAPTER 4:
"LOVE KNOWS NO DISTANCE"

The next day, Nava messages Rajveer, letting him know that she has boarded the train back home. The journey will take 48 hours for her to reach. Rajveer sinks in the emotions of her absence, the uncertainty of him seeing her again bothers him. But what can he possibly do? Long distance relationships come with their own set of challenges.

Once Nava reached Bhuvaneswar, she texted Rajveer. A wave of relief washed over him, as she reached home safely. They continued chatting over WhatsApp perpetually, and after a couple of days Rajveer realises the actual void inside him. In practical life, he is lonely without her, he has to rely on his phone for any kind of communication with Nava, it was difficult for him to adjust, but as the time went by, he got used to it. They got back to their routines, Rajveer still felt alone after work and gym. So, he decided that he will join boxing classes during the weekends and twice during weekdays. He works for a multinational company, so after a week or so he applies for a leave three months in advance. He was glad to the fact that his nine-day leave was approved. At least now, he has something to look forward to. Later that week on a video call, he informs Nava about the dates. She is thrilled by news as in the month of April 2010, she will be with Rajveer once again. Three months wait is a long time, considering the fact that they met only three times before she went back. These were the testing times in their relationship. After a month long of relationship, Rajveer's feeling remained strong as ever. Rajveer decided to tell his family about Nava.

One evening, as his mother prepared dinner, Raj approached her.

Rajveer: Maa, I need to tell you something.

Shubhangi: (Smiled) What is it, beta? You look nervous. Is everything alright?

Rajveer: Yes, Maa, everything is amazing! Actually... I met someone.

Shubhangi: (Eyes widened) Oh Ho! Tell me everything! Who is she? What's her name?

Rajveer: Her name is Nava. We met on New Year's Eve, and Maa It was... magical. We went on two dates after that, and honestly, Maa, I love her.

Shubhangi: (Beamed) Oh, Rajveer! I'm so happy for you. Tell me more about her. What's she like?

Rajveer: She's... she's incredible. Intelligent, kind, funny, and she has this infectious laugh. I haven't felt this way in a long time.

Shubhangi: (Softly) I can tell.

Rajveer: But... there's a catch. Nava lives in Bhuvaneshwar.

Shubhangi: (Smile faltered slightly) Oh.

Rajveer: I know, Maa. It's long distance. I know it won't be easy. But I... I want to make it work.

Shubhangi: (Placed a hand on his shoulder) Rajveer, I've always taught you to follow your heart. If you feel this strongly about her, then you should pursue it.

Rajveer: You really think so?

Shubhangi: Of course, I do. Love knows no boundaries, beta. Distance can be tough, but if your love is true, you'll find ways to overcome it.

Rajveer: Thank you, Maa. You're the best.

Shubhangi: (Hugged him) Always remember, my son. Love is a journey, not a destination. Cherish every moment, and never give up on something that makes you happy.

Rajveer: I won't, Maa. I promise.

Meanwhile, his siblings Anya and Reyansh, overheard the conversation. Feeling curious, the exchanged glances.

Rajveer entered the bedroom, a slight smile playing on his lips. Anya, a finance student, was engrossed in a book, while Reyansh, the youngest of the family with his mischevious and playful act, was building a tower of blocks.

Rajveer: Hey guys, you wouldn't believe

what happened.

Anya: (Looked up from her book) What's that, Raj? Did you finally beat Monty in a boxing match?

Rajveer: (Chuckled) No, something better. I met someone.

Reyansh: (Balanced precariously on a chair) Someone? Like a new friend?

Rajveer: More than a friend, Reyansh. Her name is Nava.

Anya: (Intrigued) Nava? Who's Nava?

Rajveer: She's... she's amazing. Smart, funny, and incredibly kind. We spent two days together, and I haven't felt this way in ages.

Reyansh: (Climbed down from the chair) Did you give her a flower? Like in the movies?

Rajveer: (Smiled) Not exactly. But I did ask her out on a date.

Anya: (Eyes widened) A date? Oh my god, Raj!

This is huge!

Reyansh: (Jumped up and down) A date! A date!

Rajveer: (Laughed) I know, I know. I'm still a little nervous, to be honest.

Anya: Don't be! You're Rajveer. You've got this.

Reyansh: Yeah! Show her your boxing skills!

Rajveer: (Smiled) Maybe. But I'm more interested in just getting to know her more.

Anya: Well, whatever happens, we're all rooting for you, Raj.

Reyansh: Yeah! And if she's mean to you, I'll... I'll build a really tall tower and knock it down!

Rajveer: (Chuckled) Thanks, guys. You two are the best.

Rajveer gets back into his routine—work, gym, boxing classes on Friday, Saturday and Sundays.

The pain he felt because of her absence was too much.

Just three months into boxing, Rajveer had taken a liking towards the sport. He liked it when he was being physically challenged, took his power and concentration to the next level. He thrived on adrenaline rush inside the ring. It was his first match today, against the experienced Monty. But there was fire inside Rajveer, which made him unstoppable.

The air crackled with anticipation as the bell rang, signalling the start of the epic showdown between Rajveer, the rising star, and Monty, the seasoned veteran champion. The crowd roared as the two warriors circled each other, a silent battle of wills preceding the physical clash.

Rajveer, a whirlwind of youthful energy, danced around Monty, his punches swift and accurate. Monty, however, absorbed the blows like a rock, with his granite chin and retaliating with powerful hooks that sent tremors through Rajveer's frame. The first round was a fierce exchange, a tantalizing preview of the intensity to come.

As the fight progressed, the tide began to turn. Rajveer, fuelled by adrenaline and a burning desire to dethrone the champion, unleashed a barrage of combinations, his punches finding their mark with increasing frequency. Monty, his face bloodied and his movements slowed, struggled to keep up with Rajveer's relentless assault.

In the final round, Rajveer, sensing victory within his grasp, unleashed a flurry of punches that sent Monty reeling. The champion, dazed and battered, could only manage a feeble defence as Rajveer rained down a storm of blows. Finally, with a thunderous right hook that sent Monty crashing to the canvas, Rajveer emerged victorious, the roar of the crowd echoing his triumph.

As Rajveer raised his arms in celebration, the club witnessed the birth of a new boxing legend, a testament to his skill, determination, and unwavering spirit. His victory over Monty was more than just a win; it was a defining moment in his career, a turning point that propelled him to the pinnacle of boxing glory.

He was thrilled after winning a nail-biter, called Nava on Sunday and told her about

his win. Wow! Congratulations, Rajveer. She was happy but worried as he was physically hurt. he assured her in response , "Don't worry, my love. I will be with you tomorrow, and all my scars will heal. I'm excited to see you."

CHAPTER 5:
"BHUVANESHWAR BOUND"

Rajveer's flight to Bhuvaneswar was from Mumbai, and excitement coursed through him. First of all, he was traveling via flight for the first time, he was about to see Nava after months, and he had just won a boxing match—he was on top of world. He stayed overnight with his friend Alvis in Mumbai, they were partying the whole night. Alvis insisted on showing Rajveer the Mumbai night life. They enjoyed a lot, and went to Juhu beach at night, spend hours talking. Sleep was the last thing on Rajveer mind. He was flying for the first time and was going to see Nava. His adrenaline was at all-time high. Rajveer's flight was at 5 am, he reported to the airport at 3 am, Alvis dropped him and wished him luck on the trip.

Boarding the flight, he was both exhilarated and nervous. The moment the plane took off, a wave of exhilaration washed over him. He peered out the window, mesmerized by the city shrinking below. It was a sight he'd never forget.

He decided to strike up a conversation with one of the air hostess, a friendly woman with a warm smile. He nervously asked her about her experience in flying, and she, in turn, shared fascinating anecdotes about navigating storms and encountering unusual passengers. Rajveer was captivated by her stories, his initial nervousness fading away.

The flight passed in a blur of excitement and conversation. Rajveer savoured every moment, from in-flight meal to the smooth landing in Bhuvaneswar. He stepped off the plane, a traveller in spirit, his first flight experience etched forever in his memory.

Finally!!! After landing on Biju Patnaik International Airport, Bhuvaneshwar, Odisha, Rajveer's happiness had no bounds. His heart was beating fast, excited to meet the love of his life after months. He called Nava around 9 am, to let her know that he had landed. Nava had promised Rajveer to pick him up and then they will have breakfast together. Nava picked the call and said she is still stuck in college and will take half an hour to reach the airport. Rajveer swallowed his disappointment, he hadn't slept yesterday, he was hungry, and patience was not his biggest strength.

He went outside the airport, and immediately felt the heat. Rajveer was from Pune, the weather was dry and pleasant. In Bhuvaneshwar, the weather was hot and humid, which Rajveer was not used to. He made sure that he was presentably aware of the fact he was meeting Nava after months, but it was going down the drain. The sweat had entirely consumed him, he kept wiping his sweat using his handkerchief, but soon it was soaked. He was not used to such heat and humidity and it was just 9:30 in the morning. He called Nava again, she said she will reach in 20 minutes or so. Rajveer disconnected the call in disappointment. They had planned the dates according to Navas college schedule, where she could bunk for at least for four days and spend the entire morning, afternoon and some part of the evening together. e At 10:15 am, Rajveer called Nava again, this time she disconnected the call. Rajveer was frustrated and hungrier as he just had to wait for Nava. He was new to the city, he didn't know the local language, and he felt like he was stuck. He thought of going to his hotel to eat and rest. When he informed her, Nava called him back. "Raj, don't go until I come to pick you up, the auto drivers will overcharge since you're new here. Just wait for me, okay?" Rajveer was exhausted and tired. But more than anything, he wanted to see Nava. He had been waiting for this moment for what felt like an eternity—finally, he was going to meet Nava, the love of his life. Months of longing, countless phone calls, and endless text messages had all led up to this moment.

As he scanned the crowded airport, Rajveer's eyes shone with anticipation. He couldn't wait to lay eyes on Nava, to hug her tight, and to feel her warmth. He had imagined this moment countless times, and now that it was finally here, he could barely contain his excitement.

But as the minutes ticked by, Rajveer's excitement began to give way to worry. Nava was supposed to meet him two hours ago, and yet, there was no sign of her. Rajveer checked his phone for what felt like the hundredth time, but there were no messages from Nava.

Rajveer's mind began to wander, conjuring up all sorts of worst-case scenarios. Had something happened to her? Had she changed her mind about meeting him? He tried calling her, but she didn't answer.

As the waiting continued, Rajveer's emotions seesawed between excitement and anxiety. He paced back and forth, his eyes scanning the airport for any sign of Nava. Where was she? Why was she late? And most importantly, was she okay?

Despite the uncertainty, Rajveer's love for Nava remained unwavering. He was willing to wait forever if it meant being with her. And so, he stood there, his heart beating with anticipation, his eyes fixed on the entrance, waiting for the moment when Nava would finally walk through those doors and into his arms.

He kept walking inside the airport, he had given up on the fact that he was perpetually sweating. He was drained, hungry, and even angry at the circumstances.

It was 12 pm now, he was still waiting, now he had lost it, he couldn't bear the heat, he was drenched in his clothes, extremely hungry, frustrated and angry. He called her again, Nava said the same thing again, she was stuck and will take more time to come. Rajveer barked in a loud voice,"I have been standing here for three hours. I'm done waiting. I'm getting the first cab or auto I see and heading straight back to the hotel." Nava pleaded," Please don't do it..." He already disconnected the call. Moments later, He got an auto rickshaw. He told the name of the hotel, the driver didn't understand Hindi, and Rajveer did not understand Odia language. Frustrated, he gave the name of the hotel and sat inside, after ten minutes, Nava kept calling Rajveer, he refused to pick up. He had no idea where the hotel is, how long it would take, but Nava had told him over the phone that it was 15-20 minutes away from the airport. After 25 minutes, the driver kept taking Rajveer in circles, Rajveer tried to ask how much time more in Hindi, Marathi, and English. The driver didn't have a clue. Around 12 :40 pm, Rajveer finally picked up Nava's call.

Nava: Where on earth are you?

Rajveer: I have no idea! I am in the auto for 25 minutes and I don't see the hotel nearby. This chap doesn't understand any language I know. You speak with him and ask where we are, and tell him to drop me here at this instance. You come to pick me up from wherever I am.

Nava: (Angrily) Who the fuck asked you to get out of the airport without me?

Can't you be a little patient?

Rajveer: (Frustrated) Like a fool I was waiting for you at the airport, for three fucking hours. Do you call that not having patience? I am giving the phone to the driver, tell him what I told you.

Rajveer's handover the phone to the driver.

Nava asks in Odia language, about their whereabouts and tells him to drop him at this instance and leave. Driver drops Rajveer, hands him the phone and ask for ₹300 for his services. Clueless Rajveer pays him, takes his luggage out and continues his wait for Nava in the middle of nowhere.

Nava: Raj, baby. I am so sorry. I am coming where you are don't worry. I know the place it will take half an hour more, please be where you are until I get to you.

Rajveer :(In a weak voice). OK, what other choice do I have?

Rajveer continues his unending wait, and starts thinking of going back to Pune after meeting Nava once.

Finally, around 1:10 pm, Nava arrived. She jumps out of the car and rushed towards him.

Nava: Hi baby, I am so sorry.

Rajveer tried to control his anguish, and stayed quiet.

Nava: Let me take you to a restaurant, you must be starving.

The moment the waiter placed their food down. Rajveer slammed his fork down with a loud clang. Rajveer: I can't believe this! Four hours! Four hours I waited in that godforsaken airport, sweating like a pig. And then that auto-rickshaw driver, takes me on some detour to "show me the sights." Sights my backside! I'm exhausted, starving, and honestly, Nava? I just want to go back to Pune.

Nava: (Calmly) Rajveer, please. You just landed. We're here. Let's at least try to enjoy this one evening. We can order some food, relax, and tomorrow we can figure things out.

Rajveer: Enjoy? I don't think I can enjoy anything right now. My mood is completely ruined. This whole trip is off to a disastrous start. I should have just stayed home.

Nava: Come on, don't be like that. It wasn't anyone's fault. My professor kept giving me work, I couldn't just walk away. I did not expect this at all. These things happen. Look, the food here is amazing.

Eat some Idli and vada. You'll feel better after this.

Rajveer: (Scoffed) Idli and vada? I'm craving a proper meal, something substantial. And frankly, I don't think I can stomach anything right now.

Nava: Okay, okay. We'll order something else. But please, try to relax. We're here now. Let's make the most of it. We can visit the temples tomorrow, explore the old city, and maybe even try some local street food.

Rajveer: Temple? Street food? I don't think I'm up for any of that. I just want to go back to my air-conditioned room, have a cold shower, and maybe order some room service.

Nava: (Sighed) Rajveer, you're being unreasonable. You came all this way, for me. I was so looking forward to this.... Us.

Rajveer: I know, Nava. I know. And I feel terrible about it. But I'm just so frustrated right now. I need some time to calm down.

Nava: (Softly) Okay. Let's just finish our drinks. Then we can go back to the hotel. Maybe tomorrow morning, you'll feel better.

Rajveer: (Looked at Nava, a hint of guilt in his eyes) I hope so. I really do. I hate to ruin this for you.

Nava: (Smiled gently) It's okay, Rajveer. We'll figure it out.

After lunch, they headed towards the four-star hotel Rajveer had booked in advance. At the reception, they showed each other's ID cards upon request. Within minutes, they had the room keys, and made way to the room. After looking at room, Nava says in disappointment that they had booked a suite and this room is nowhere near a suite. They both headed back to the reception.

Receptionist: I am so sorry, mam. The suite you booked will be available in a couple of hours. If I can request you both to rest in the temporary room allocated to you. Once ready, we will shift you both to your suite.

Nava and Rajveer:(Impatiently) It's fine. Please do let us know once it is ready. We came two hours later than our actual check-in time and still have to go through this? Just make it available on priority and let us know.

Still frustrated, the couple went back to the temporary room.

Rajveer: I am going to take a shower; Nava please turn the air conditioner on, the heat is killing me.

Nava: Sure baby, I will be waiting for you.

Stepping out of the cold shower, the chill of air conditioner bought him much-needed relief. He looked at Nava. He walked over and wrapped his arms around her.

Rajveer: Babe, I am sorry. This heat, hunger, and endless waiting pushed me over the edge. I had already waited for four months to see you, had to wait for four more hours. I was insecure in the new city, and took it out on you. Please, forgive me love.

Nava: (Cried) You are not the only person who was waiting. I was looking forward to be with you today, but I am glad that you stayed back. I thought you would go back to Pune which would have broken me. Let's leave this behind.

The air crackled with unspoken words as Nava and Rajveer stood face-to-face, the aftermath of their fierce argument still hanging heavy. Four long months had passed, a chasm of hurt and resentment separated them. But the sight of him, his eyes mirroring the same desperation, shattered the fragile peace.

He reached out, his fingers tracing the line of her jaw, a tremor running through him. "Nava..."

She leaned into his touch, the familiar scent of his cologne washing over her, a potent drug. "Rajveer."

Words were unnecessary. The unspoken yearnings, the pent-up passion, ignited a fire between them. He pulled her close, his lips finding hers in a desperate, soul-baring kiss. It was a collision of longing, a desperate reclaiming of the love they'd almost lost.

They stumbled back, their bodies entangled, hands exploring, seeking comfort and solace. He tasted her tears, salty and sweet, a poignant reminder of the pain they'd inflicted on each other. But amidst the pain, a fierce joy erupted—a celebration of their enduring love.

A loud knock shattered the moment.

It was the Room attendant: Sir, your suite is ready. I am here to help you shift.

Rajveer annoyed by the interruption, gathered his composure enough to say, "We will be out in a minute."

After settling into the suite, Rajveer handed a ₹100 note to the room attendant. He thanked him, and informed that they do not need anything else. They would appreciate the privacy and there has to be no more disturbance under any circumstances.

The room attendant agreed and walked away.

Rajveer: So, where were we?

He stripped away her clothes, his touch reverent, each touch a whispered apology. She mirrored his actions, her hands

trembling as they explored the contours of his body. The months apart had only intensified their desire, their bodies aching for the familiar warmth, the comforting weight of the other.

They moved with a desperate urgency, their bodies a symphony of rhythm and need. Gasps and moans filled the air, a testament to the raw, unbridled passion that consumed them. In that moment, there was nothing but the two of them, their love a raging inferno, burning away the remnants of their fight.

As they climaxed together, a wave of euphoria washed over them, leaving them breathless and spent. They lay entwined, the aftermath of their passion a sweet exhaustion. But more than that, it was a reaffirmation of their love, a testament to its enduring strength, a promise that they would overcome any obstacle.

Rajveer: Baby, was it anywhere near as to what you had imagined it to be? How was it?

Nava: It was beautiful baby. I am so happy to be with you, to touch you, to feel you.

Rajveer: (Smiled) Let's order some cold coffee and fries. what do you say?

Nava: Sure, I would like that.

They fed each other, lost in each other's eyes. After the refreshments were over, Nava says she has to get back home, her parents would be worried.

Rajveer: You really have to go? We just got here!

Nava: Unfortunately, yes. But I will be back tomorrow morning, we have the entire week to ourself. We can explore Bhuvaneswar tomorrow, stay in, and do whatever you want.

Rajveer: I want to explore more of you tomorrow,

Nava: (Giggled) I am glad. Chalo drop me to my cab.

Rajveer: OK, let's go.

While dropping Nava, Rajveer felt few droplets of his tears cascading down his face. He tells Nava to ride safe and message him once she reaches home safely. Nava nodded and she rode away.

20 minutes later, Rajveer gets back to his suite. Nava messaged him that she has reached home.

From his balcony, Rajveer watched the storm gather. Dark, menacing clouds, like bruised giants, blotted out the sun. The wind howled, whipping through the palm trees below, and the air hung thick with the scent of petrichor. Distant thunder rumbled, a low and ominous growl that echoed through the city.

Rajveer sighed in relief—thankfully Nava reached home before this unexpected change of atmosphere and weather. Excited to see her tomorrow morning, he called his family and let them know that he was safe and was with Nava. Then he waited for the rain to stop, so that he can go out nearby to explore a bit, find new restaurants for dinner.

The rain had other plans. Rajveer ordered some food in his suite, had a brief chat with Nava before retiring.

The next morning, Rajveer woke up to persistent drumming on the window. He freshened up and went down for breakfast. He called nava, she didn't answer, so he texted her instead.

Rajveer: Good Morning. When are you coming?

After half an hour later, Nava

responded saying that it is still raining heavily, she is waiting for the rain to ease out, before leaving.

After breakfast, Rajveer headed back to his room. He opened the curtains aside, to his disappointment it was still raining heavily, his heart sinks. He was sitting numb, at the same instance, he gets a call from Nava.

Rajveer: Hello babe, what's going on?

Nava: This stupid rain is not easing down, and I can't step out of the house.

Rajveer: How far is the hotel from your house?

Nava: May be about 20-minute ride.

Rajveer: Just take a cab or an auto and come baby, I am missing you a lot.

Nava: Honestly, my father isn't allowing me to go out in this weather. He wants me to stay until it settles.

Rajveer: Huh! Okay. I guess I will wait for the rain to stop then. It is raining like cats and dogs, so it's better if you stay home.

Nava: Thanks love for understanding, I will be there as soon as I can. Bye now.

She hungs up.

Rajveer stared outside, looking helpless. He doesn't like things when he has no control over them, but there was nothing he could do as of now. He was aware that his girlfriend was just 18 years old, she had family restrictions and she wasn't financially independent. So even after planning everything beforehand, these things were bound to happen. He decides to hit the gym and practice boxing.

Soon it was lunch time, it was still pouring outside. After the call with Nava, Rajveer called his mother, updating the situation. She advised him to stay patient.

By evening, Rajveer was done sitting in his suite. He decided to go out; as he was exploring around the nearby area, he was glad that every necessary shop was available. He spots a restaurant, orders three chicken and egg rolls on the go, and then stopped at a wine shop. He picked his favourite Ballentine which was surprisingly cheap, and headed back to his room. That night, he poured himself a drink, unwrapped his roll, and called his friend Parag, who is now back in the USA for his job. They chatted about Bhuvaneswar, and by the time the called ended, he drifted back to sleep.

Next morning, he checked his phone and he had 'n' number of missed calls from Nava. Feeling guilty, he called her back.

Nava: Where on the earth are you? I called you so many times yesterday. You didn't answer my calls?

Rajveer: Sorry, babe. I slept off early, had to exhaust myself in the gym and boxing practice. I had early dinner and I guess I just crashed.

Nava: Baby, at least inform me about your whereabouts as you are alone in the city. It gets me worried.

Rajveer: Sure, I will my love, what is the situation outside?

Nava: It's bad, water has started clogging a little. It has been pouring in the last two days, what's the situation there?

Rajveer gets up and pushed the curtains aside, but the situation is unfavourable than yesterday.

Nava: Babe I am so sorry, you spent so much money and time to be with me, and now the rain is not favouring us. My dad won't even let me step outside.

Rajveer swallowed his frustration. He couldn't let her feel guilty for something beyond her control.

Rajveer: I understand, babe. Your safety is my upmost priority too. Stay home and stay safe.

Nava: Due to all this stress, my periods have come early, just letting you know.

Rajveer: Please take care of yourself, baby. Let me know if you need anything.

After the call, Rajveer got up, freshened up, and went down for his breakfast. The day ended up with same routine. Rajveer was far away from home, far away from Nava as well. His heart broke, but no one can overpower nature, he can only hope tomorrow might be better.

Next day, the situation was the same as yesterday. Rajveer kept himself busy with his morning schedule, he was trying to get exhausted as much as possible so he could not feel the void inside him. Days passed by, he had spent hardly any time with Nava. In the evening, the rain eased a bit, he took his umbrella and went for a walk in the streets clogged with water. It didn't bother him, staying alone in his room was haunting him. He didn't like watching TV much, no matter how many calls he made to his family, friends, and colleagues, there was still time to kill. Coming so far away from his hometown, just to end up alone, was breaking. Nava tried giving him time as much as she could over the phone, but it wasn't good enough as he was just 20 minutes away from her. Her parents didn't know about their relationship,

Rajveer saw it as a red flag. He had informed his family, spent nearly ₹50000 for flight tickets, hotel booking, food, and booze etc. It all came down to the amount of time they spend with each other was less compared to the time, effort, and money it had taken for him to come here. He had travelled 1615 kms for her, and she couldn't travel seven kilometres to be with him. He kept asking himself, has he fallen in love with a wrong girl? Spending three days alone here on heavy rainfall had taken a toll on his mental health. His subconscious mind questioned everything. His heart was still longing for Nava, but once a girl decides not to show up, regardless of any reason, what can a guy do? After swift walking aimlessly, he found himself in front of a Iskcon temple. He went inside to calm down the storm which was brewing inside him. Inside the temple, he questioned his every choice. He got out of the temple after half an hour of silent prayer, and started walking in the opposite direction of his hotel with same intensity. His phone rang and it was Nava, in a cold stern voice he picked up the call.

Rajveer: Hello

Nava: Where are you? What are you

doing?

Rajveer: Just taking a walk.

Nava: In this rain, and with water all around? Are you crazy?

Rajveer: I don't make fuss out of nothing. You just want me to sit idle in my room! It's really not that bad outside, people are out in raincoats, business are running, temples are open.

He didn't wait for her to answer.

Why is your father being unreasonable and not allowing anyone to go out? Why don't you tell your father about us? Shall I come meet your family?

Nava: Baby! I know it's frustrating. Even I miss you, but I come from an orthodox family. I know my father, he doesn't like all this. He is very protective and I will tell my family when the time is right. I did try to convince my father to step out for an hour he is not listening. What should I do? I am giving you time over the phone as much as possible, aren't I?

Rajveer: (Frustrated) Phone call? We do that when I'm in Pune. I didn't travel all the way to talk on the phone. I know it is not entirely your fault, but if you know your family, then maybe you should not have fallen in love with me. I don't know anyone here, I am stuck and I can't leave for another three days. Forget it, I don't want to vent out my frustration on you, but you calling me is not making things any easier. You know what, I have given up on you. Whether you meet me or not, I don't care.

He hung up.

Nava called again. He ignored it. She tried several more times. Finally, Rajveer switched off his phone.

He kept walking, oblivious to the surroundings, until he spotted a bar on the left side.

What else can go wrong?

He ordered whiskey and finished 180 ml of it in an hour. He noticed a guy across the room. He was drinking fast, barely checking his phone.

The stranger stumbled towards the bar and took the seat next to him.

Excuse me, bro. Mind if I squeeze in next to you? This place is packed.

Rajveer: (Slurred slightly) Not at all. Join the party.

Stranger: (Slided onto the stool) Cheers to that. (Raised his glass) So, what brings you to this fine establishment?

Rajveer: (Chuckled) Lost count of the reasons, to be honest. Just needed to drown out the noise in my head.

Stranger: (Nodded understandingly) I hear you. Work, eh? Women? Life in general? The usual suspects.

Rajveer: (Laughed) You hit the nail on the head. All of the above. What about you?

Stranger: (Grinned) Similar story. But with a dash of existential dread thrown in for good measure.

Rajveer: (Raised an eyebrow) Existential dread? At this hour? You sound like a philosopher.

Stranger: (Scoffed) More like a drunk philosopher. But hey, who needs logic when you have whiskey?

Rajveer: (Grinned) You're alright, you. What's your name and What do you do for a living, if you don't mind me asking?

Dhruv: I'm Dhruv. I'm a writer. Trying to write a novel.

Rajveer: A writer, huh? That's cool. I'm Rajveer by the way. What's it about?

Dhruv: It's... well, it's about a guy who loses everything and tries to find himself again. Sounds deep, right?

Rajveer: Sounds relatable. I think we all lose ourselves sometimes.

Dhruv: Absolutely.

(They both took a long sip of their drinks, a comfortable silence falling between them.)

Rajveer: You know, I think we're going to be friends.

Dhruv: (Smiled) I think so too.

Rajveer: (Pulled out his phone) Here, give me your number. We should do this again sometime.

Dhruv: (Grinned) Absolutely.

Rajveer: (Raised his glass) To new beginnings.

Dhruv: (Clinked glasses) To new beginnings.

(They both took another long sip, the conversation continuing late into the night, the worries of the world fading away with each passing drink.)

Next day, Rajveer wakes up with a pounding headache, he remembered the unpleasant conversation he had with Nava yesterday, but he pushed them away. He kept checking his phone and replied to necessary messages, just as it buzzed—Nava.

Nava: Where the hell have you been since yesterday? I am been worried sick. Why didn't you bother picking up my calls and reply to my texts?

Rajveer: If you were so worried about me, you would have been here! I was trying to avoid an unpleasant conversation, so I didn't respond. Are you coming today?

Nava: Did you drink yesterday? Why are you so rude?

Rajveer: One has to kill time somehow.

Nava: You know how much I hate drinking.

Rajveer: I am not drinking now, are you coming?

Nava: I am not sure. Let me check with my father. If he allows me, I may co—.

Before she could finish, Rajveer disconnected the call. He shot her a message: If you decide to come, you know the way.

Then he remembered Dhruv, he pulled up his chat and sent a message. They planned to meet at the same bar. Dhruv offers to pick him up, he agrees, and goes back to sleep.

Rajveer got up to freshen up in the afternoon, orders room service with lemon water, and sleeps again.

In the evening, Dhruv waited at the hotel entrance. Rajveer slids into Dhruv's car, and they sped up to pulsating nightclub.

Inside, the air was pumping with energy. The music was loud, lights flashed, and the crowd moved with ease. Rajveer and Dhruv hit the floor, clearly having a blast.

Rajveer: (Grinning, he shouted over the music) This is insane, Dhruv! I haven't had this much fun in months.

Dhruv: (Laughing, took a swig from his drink) Tell me about it! This place is electric. Let's lose ourselves in the rhythm.

Rajveer: (Grabbed Dhruv's hand and pulled him closer) You know, I was thinking... we should do this more often.

Dhruv: (Winked) I'm in. Let's make it a regular thing.

Rajveer: (Leaned in close, his voice dropping) Maybe we could even... explore other things besides just dancing.

Dhruv: (Eyes widened playfully) Now you're talking.

Rajveer: (Grinned) Just a thought. But seriously, you're amazing.

Dhruv: (Smiled)

Rajveer: (Threw his head back and laughed) Let's keep this party going!

Dhruv: (Raised his glass) To new beginnings!

Rajveer: (Clinked his glass against Dhruv's) To new beginnings!

They both took a long drink and dove back into the music, lost in the moment.

At the same moment, a group of girls came near Rajveer and Dhruv, they started dancing and partying together. The music intensified so does their mood. Everyone was in high spirits, a girl dancing besides Rajveer came closer. He can smell her fragrance, her hot body touching him slightly, she was hot with tempting curves. He gets pulled into the aura she had created, and she starts grinding towards him. He holds her from behind, they both were breathing hard and heavy, and they looked at each other, instantly they start kissing each other like animals. She grabbed his hands and rested them on her perfect boobs, pressing hard against his excitement and his hard body. They continued for a moment, before pulling themselves to the corner of the bar. Inside he saw Dhruv with another girl from the group, making out passionately. Rajveer calls out for Dhruv," Get inside another booth before someone catches you." Dhruv shot him a playful glare but complied. The women in Rajveer's arm wasted no time, she slammed him against the wall and bites his neck, starts kissing Rajveer passionately, he kisses back in the same motion. His hands roamed around unhooking her bra, presses her boobs hard, surrending to temptation. Then suddenly everything stopped. Guilt washed over him, *what am I doing?* He suddenly goes pale and completely withdrawals from her, he apologies to her and runs away from the club. He ran as hard as he could, towards the hotel, his guilt had taken over him, he was crying, guilty of diving into the temptation when he was lonely. He ran harder towards the hotel in the pouring rain, after a while, he gets exhausted. Jogging, he thanked god as it rained, so nobody could notice his tears. He went into the wine shop near the hotel and bought a bottle of whiskey, then made a detour to pan shop for cigarettes.

Back in his room, he shed his clothes and collaped onto the bed. His body trembled, not just from the cold, but from guilt. He opened the whiskey bottle, poured a glass, and gulped it down in one go.

Another.

Another.

He lit a cigarette, letting the smoke fill his lungs. As he calmed himself down, he crashed on his bed.

Unaware of the time and knocking himself out senseless.

Next Day, a relentless ringing jolted Rajveer awake. His heart pounded as he reached for his phone, only to find it in offline.

Yet the sound persisted, a hammering sound against his skull. Irritated, he realised it was the door. As he opened the door and saw Nava in front of him. She entered as he flipped the Do Not Disturb sign on the door.

The room was a mess—empty bottles strewn across the floor and crumpled clothes everywhere. Cigarette buds flooded the ashtray, food sat untouched on the table. Rajveer, unshaven, sprawled on the bed, looking pale and miserable. Nava, her face a mixture of anger and worry.

Nava: Rajveer! Where were you? I called you a hundred times.

Rajveer groaned and buried his face in the pillow.

Nava (Kneeled beside him)

Are you alright? You look terrible.

Rajveer: (Muffled) Just... hungover.

Nava (Scoffed) Hungover? That's all? You disappeared yesterday! I was so worried. I should have come to you. I know you wanted me there.

Rajveer: (Sat up, rubbing his head) Don't. Don't blame yourself. It's... complicated.

Nava: Complicated? What's so complicated? You won't even tell me what's wrong.

Rajveer: (Avoided her gaze) I can't. Not now.

Nava: (Stood up, voice rising) Why not? What is this, some game? You come here, disappear, and then expect me to just sit around and wait?

Rajveer: (Frustrated) I'm sorry, okay? I'm sorry I worried you. I'm sorry I couldn't be there for you over the phone.

Nava: (Voice softened) Rajveer, what is it? You know you can tell me anything.

Rajveer: (Looked at her, his eyes filled with a mixture of guilt and pain) I can't. You don't deserve this.

Nava: (Confused) Deserve what?

Rajveer: (Shook his head) Nothing. Just... forget it.

He turned away from her, buried his face in

his hands. Nava watched him, her anger slowly replaced by concern. She knew something is deeply wrong, but Rajveer is clearly not ready to talk.

Nava: (Softly) Alright. We'll talk later. But you need to take care of yourself.

She moves towards the door, then pauses.

Nava: (Looked back at him)

I love you, Rajveer.

He doesn't respond, but she sees a flicker of something in his eyes - guilt, maybe? Or perhaps something deeper. Nava tried to leave the room,

in that instant, Rajveer jumped out of his bed, realized how much he missed and loved her. He took hold of her hand and smoothly dragged her back to him, holding back his tears he hugged her tightly. Days without her felt like an eternity, now having her in his arms, the weight of everything came crashing down.

Rajveer: I am sorry I got drunk every night and didn't tell you. Even after working out so hard I couldn't be in peace with you not being here. I am sorry I lied.

Nava: Baby, as much I hate drinking, it's okay. It's my fault I wasn't able to come to you, but trust me my love, I did miss you a lot. I am here now, let me take care of you.

First, go take a shower you stink like a pig, and let me shave that beard of yours.

Rajveer: Whatever you say, my love. Let me just order some food—all your favourites—and I will ask the housekeeping to clean up, is that okay? (He Removed the DND sign from the door)

Nava: Sure, order some shawarma rolls for me. And you?

Rajveer: Lots of lemon water for me.

After an hour or so, the room was clean, smelled better, food was on the table, the couple were on their own.

Nava: Let's go to the bathroom.

He gleefully followed her.

Sunlight streamed through the window, illuminating the dust motes dancing in the air. Nava stood on the edge of the stool, carefully shaving Rajveer's face with a razor. He leaned back, eyes closed, a contented sigh escaping his lips.

Nava: (Softly) Almost there...

The razor glided smoothly over his skin. Nava's touch was gentle, almost reverent. Rajveer opened his eyes, caught her in the act of admiring his face in the mirror. He smiled, a slow, lazy curve of his lips.

Rajveer: You know, I think I'd let you shave me every morning.

Nava: (Chuckled) Only if you promise to stop growing this ridiculous beard.

Rajveer: (Grinned)Deal. But only if you promise to shave me every morning.

He reached up and gently cupped her face, his thumb tracing the outline of her jaw.

Rajveer: (Voice husky)

You're so beautiful, Nava.

Nava's eyes softened, and she leaned in to kiss him, a long, slow kiss that spoke volumes.

Nava: (Smiled) And you, my love, are impossible.

She finishes shaving him.

Nava: Now, let's get you cleaned up.

Rajveer: (Grinned) Sounds like a plan.

The steamy shower relaxed them both. Nava washed Rajveer's hair, massaging his scalp gently. He returned the favor, lathered her with soap and traced patterns on her skin.

Rajveer: (Whispered) This is perfect.

NAVA: (Smiled) It is.

They lingered in the shower, enjoyed the intimacy of their shared space. As they stepped out, wrapped up in towels, Rajveer pulled Nava close and buried his face in her hair.

Rajveer: I'm so lucky to have you.

Nava: (Pulled back to look at him) And I, you.

She kissed him again, a passionate kiss that left them breathless.

Rajveer: (Held her close) Never let me go.

Nava:(Smiled) I never will.

They pulled apart, their eyes locked. Rajveer knew he can't tell her about last night. Not yet. Maybe never. But in this moment, surrounded by the warmth of her love, he felt a sense of peace he hasn't felt in a long time.

Rajveer and Nava settled down with their food. The aroma of shawarma roll filled the air.

Nava: (Smiled) So, I told my family I'm staying at Priya's place tonight. Said we have a big project due tomorrow.

Rajveer: (Eyes widened) Really? You did it!

Nava: (Took a sip of her lemon water) Yep. It wasn't easy. My father kept asking a million questions, but I somehow managed to convince him.

Rajveer: (Beamed) I'm so proud of you. And so, so happy.

Nava: (Blushed) Me too. I can't believe we're actually doing this.

Rajveer: (Took a bite of his shawarma) It's like a dream come true. We'll have the whole evening and night to ourselves.

Nava: (Giggled) I know, right? We can watch a movie, talk for hours, maybe even star gaze.

Rajveer: (Gazed at her) Or we could just spend the time holding hands and talking about everything and nothing.

Nava: (Leaned closer) I like that idea too.

Rajveer: (Smiled softly) You know, I'm so lucky to have you. You're amazing, Nava.

Nava: (Smiled back) And I'm lucky to have you, Rajveer. You make me feel like I can do anything.

Rajveer: (Took her hand) I can't wait to spend the night with you. It's going to be perfect.

Nava: (Smiled dreamily) Me neither.

Rajveer: (Leaned in to kiss her forehead) You have no idea how much this means to me.

Nava: (Wrapped her arms around him) I know, Rajveer. I know.

Rajveer: Babe, we've been together for months now. Shouldn't we tell your parents?

Nava: (Hesitated, sipping her lemon juice) Rajveer, you know how my father is. He's so protective, so orthodox. He wouldn't approve. I'm just 18, barely an adult.

Rajveer: But we're adults now. We're serious about each other. Your parents deserve to know.

Nava: I know, but... what if they forbid us from seeing each other? What if they ground me for months?

Rajveer: We can talk to them, explain how we feel. We can assure them that we'll respect their wishes, but we can't live our lives hiding.

Nava: What if they disown me? I can't lose my family, Rajveer.

Rajveer: They won't disown you. They love you. They just need time to adjust to the idea that their darling daughter has a boyfriend.

Nava: I can tell Di. She'll understand. She'll support us. And then, when the time is right, I'll talk to them.

Rajveer: But why wait? Why not tell them now?

Nava: Because I'm scared, Rajveer. I'm scared of losing their love, their acceptance.

Rajveer: I understand. But we can't build a future on fear. We need to be honest with each other and with our families.

Nava: (Sighed) You're right. But please, give me some time. Let me talk to Di first.

Rajveer: Okay, I'll wait. But promise me you'll talk to them soon.

Nava: I promise.

(They shared a long, meaningful look.)

Nava: (Smiled softly) Thank you for understanding, Rajveer.

Rajveer: Always, babe. Always.

Rajveer: I told my mom and my siblings about you.

Nava: You did?! How did they react?

Rajveer: They were so happy! My mom gave us her blessings. She said she always knew we'd make a wonderful couple.

Nava: (Smiled) That's wonderful, Rajveer! What about your siblings?

Rajveer: They're excited to meet you. They've been asking me all sorts of questions about you.

Nava: (Beamed) Oh my god, this is incredible news, Rajveer! I'm so happy!

Rajveer: I'm so happy too, Nava. I can't wait to spend the rest of my life with you.

Nava: (Hugged him) Me too, Rajveer. Me too.

(Nava pulled out her phone)

Nava: I need to call my Di. I have to tell her everything!

Rajveer: (Smiled) Go ahead. I'll be right here.

(Nava dialed her sister's number)

Nava: (Excitedly) Di! You won't believe it! I met Rajveer in Pune, we are in love and you know what! He told his family about us and they all love me!

(Nava proceeded to tell her sister everything about her conversation with Rajveer.)

Rajveer watched Nava with a loving gaze.

He is happy and content thinking at least Nava's sister knows about their relationship. All the negativity and anxiety he had when he was alone had disappeared. He felt lighter, unburdened.

When she hung up, she smiled at Rajveer radiantly.

Rajveer: do you want to meet my family over a video call?

She happily agrees.

(Video call starts)

Rajveer: Hello ma. Look who is here.

Shubhangi: (Smiled warmly) Hello Nava! It's so lovely to finally meet you!

Nava: (Smiled) Hello Aunty! It's a pleasure to meet you all too.

Anya: (Excitedly) Hi Nava! Rajveer talks about you all the time! You're even prettier in person!

Nava: (Blushed) Thank you, Anya! You're so sweet.

Reyansh: (Ran towards the screen) Hi! Are you Nava? Rajveer says you are the best Classical dancer!

Nava: (Laughed) Hi Reyansh! Yes, I am still learning right now, but your brother keeps praising me.

Rajveer: (Smiled) She is the best classical dancer, Reyansh.

Shubhangi: Nava, you seem like such a wonderful girl. We're so happy for Rajveer.

Nava: Thank you, Aunty. I'm very happy with Rajveer too.

Anya: So, can you show us some of your moves please?

Reyansh: Can you show us some of your moves Please?

Nava: (Smiled) Of course.

(Nava quickly showed her hand gestures in Bharatnatyam like shakata and kartari-swastika.)

Reyansh: (Danced excitedly) Wow! You're amazing!

Anya: You're so talented, Nava!

Shubhangi: This is beautiful, Nava. Thank you.

Nava: (Smiled) You're welcome.

Rajveer: (Looked at Nava lovingly) She's

the best, isn't she?

Shubhangi: (Smiled) Indeed, she is, Rajveer.

Shubhangi: What do you study Nava?

Nava: Psychology, I want to pursue my masters in the same field.

Shubhangi: Tht's wonderful. There are top colleges in Pune. I can help you get an admission for your masters.

Nava: Wow, Aunty! You are the best. I'd love to come to Pune for my masters.

Shubhangi: That would be great, what does your parents do?

Nava: My ma and baba run a school here in Bhuvaneswar, and my Di is pursuing her masters.

Shubhangi: That's nice. Even I'm in the education field too. I am a professor at a college.

Nava: That's how you have contacts! Well, that's great.

Shubhangi: Always happy to help. It was nice talking to you for the first time. Please make sure to come to our house, next time you visit Pune, OK.

Nava: Definitely, Aunty! I am excited to meet you all in person.

After the video call and lunch, the couple rested for a while. By 4 pm, they left for Udayagiri and Khandagiri caves.

The Udayagiri and Khandagiri caves date back to the 2nd century BCE, were built during the reign of King Kharavela of the Mahameghavahana dynasty.

The Udayagiri caves, also known as the "Sunrise Hill," consist of 18 caves. These caves are carved out of sandstone and feature intricate carvings, sculptures, and inscriptions.

The largest and most impressive cave is Rani Gumpha, also known as the "Queen's Cave." It features a spacious courtyard, a pillared hall, and several cells.

The Khandagiri caves, also known as the "Broken Hill," consist of 15 caves. These caves are smaller than those at Udayagiri, but are equally impressive in terms of their carvings and sculptures.

Both Udayagiri and Khandagiri caves feature ancient Indian architecture, with intricate carvings, sculptures, and inscriptions. The caves are carved out of sandstone and feature a mix of Jain and Hindu sculptures.

The Udayagiri and Khandagiri caves are significant not only for their architectural and sculptural beauty but also for their historical importance. They provide valuable insights into the history and culture of ancient India, particularly the Mahameghavahana dynasty.

Nava: Rajveer, look! These carvings are incredible. The detailing is just amazing.

Rajveer: I know, right? It's like they've captured a moment in time. Imagine the skill and patience it took to create these sculptures. They must have spent years working on them.

Nava: And the stories they tell! I wonder what life was like back then.

Rajveer: These caves weren't just homes, Nava. They were places of worship and art.

Nava: It's truly fascinating. I feel like I'm stepping back in time.

Rajveer: Me too. This is definitely one of the most impressive archaeological sites I've ever seen.

Nava: We're so lucky to be able to experience this.

Rajveer: Let's explore some more. I'm sure there are more wonders to discover.

Rajveer: (Gazed at the intricate carvings on a cave entrance) Wow, Nava, look at this! These caves are incredible. I can't believe people lived here centuries ago.

Nava: (Traced her hand along the smooth rock wall) Me neither! It's hard to imagine the life these Jain monks led.

Rajveer: (Read from a guidebook) "The caves served as residences for Jain ascetics, providing them with a place of meditation, study, and community living away from the distractions of urban life." So, essentially, it was like a retreat centre for them.

Nava: That makes sense. Imagine the peace and tranquillity they must have found here, surrounded by nature. No noise, no crowds... just the sounds of the forest.

Rajveer: (Pointed to a small, carved niche) Look, Nava! This must have been where they kept their belongings. And see those inscriptions? They probably recorded their spiritual progress or important events.

Nava: It's fascinating to think about their daily routines. Did they spend all day meditating? Did they grow their own food?

Rajveer: (Looked around) I wonder how they managed during the rainy season. These caves must have been quite damp.

Nava: Perhaps they had special drainage systems, or moved to higher ground during the monsoon.

Rajveer: (Sat down on a rock ledge) You know, Nava, it's amazing how these caves have survived for so long. They offer such a valuable glimpse into the past.

Nava: (Nodded in agreement) It's a reminder that even in the midst of bustling modern life, there's always a need for quiet contemplation and a connection with nature.

Rajveer: Absolutely. These caves are a testament to the enduring human desire to find peace and meaning.

As they exit the caves, Rajveer stretched and looked at Nava.

Rajveer: Babe, where should we go for dinner?

Nava: Let's go back to the suite, Raj. What if someone sees us outside? You know I have told them that I am at a friend's place.

Rajveer: Yes, that's correct. I don't want you to be in trouble unnecessarily. Let's go back—we can order room service.

They took a cab and headed back to their hotel.

Nava: Udayagiri and Khandagiri caves were indeed beautiful and mesmerising.

Rajveer: I agree with you baby. The caves were magnificent and informative.

What would you like for dinner?

Nava: Let's go for a pizza, what say?

Rajveer: I will order room service.

He dialled the number and ordered two chicken and cheese medium size pizzas with two garlic breads and two cokes, and he cuts the phone.

Their order arrived in 20 minutes or so, the couple started having their pizza in excitement.

Nava: (Smiled) This pizza is amazing! You know, I've been thinking...

Rajveer: (Looked at her intently) Thinking about what, my love?

Nava: About us. About our future. I really want to get a job in Pune.

Rajveer: (Excited) That's fantastic, Nava! It would be amazing to have you there.

Nava: I know, right? And then... well, we can finally start planning our life together.

Rajveer: (Took her hand) That's exactly what I've been thinking about too.

Nava: (Smiled) You have?

Rajveer: Of course! I want us to be together forever, Nava.

Nava: (Blushed) Me too, Rajveer. Me too.

Rajveer: So, once you get that job in Pune...

Nava: (Leaned closer) We'll get married.

Rajveer: (His eyes twinkled) That's the plan.

Nava: I know it might seem a little soon, but I can't wait any longer.

Rajveer: (Smiled) It's not soon at all, we still have four years at most, Nava. I want to spend the rest of my life with you.

Nava: (Thoughtful) But what about your house?

Rajveer: (Took a deep breath) That's the next step. I'm working towards it. I want to buy my own place before we get married.

We will stay at my family house, but having one more house in the outskirts of Pune would be a good option.

Nava: (Hugged him) You don't have to rush it, Rajveer.

Rajveer: I know, but I want to give you the best. I want to build a home for us.

Nava: (Looked into his eyes) You already have, Rajveer. You've built a home in my heart.

Rajveer: (Kissed her forehead) And you've built one in mine.

Nava: I love you, Rajveer.

Rajveer: I love you too, Nava. More than words can say.

Nava: (Voice trembled) I'm so sorry, Rajveer. I know these past few days haven't been ideal. The rain... it just wouldn't stop. And my parents... they were so worried. I feel terrible that you were here all alone.

Rajveer: (Smiled gently) Hey, it's okay, Nava. I understand. The weather was crazy. No one could have predicted this. And your parents, they were just looking out for you.

Nava: But you waited for me. For four whole days. I feel so guilty. I should have tried harder.

Rajveer: (Took her hand) Don't even think like that. It wasn't your fault. You had no control over the situation. And besides, today... today was perfect. Spending the whole day with you, exploring the city, laughing together... it made me fall even more in love with you.

Nava: (Tears welled up) I know. Me too. I feel so lucky to have today. I wish... I wish we had more time.

Rajveer: (Held her close) I know, me too. But we'll make it up to you, I promise. I will come back here again soon. And maybe next time, the weather will be kinder to us.

Nava: (Looked up at him) I hope so. I hate the thought of you leaving tomorrow.

Rajveer: (Kissed her forehead) I hate it too. But I already booked my flight, and my leave is almost over.

Nava: I know. I understand.

Rajveer: Don't worry, love. I'll be back soon. And in the meantime, we'll talk every day.

Nava: (Smiled through her tears) Promise?

Rajveer: I promise. Now, let's make the most of the little time we have left.

Then they started getting ready for bed, Nava switches on the TV and kept changing the channel aimlessly. Her mind was on Rajveer and the very limited time they had left. She wasn't sure when he would be back. But there was nothing she could do about it now. His flight is scheduled for tomorrow evening at 6p m and time was running out.

Nava: (Felt drowsy) You know, I never thought I'd find someone who could make me feel this safe.

Rajveer: (Held her closer) Me neither. I used to think love was just a fairytale, something that only happened in movies.

Nava: (Nuzzled into his chest) But then you came along, and suddenly, every fairytale seemed real.

Rajveer: (Kissed her forehead) And you, my love, you're the most beautiful fairytale I could ever dream of.

Nava Blushed.

Rajveer: (Chuckled) I know. Now close your eyes, princess. It's time to sleep.

Nava: (Yawned) But I don't want to sleep. I want to stay here with you forever.

Rajveer: (Whispered) We will, love. We will.

Nava: (Smiled contentedly) I love you, Rajveer.

Rajveer: (Held her tighter) I love you more, Nava.

(They fell asleep peacefully in each other's arms.)

In the morning, they woke up smiling at each other and cuddled. It was their first sleepover, they both felt special and loved that they belong with each other.

The couple knew that it was their last day on this trip, just a few more hours to spare. They lingered in a bed for a few more moments, savouring each other's warmth. The thought of leaving stirred something inside them.

They went out for breakfast, and chose english breakfast with pan cakes, egg whites, orange juice and coffee. They enjoyed their meal, teasing and laughing as they stole bites from each other's plates.

Rajveer: So, what's the plan after breakfast?

Nava: Whatever you say, Raj.

Rajveer: Hmmm....There is a swimming pool and table tennis. We can indulge in any activity you want.

Nava: I don't know how to swim, but I bet I can beat you in table tennis.

Rajveer: Is that so? Huh! Let's play then.

Nava: (Playfully) Let's go.

Rajveer and Nava squared off for their table tennis match. Rajveer, known for his aggressive style and powerful forehand, was a formidable opponent. Nava, on the other hand, was a master of deception, with subtle spin and unpredictable shots that often-caught opponents off guard.

The first few points were a fierce exchange, with both players matching each other stroke for stroke. Rajveer's thunderous forehands were met with Nava's deft touches, the ball a blur of motion across the net. But slowly, Nava began to gain an edge. Her deceptive serves, with subtle spin, threw Rajveer off balance, and her backhand slices were impossible to read.

Rajveer fought valiantly, digging deep to retrieve seemingly impossible shots. He unleashed a barrage of powerful drives, hoping to overwhelm Nava, but the latter remained composed, returning each shot with precision and finesse. As the score climbed, it became clear that Nava was in control.

Finally, at 21-19, Nava secured the victory with a perfectly placed drop shot that caught Rajveer off guard.

Rajveer, despite the loss, shook hands with Nava, a broad smile on his face. "That was incredible, Nava," he exclaimed. "Your spin and placement were simply brilliant. I learned a lot from playing you today."

Nava, modest in victory, thanked Rajveer for the challenging match. "You pushed me to my limits, Rajveer," he said. "Your power and aggression were a constant threat."

Rajveer: Another game?

Nava: Nah babe, we hardly have time let's spend some quality time together upstairs.

The air crackled with unspoken words and the promise of a time they wouldn't soon forget. Rajveer's eyes, dark and intense, roamed over Nava's face, tracing the curve of her lips, the delicate arch of her brow. He reached out, his fingers brushing against her cheek, sending shivers down her spine.

Nava leaned into his touch, her breath catching in her throat. She knew this was it - a last dance before an uncertain future. Fear mingled with an exhilarating sense of freedom, a reckless abandon that urged her to seize the moment.

Their lips met, a fierce, desperate claim, a hunger that had been simmering beneath the surface for far too long. Rajveer groaned, pulling her closer, his hands exploring the contours of her body. Nava

responded with equal fervour, her nails digging into his back, urging him on.

They moved with a primal urgency, their bodies a symphony of movement, a desperate attempt to imprint themselves on each other's memory. The room seemed to shrink, the world outside fading away as they were consumed by the intensity of their passion.

Nava arched beneath him, her cries mingling with his own as they reached for a crescendo, a release that left them breathless and spent. They lay entwined, their bodies slick with sweat, their hearts pounding in unison.

Rajveer traced lazy circles on her skin, his gaze filled with a love both profound and bittersweet. "I don't know when I'll see you again," he murmured, his voice rough with emotion.

Nava turned her head, her eyes glistening

with unshed tears. "Me neither."

He pulled her close, burying his face in her hair, the scent of her intoxicating him. "But I'll never forget this," he whispered, his voice thick with longing.

Nava clung to him, savouring the warmth of his body against hers, the feel of his heartbeat against her own. In that moment, nothing else mattered. Only the two of them, lost in the aftermath of their passion, clinging to the memory of a love that burned bright, even in the face of uncertainty.

After having some liquids, they made love again. After gathering their breaths and cuddling for a while, they ordered chicken biryani and cold drinks for lunch. The clock was ticking, soon after lunch they had to leave for the airport as the reporting time was 4 pm.

Nava: (Looked at the clock, her voice trembled slightly) An hour.

Rajveer: (Tried to be strong, but his voice catches) An hour.

(Silence hung heavy between them. They both avoid eye contact, lost in their own thoughts.)

Nava: (Finally looked up, her eyes brimming with tears) I still can't believe you're leaving.

Rajveer: (Swallowed hard) Me neither. This feels surreal.

Nava: (Voice cracked) I wish this wasn't happening. I wish we could just stay here, like this, forever.

Rajveer: (Reached out to hold her hand, his voice thick with emotion) I wish that too, Nava. More than anything.

Nava: (Buried her face on his shoulder, sobbing) I'm going to miss you so much.

Rajveer: (Held her close and whispered) I'm going to miss you too, more than words can say.

Nava: (Pulled back and looked at him with tear-filled eyes) Promise me you'll call me. Every single day.

Rajveer: (Nodded solemnly) I promise. Every single day. I will.

Nava: (A small smile graced her lips) I'll wait for them. Every single one.

Rajveer: (Cupped her face and wiped away her tears) Don't cry, Nava. I'll be back. I promise.

Nava: (Shook her head) It's not easy. Leaving like this, without knowing when we'll see each other again.

Rajveer: (Kissed her forehead) I know. But we have to be strong. This is just a temporary goodbye.

Nava: (Looked into his eyes, searching for reassurance) You'll come back, right?

Rajveer: (Held her gaze) I swear. I'll come back to you.

(They share a long, lingering kiss, savouring every moment. The clock ticked away, each second felt like an eternity. Finally, Rajveer pulls away, his heart aching.)

Rajveer: (Tried to be cheerful) We should go. Don't want to miss my flight.

Nava: (Nodded, her voice barely a whisper) Yeah. Let's go.

(They walked towards the door, their hands intertwined, their hearts heavy with the weight of their impending separation. As they leave, they steal one last glance at each other, a silent promise echoing in their eyes.

CHAPTER 6:
EMOTIONAL TURMOIL.

A moving moped glides down the street, the city buzzing around them. Rajveer gripped the handlebar, driving smoothly as Nava sits behind him, holding on.

Rajveer: (Smiled) You know, I met this guy, Dhruv. Really interesting guy.

Nava: (Startled) Dhruv?

Rajveer: (Nodded, accelerating slightly) Yeah, Dhruv. He is a writer, we just clicked. We spent two evenings drinking together, talking about everything and nothing. He's a cool guy.

Nava: (Voice trembled slightly) What did you... what did you talk about?

Rajveer: (Unconsciously sped up) Oh, you know, the usual stuff. Music, movies, travel... he's a bit of a philosopher, actually. Keeps talking about finding your true self and all that.

Nava: (Eyes glued to the road, heart pounding) And... and what did you do?

Rajveer: (Hesitated) We were... just drinking and talked. Went for the night club, danced.

Nava: (Tried to sound casual) Did you... did you like him?

Rajveer: (Smiled) Yeah, he's a good guy. Really easy to talk to.

Rajveer: (Broke the silence) Hey, we're here.

Nava: (Got off the moped, feeling dizzy) Okay.

Rajveer: You sure you'll be alright?

Nava: (Forced a smile) Yeah, I'll be fine.

Rajveer: (Looked at her, concerned) You seem a bit off.

Nava: (Avoided his gaze) It's just... a long drive. Have a safe flight baby. I'll be fine.

Rajveer: (Reached out to touch her arm, but stops) Okay. Take care.

Nava: (Turned away) You too.

Rajveer watched her turn away her moped towards the airport exit.

He saw her hesitate just for a second. As if making a decision, Nava turned back, her eyes were wide with a mixture of fear and disbelief. Before he can say anything, she spins around and drives away, disappearing into the crowd.

Rajveer started walking towards the airport with his luggage. Something about the way Nava looked at him unsettles him. He knows he should have told her the truth, his heart was heavy with guilt, but he knew it would break Nava's heart. He was not in his senses and was unsure about Navas intentions towards him. He was alone for four days, still he knew what he did was not right. Did she suspects something? Did she already know? After he cleared the security check, he had an hour left for the flight back home. Firstly, he called his mother, informed her that he has reached the airport and will board the flight on time.

Then he decides to call Dhruv.

Dhruv: Hello

Rajveer: Hi, I'm at the airport, going back to Pune. Just called to say bye and thanks for the time together, it was fun. Next time I'm in Bhuvaneswar, we should catch up.

Dhruv: Have a safe flight. By the way, where on this earth did you disappear from the night club. I called you so many times, you didn't pick up? You just... vanished.

Rajveer: It's a bit complicated, Dhruv. I wasn't supposed to do what I did under the influence, you know!

Dhruv: Why not, my man?

Rajveer: I have a girlfriend. I came here to spend time with her, she couldn't meet me for few days and I was alone. Then I met you...well you know the rest.

Dhruv: Did she meet you finally?

Rajveer: Yes, on my first day and last two days we were together. Just those four days, when it was raining like cats and dogs, she couldn't come out to meet me.

Dhruv: What's her name? If you don't mind me asking!

Rajveer: (A little thrown off) Nava.

Dhruv: What!!!!??? What is her last name?

Rajveer: (Tried to recall) I know, but I don't recollect exactly, but it starts with a B, she has a difficult last name.

Dhruv: Is it Bahrami?

Rajveer: Wow. How did you guess? That's the one.

Dhruv: You idiot! I didn't take a guess, I know her, she is my neighbour. Wait, I will send you a picture, check it now.

Rajveer: (Looked at the picture) It's her.

Dhruv: Bro, are you in love with her?

Rajveer: (Without hesitation) Yes, we love each other.

Dhruv: Have you ever asked about her past?

Rajveer: (Confused) Not really, I thought she is 18. Her father is strict and her family is a orthodox one, that doesn't leave any room for you know... boyfriends and stuff.

Dhruv: You are so naive! Do you know the fact that the stricter the parents are, the more child tends to break rules and acts out against her parents?

Rajveer: (Shook his head) No, she is innocent, kind and loving. She cares for me and my family. It never occurred to me that she—what are you trying to tell me Dhruv?

Dhruv: Rajveer, it's best if you ask her about her past before reaching any decision.

Rajveer: I don't care about the past. Is there something I should know about her, or what she did in the last four months or so?

Dhruv: (Sighed) I don't know how to say it, but there is only one way to do it. I will tell you the naked truth my friend, because I think you deserve to know, rest is up to you.

Rajveer griped his phone tighter. His pounded in anticipation.

She is a sex addict. She has been going around with guys over the past two years. I am telling you what I know, she is the prettiest girl in our neighbourhood, the hottest. She never lacked any male attention, boys here are ready to kill for her. When it comes to me our equation is only physical, we hooked up a lot than few times. Her parents know me, I can come and go anytime at her place, they think we study together, they trust me. She confides in me, I am like a 'friend with benefits' but there isn't any love involved.

Rajveer: (His heart beat so fast that he can actually hear it, tears rolled down from his eyes) When was the last time you guys hooked up?

Dhruv: Hmmm.. Two days before I meet you.

His chest tightened from the weight of betrayal.

Rajveer: It is my humble request Dhruv. Please don't meet nor contact Nava anymore!

Rajveer disconnects the call.

Rajveer felt a wave of nausea wash over him, the news hit him like a physical blow. His stomach churned, bile rised in his throat. Nava, the love of his life, the woman who held his heart, had been with another man. And not just any man, but Dhruv, a man he barely knew, a man he'd met only twice.

The image of Nava and Dhruv together, intimate and close, replayed in his mind on an endless loop. Each replay brought with it a fresh surge of pain - a searing, agonizing pain that seemed to grip his chest and squeeze the life out of him. He

felt a profound sense of betrayal, a deep, aching loneliness that mirrored the emptiness he'd felt those four days ago, waiting for her, alone and vulnerable.

Anger, hot and furious, threatened to consume him. How could she? After everything they'd shared, after all the promises whispered in the dark, after months they'd spent building their love? He felt a crushing sense of rejection, as if his worth, his very essence, had been deemed insignificant.

Tears welled up in his eyes, blurring his vision. He tried to blink them back, to maintain a semblance of control, but the dam had broke. He wept uncontrollably, the sobs racked his body, each one a testament to the shattered pieces of his heart.

Rajveer felt utterly lost, adrift in a sea of despair. The world around him seemed to fade away, replaced by a suffocating silence, broken only by the echo of his own grief. He questioned everything – their love, his own self-worth, the meaning of it all. The future, once a vibrant tapestry woven with dreams of them together, now seemed bleak and uncertain, a desolate wasteland stretching endlessly before him.

Rajveer sat there in silence, when he heard the announcement, he walked through the motions in a daze. His phone continuously buzzed with incoming message from Nava, he ignored them all. Finally, he switched off the phone. After two and half hours, he landed on Mumbai airport. The moment he turned his phone on, his screen lit up with more missed calls and messages. He ignored them all. Instead, he called his mother, "Ma, I just landed. I'll be home soon."

Mechanically, he walked towards the taxi stand. The taxi ride was a blur. The driver tried, to make a conversation, all he got in return was silence. When he saw his passenger face in the mirror—red-rimmed eyes, tear-streaked cheeks. After three hours, Rajveer found himself infront of his gate. He unlocked the door and relieved to find no one was at home. He got to his room, and set up an alarm for tomorrow, and tried to sleep.

Next day, Rajveer woke up and went to work, but his mind and heart was in Bhuvaneswar. He struggled to focus on, and somehow managed to complete the tasks which were a priority. He needed clarity, a second opinion. After work, he called Parag.

Rajveer: (On the phone) Parag, you won't believe what I just found out!

Parag: What happened, man? Spill the beans!

Rajveer told his friend everything— the trip, the days of waiting, an unexpected friendship with Dhruv, and the betrayal.

Parag: Man. I'm sorry.

Rajveer: You know what Dhruv said, "Man, Nava was crazy hot. I mean, any guy would love to be with her.

Parag: Wait, what? What did he mean by that?

Rajveer: He basically said that they hooked up. Like, seriously hooked up.

Parag: Are you sure? Dhruv sounds like a bit of a... exaggerator, you know?

Rajveer: You think he made it up?

Parag: No entirely. Rajveer, I understand you're hurt, but don't jump into conclusions. Dhruv may have made up these colourful stories to keep you away from her.

Rajveer: But what if it's true? What if she used me?

Parag: Look, I know this is hard, but the best thing to do is talk to Nava. Hear her side of the story.

Rajveer: You think I should confront her?

Parag: Not confront, Rajveer. Just talk to her calmly.

Rajveer: I don't know if I can. I'm scared of what she might say.

Parag: I know it's scary, but you deserve to know the truth. You can't build a relationship on assumptions and doubts.

Rajveer: You're right. I need to hear from her directly. Thanks, Parag. You're a true friend.

Parag: Anytime, man. I'm here for you.

Rajveer: Thanks. I'll talk to you later.

Parag: Take care.

Rajveer checked his phone, there were numerous calls and messages from Nava, all of them which he ignored. He took a screenshot of Dhruv's display picture from WhatsApp and sent it to Nava.

Rajveer video called her.

Rajveer: Hey Nava, how are you?

Nava: Hi Rajveer, I'm fine. How are you?

Rajveer: I'm good. I have sent you a picture of Dhruv. Who is he?

Nava: (Looked at the picture) He's my neighbour. Why?

Rajveer: I just wanted you to see him. So, how's it going with you two?

Nava: (paused) We're good.

Rajveer: When did you guys last... you know... hook up?

Nava: (Hesitated) A while ago. Why?

Rajveer: Dhruv told me it was raining that day— the same day you couldn't meet me for four days. And you hooked up with him?

Nava: (Slightly annoyed) That's not true, I consider him as my friend, we use to hook up in the past. But after I met you, I stopped.

Rajveer: He seemed pretty sure about it.

Nava: Look, Rajveer, I know I've done some stupid things in the past. I like sex, I'm not going to deny that. I hooked up with Dhruv before I met you. But I truly love you.

Rajveer: I know, Nava. I never asked you about your past! I trust you. It's just... I don't want to feel like I'm being lied to. Does Dhruv has feelings for you?

Nava: I wouldn't lie to you about something like this. I don't know about Dhruv, maybe yes. Or he just can't digest the fact that I have a boyfriend and I'm committed to you. Now that I cut him off, he might be jealous and acting out.

Rajveer: Okay, I don't know whom to believe. I saw the look on your face when I mentioned Dhruv's name, that look wasn't so assuring. You looked guilty.

Nava: It was because you never asked me about my past. All of a sudden, you meet him, partied with him, he is my friend and was more than a friend before you came in my life. I was shocked. I pursued him in the past but since he didn't feel that way, I moved on.

Rajveer: I get that. Maybe he wants you now. But I also need to be honest with you. In Bhubaneswar, at that nightclub... I danced with someone, grinding, and touching her.

Nava: (Sighed) I know. Dhruv told me about you and Soniya.

Rajveer: He did?

Nava: Yeah. He said you two were getting close.

Rajveer: We were just having fun. Nothing serious.

Nava: I don't know, the way Dhruv explained it to me, it didn't seem casual. Anyway, one problem at a time.

Rajveer. We both seem to be getting information from Dhruv that makes us suspicious of each other. I think he might be trying to create problems between us.

Maybe We should talk to him about it.

Nava: Nah. Let's not give him that much importance. I will ignore him, block him and you should too.

Rajveer: I have already told Dhruv to stay away from you. But, he is your neighbour. Your parents let him into your house, into your room. You are easily accessible to him, while I am far away The situation is not assuring at all. I'm sorry, Nava. I don't want to fight with you.

Nava: Me neither. I love you.

Rajveer: I love you too, but please promise me that you will not entertain Dhruv under any circumstances.

During the conversation, Rajveer received a picture of Soniya from Dhruv, with a caption that said, 'She misses you', and sent her number. Rajveer, annoyed, forwarded the message to Nava.

Rajveer: This guy really wants me to be with Soniya and leave you alone. He is addicted to you baby, I trusted him with something, and I wasn't aware he was your neighbour. Dhruv has taken complete advantage of the situation and created problems between us that was almost successful. Today, I had called to end things with you initially. But after knowing the facts, I am glad I didn't act on it.

Nava: (Furious) Called to end it with me ha? Like a fool, I was called you non-stop since yesterday. You didn't even bother to respond. Then I got to know that when I was stuck in my house, you were busy drinking with Dhruv and his friends— touching the other girl. Don't you think that you made a mistake? First, you believed Dhruv, acted on it without knowing the facts, second, you fooled around behind my back, while we are in a relationship, and have the audacity to end it with me. Tell me, am I a fool for being loyal to you? For lying to my parents to be with you? I don't like this behaviour at all. How can I trust you that you won't repeat this behaviour again in Pune?

(Rajveer felt guilty, but at a same time, felt relieved. He responded after a long silence.)

Rajveer: Baby, I am extremely sorry. But I love you so much that my heart was crushed after talking to Dhruv. He kept adding shock after shock, it took me time to get a grip on myself. I was shattered and cried the entire trip home. The night club thing... it wasn't planned. I am not trying to defend myself but telling you what I was going through. I accept it was my mistake, I'm ready to accept any punishment from you. But first please hear me out, I was alone for those four days and missed you like crazy. For the first two days, I tried to understand your situation, but it kept getting worse. I come from a liberal family, I couldn't completely understand what you were going through as why you weren't honest with your father. I had doubts about your intentions on me.

Nava :(Interrupted) I kept calling you, didn't I? Even when I was not able to be with you physically?

Rajveer: Did I fly across states just to talk to you over the phone? That can be done from Pune as well. I spent my time, energy, and money to be with you. Do you even know that I have to wait for minimum six months before I can get leave again. I don't want to be away from you even for a split second. But we were stuck for four days, unable to see you, I got frustrated. I accidentally met Dhruv in a bar, and the next night, he suggested we go to the nightclub. That's when it happened. I was drunk, lonely, and she came to me. I caved in, it's my fault.

Nava: (Softened) Rajveer, I know—

Rajveer: Did you tell Dhruv I was in town? That we were together?

Nava: Yes. I saw him as a friend, and confined in him. Soniya is his friend, will do anything if offered free booze and party. They know each other for a while.

She sent a picture to Rajveer.

(Rajveer looked at the picture, Dhruv and Soniya taking a selfie, in high mood.)

So, my dear, naive Raj. She wasn't attracted to you instantly, it was a setup. Soniya chosing you was a trap. He created misunderstandings and was almost successful in breaking us up.

Rajveer: I am sorry, my love. I'd would anything that you say.

Nava: I don't want you to do anything. I love you and don't want to lose you. I will keep Dhruv away from me, he is clearly obsessed. I will take help from my father if required, you better behave yourself in Pune.

Rajveer: Yes, my princess. Your wish is my command. I will cut down on drinking and focus on improving myself, physically, mentally, and financially, so we can lead a happy life together. Long-distance relationships are hard, but we are a team, you and me against this mean world.

Nava : I have sent you my Di's number. She knows everything about my life. Dhruv didn't even enter my house during those four days. You can cross-check with my sister, she doesn't lie, even if it is for herself. Soon, I will send you my mother's number after I talk to her. Baby, what we have is special, I am attached to you, I feel secure around you, I don't mind waiting for six months to be with you again. This time, we will plan the trip properly—no more rainy days. I agree I have been stupid and immature in the past, but that's behind me.

You are my present and future, I am all yours. You have my heart, my soul, and my body.

Rajveer: (Eyes welled with tears) I will never let you down my love. You are my life, you are my everything. I love you from the bottommost part of my heart.

They blow flying kisses to each other before hanging up.

Rajveer texts Parag, "Eerything is sorted. Thanks a lot for the advice, it saved us. Miss you bro, talk to you soon.

CHAPTER: 7:
"RAJVEER'S RECKONING"

Next day, Rajveer goes to work with a sceptical mind. The storm brewing inside him refused to settle. He was confused and wanted to make a decision. He didn't take Dhruv's actions lightly and wasn't able to let go. He wanted to teach him a lesson and also was worried about Nava. He might might try something stupid to get her attention.

Then, Rajveer went to speak with his boss.

He told him that he has a family emergency, he needs to be with family on coming monday. His boss hesitated at first, before approving his one-day leave, and informs about his lack of leave for at least six months.

After work, he goes to gym for training. After reaching home, he booked his flight from Mumbai to Bhuvneshwar for Friday evening, returning Tuesday morning. He even booked the same hotel again. The last-minute plan cost him a fortune, but he didn't care.

He followed his routine—work, gym, and boxing—while being in touch with Nava. He didn't tell her about his plans. He called Soniya and told her he wanted to meet her in person. They planned to meet on Saturday. He wasn't interested in Soniya, it was a test. He wanted to check if this information reaches Nava through Dhruv. If Nava didn't mention it, that means she had cut him off.

On friday, he boarded his flight and didn't tell anyone apart from Soniya.

Rajveer lands in Bhubaneshwar. At the exit gate, Soniya was already waiting for him, with a smile on her face. Rajveer's previous experience on the airport was daunting, seeing Soniya on time he felt relieved. They hugged each other in friendly manner. Soniya caught Rajveer's arm as they walked towards the exit, she was visibly attracted to him. Rajveer was uncomfortable but didn't say anything. Soniya helped him place his luggage in her car before taking driver's seat. Rajveer sat beside her.

Rajveer: Hi Soniya, do you know where I can find Dhruv? I need to talk to him about something important.

Soniya: (Beamed, a little flustered) Oh, hi Rajveer! Dhruv... well, usually at the park near his house. The one with the big old banyan tree? We meet there quite often.

Rajveer: Listen, could you do me a favor? Could you call him and tell him to meet you there? I want to surprise him.

Soniya: (Eyes sparkled) I could... but... (She hesitated, a playful glint in her eyes) Remember the night at the club? The... the thing we started?

Rajveer: (Blushed slightly) Uh... yeah.

Soniya: I'll call Dhruv for you... if you, you know, continue what we started.

Rajveer: (Cleared his throat) Soniya, I... I should probably tell you. I have a girlfriend. We've been together for a while now.

Soniya: (Her smile faltered for a second, but she recovered quickly) Oh. Okay. Well... (She shrugged) My lips are sealed. I won't say a word to anyone.

Rajveer: (Was grateful) I appreciate that, Soniya, but I can't. It wouldn't be right. But I really do need to talk to Dhruv. Could you please call him for me?

Soniya: (Sighed dramatically, but her smile returned) Fine. You're no fun. (She pulled out her phone and dialled a number) Hey Dhruv, it's Soniya. Can we meet at the park near our house, by the big banyan tree? Okay, see you there. (She hung up)

Soniya: He will be there soon.

Rajveer and Soniya reached the deserted park in Bhubaneswar. The late afternoon cast long shadows across the ground, leaving the park haunted.

Rajveer: Please call Dhruv again. And tell him, you have reached here.

Soniya: (Ignored his request) You know,

you could have stayed that night. I wanted you to—

Rajveer: Soniya, this isn't about that. I need your help with this.

Soniya: (Stepped closer, her eyes fixed on him) HHMMM

Rajveer: (Felt overwhelmed) I... I just need you to call him here. That's all.

Soniya: (Leaned in closer, her breath fanned his face) Or... we could do something else. Something a little less... business-like.

Rajveer: (Stepped back) Soniya, please. This isn't the time for this.

Soniya: (Frustrated) Why not? I want you.

Rajveer: (Looked away) I... I can't. I shouldn't.

Soniya: (Her voice hardened) You know, you're playing a dangerous game. I'm not someone you can just use and discard.

Rajveer: (Sighed) I know. I'm sorry. But this is important.

Soniya: (Eyes narrowed) Fine. If this is so important, I'll call him. But you owe me.

Rajveer: (Relieved) Thank you.

Soniya: (Took her phone out) Alright, let's get this over with. (Called Dhruv)

Dhruv: (On the phone) Hey, Soniya. Have you reached?

Soniya: (Smiled) Hey, Dhruv. Yes, I have.

Dhruv: (Surprised) Sure, I'll be there in ten minutes.

Soniya: (Hung up) He's on his way.

Rajveer: (Looked at her) Thanks, Soniya. I really appreciate it.

Soniya: (Smirked) Don't worry, I haven't forgotten about our... little agreement.

Rajveer: (Avoided her gaze) I know.

Soniya: (Watched Dhruv approach) Now, let's see what happens.

Dhruv stepped into the park, his confident stride faltered, when he saw Rajveer with Soniya.

Dhruv: Hey Rajveer! Long time no see. You look... intense.

Rajveer doesn't look up,

Rajveer: (His voice low, dangerous)We need to talk, Dhruv.

Dhruv smile faltered a moment before he chuckled.

Dhruv: What's up, Rajveer.

Rajveer: Don't play games with me, Dhruv. You know exactly why I'm here.

Dhruv (Stammered) I... I don't know what you're talking about.

Rajveer: (Leaned forward, his eyes blazed) You used me. You lured me towards Soniya, fed Nava all my secrets, tried to drive a wedge between us. You betrayed my trust, Dhruv.

Dhruv shrinked back, his eyes wide with fear.

Dhruv (Voice trembled) I... I didn't mean to. I was... I was just confused.

Rajveer (Scoffed) Confused? You manipulated me, played me like a puppet. For what? To get to Nava?

Dhruv looked away, unable to meet Rajveer's gaze.

Dhruv (Muttered)

I love her, Rajveer.

Rajveer (Voice laced with sarcasm)

Oh, you love her? Then why did you push her away when she wanted to get serious?

Dhruv clenched his fists, his face contorted with anger.

Dhruv: (Yelled) Because I was stupid! I was scared! And then you came along... and she was happy.

He paused, his anger rising.

But I won't let you have her, Rajveer.

Rajveer stares at him, disbelief etched on his face.

Rajveer: (Voice calm, but deadly)

What are you going to do, Dhruv?

Dhruv lunged across, grabbed Rajveer by the shirt.

Dhruv: (Roared) I'll do whatever it takes to get her back!

He pushed Rajveer back, landing a hard punch to his stomach. Rajveer gasped for air, clutched his stomach in pain.

Dhruv: (Panted)This is just the beginning, Rajveer.

Then Dhruv started attacking, Rajveer doubled over in pain, his eyes filled with a cold, determined fury.

The air hung heavy with the scent of pine needles and the distant hum of the city. In the heart of the deserted park, near the Nava's residence, a silent battle raged. Rajveer, his jaw clenched, moved with the grace of a panther, deflecting Dhruv's wild swings. Dhruv, fuelled by a rage, was a whirlwind of fists and fury.

Soniya, her heart pounding in her chest, tried to intervene. "Stop it! Both of you!" she cried, rushing between them.

But Dhruv, blinded by anger, shoved her aside with a force that sent her crashing into a nearby banyan tree.

The sound of Soniya's pained gasp shattered the tense silence. Rajveer's eyes narrowed. The fight, which had been a desperate dance of défense, transformed into a brutal assault. He unleashed a flurry of punches, each one a controlled explosion of power. Dhruv, unprepared for the ferocity of Rajveer's counterattack, stumbled back, bewildered. He had underestimated his opponent.

Rajveer moved with a predatory grace, his fists a blur of motion. He rained blows upon Dhruv, each one a thunderclap against his flesh. "Never hit a girl!" he roared, his voice hoarse with fury. "Stay away from Nava!"

Dhruv, battered and bleeding, could only offer a pathetic defence. He was no match for Rajveer's skill and fury. The fight descended into a one-sided mauling. Rajveer, driven by a primal rage, continued to pummel Dhruv, his blows relentless, merciless.

Suddenly, a voice cut through the chaos. "Rajveer! Stop!"

Nava stood frozen in the entrance of the park, her eyes wide with shock and horror. The sight that met her gaze was a nightmare. Rajveer, his face contorted with fury, was raining blows upon the crumpled form of Dhruv.

Rajveer, his gaze meeting Nava's, seemed to snap out of his rage. He staggered back, his breath coming in ragged gasps. The fight, as abruptly as it had escalated, came to an end.

Dhruv lay motionless on the ground, his face a mask of pain and disbelief. Soniya, clutching her side, watched the scene unfold with a mixture of fear and awe. Nava, her face pale, rushed towards Dhruv, her voice trembling with concern.

The air hung heavy with the aftermath of violence, the only sound was the laboured breathing of the combatants and Nava's frantic cries.

CHAPTER 8: "FRACTURED BONDS".

Rajveer: (Voice low and menacing) I told you to stay away from her, Dhruv. I warned you.

Dhruv whimpered, clutching his ribs.

Rajveer: (Kicked Dhruv again)

You think you can just waltz in and ruin her life? You think you can hurt her and get away with it?

Nava's breath hitched in her throat. She want to stop him, but fear paralyzed her.

Suddenly, a figure emerged from the shadows. It's her father—Mr. Arash— with his face etched with worry. He rushed towards them, his eyes landing on Dhruv.

Mr. Arash:(Horrified)Dhruv! What happened?

Nava, unable to bear the sight any longer, runs towards her father, tears streaming down her face.

Mr. Arash: (Turned to Rajveer, voice trembled with rage)

You! You monster! What have you done to him?

Rajveer, panting, looked up to see her father's accusing gaze. He tried to explain, but the words catch in his throat.

Rajveer: (Gasping) Sir, he... he tried to...

Mr. Arash: (Cutting him off)

You will pay for this!

He pulled out his phone and dialed the emergency services.

Rajveer helped Mr. Arash to take Dhruv to a nearby hospital in Soniya's car.

Hospital- LATER

Rajveer, Nava's father, and Soniya stood next to Dhruv's bed. The rhythmic sound of the monitor is the only sound filling the tensed place.

Soniya paced frantically, trying to explain to the gruff-looking policeman.

Soniya: Officer, he defended himself! Dhruv, he pushed me hard and Raj defended me.

The policeman sighed, looking at Dhruv.

Policeman: Ma'am, I understand you're upset, but we can't just take your word for it. Your friend here seems to have taken a serious beating.

Soniya clutched her hand into a fist, raging.

Policeman (Continued): We're arresting Rajveer under Section 159 of the Indian Penal Code— voluntarily causing hurt.

Rajveer, his eyes filled with a mixture of anger and disbelief, stared at the wall. He knew he did the right thing, but justice, it seems, is blind.

Jail - day 2.

The cell was cramped, with a single, flickering fluorescent light. Rajveer—eyes filled with a desperate urgency—sat on a wooden bench, staring at the cracked concrete floor. He's been here for a day, the events of the previous night a blur of confusion and fear.

Suddenly, the cell door CLANGS open.

A gruff but kind guard gestured towards the phone.

Rajveer rushed to the phone, his heart pounding.

Rajveer:(Into the receiver) Hello?

Rohan (Lawyer): (Voice warm and reassuring)

Rajveer, it's Rohan. How are you holding up?

Rajveer: (Desperate) Rohan, I need to get out of here. What's happening?

Rohan: Don't worry, I've been working on it. Charges are minor, I should be able to get you out on bail soon.

Rajveer: (Eagerly)Bail? How much?

Rohan: (Chuckled) Don't worry, I know a judge. 100 rupees should do the trick.

Rajveer: (Relief washed over him)

100 rupees? Thank you, Rohan. You're a lifesaver.

Rohan: Just doing my job. I'll be there soon.

Rajveer stepped out of the station with his lawyer, a newfound lightness in his step. He immediately pulled out his phone, desperately tried to contact Nava. But his calls go unanswered. He tried texting, but to no avail. A wave of anxiety washed over him. Where is she? Why isn't she answering?

Rohan: (patted Rajveer on the shoulder) Rajveer, I'll see you soon.

He watched as Rohan bid them farewell. Soniya turned, a knowing smile on her lips.

Soniya: I guess now you owe me twice.

Rajveer: (Hugged Soniya in a friendly manner) Thank you very much, you are an angel. Without you, I don't know how many days I would have suffered inside. I didn't even have the courage to call my mother.

Soniya: It's okay, my dear, you defended me in front of that brat, I am grateful. I just couldn't stand the thought of you behind bars.

Rajveer: I can't stand anyone disrespecting girls and playing games with them in front of me. I am really grateful for the things you have done for me, despite me running away that night.

Soniya: (chuckled) Yeah, you did leave me behind.

Rajveer: (Rubbed the back of his neck) Huh... I'm sorry. By the way, how did you contact Rohan? Even I couldn't recall him in emergency.

Soniya: You should never underestimate my stalking skills. Kidding. I went through your IG profile to contact your friends. Luckily, you had a lawyer one. You know the rest.

Rajveer: You are wonderful. I really owe you.

Soniya eyes softened for a bit. Rajveer noticed the swift in her eyes.

Rajveer: But Soniya, you really need to understand, I love Nava.

Soniya: I really wish someone loved me with the same passion. Nava is lucky. But don't you think the age gap between you two and her orthodox family would be an issue for you in the future?

Rajveer: Love just happens without any prior indications and at unexpected time. One just doesn't have any control over it. Soniya, honestly me and Nava never thought about our age gap, we just felt as one since the first day. I know the situation has worsened now, but I will try my best to convince her father whatever it takes, whichever means possible.

Soniya :(clearly smitten by Rajveer's passion) All the best dear, I am even ready to help you out whenever and however I can.

Rajveer: I really appreciate it. I am lucky to have found a friend like you. Are you always this generous for everyone around you?

Soniya: Friend? As of now, it's okay I guess. But I am not a saint Raj, you know my feelings towards you. I don't do this for just anyone.

Rajveer: (Blushed slightly) You can count on me too.

Soniya: I am.

Rajveer: Can we go and visit Dhruv in the hospital? I am worried about him. I will never forgive him, but I am the reason he is in the hospital.

Soniya: You are kind. I would not even bother to forgive him either. He used me to break your relationship, and then pushed me on that tree. I just hate him. but I will come with you on humanitarian grounds.

Rajveer: Let me see the stitches on your head.

Rajveer gaze shifted to the stiches on her forehead. He examined her with concern.

Rajveer: Does it still hurt? Are the stiches intact?

Soniya: It does a little.

Rajveer (Playfully): You look hot with those stiches!

Soniya: Oh.I wasn't Hot before?

They both share a hearty laugh, which lightens their mood a bit. Soniya grabbed Ranveer's arm and led him towards her car, and both raced towards the hospital.

Dhruv layed on the hospital bed, clearly wincing in pain. He ribs ached with every breath.

"Dhruv, how are you feeling?" Soniya asked, her voice laced with concern. She sat on the edge of his bed.

Dhruv winced slightly as he shifted, a grimace twisting his face. "Better," he mumbled, avoiding eye contact with Rajveer. The man stood by the window, his back to them. He was still a little shaken, the memory of Rajveer's sudden, furious attack fresh in his mind.

Rajveer turned, his expression unreadable. "You gave us quite a scare," he said, a hint of something that might have been amusement in his voice.

Dhruv flinched again, pulling his arm closer to his body.

"Just... a misunderstanding," Dhruv stammered, his eyes darting between Soniya and Rajveer. He didn't want to elaborate, not with Rajveer standing there, radiating an unpredictable energy.

Soniya frowned. "A misunderstanding that landed you in the hospital, Dhruv! You should not have pushed me.

"Yeah, well..." Dhruv trailed off, clearly uncomfortable. He just wanted this conversation to be over.

Rajveer stepped closer. "Dhruv, I need Nava's address."

Dhruv's eyes widened slightly. He hesitated, his gaze flickering nervously towards Rajveer. He knew Rajveer's temper, and he didn't want to be involved in whatever he was planning. "I... I don't know it," he lied, the words catching in his throat.

Rajveer's jaw tightened. He didn't say anything for a moment, just stared at Dhruv with an intensity that made the younger man shrink back against the pillows.

Soniya placed a hand on Rajveer's arm. "Rajveer, please," she said softly. "Can't this wait? Dhruv's just been through a lot."

Rajveer ignored her. "Dhruv," he repeated, his voice low and dangerous. "Nava's address. Now."

Dhruv swallowed hard. He knew he couldn't lie to Rajveer, not when he looked like that. He was scared –

genuinely scared – of what Rajveer might do. "It's...Near the park" He finally whispered, "Number 27".

Rajveer nodded curtly. "Thanks, Dhruv. Get well soon. Stay away from Nava and Soniya." He turned towards Soniya. "We have to go."

Soniya looked from Rajveer to Dhruv, her face etched with worry. "Rajveer, wait-"

He cut her off. "We will be back later," he said, and with that, they were gone.

As Rajveer and Soniya stood outside Nava's house, the air was thick with anticipation and apprehension. The intensity was palpable, like a living, breathing entity that wrapped itself around them, squeezing tight.

Rajveer's heart raced like a jackhammer, his palms growing sweaty as he hesitated. His fingers hovering over the doorbell. He was scared, unsure of what lay ahead, and the thought of meeting Mr. Arash again made his stomach twist into knots. The possibilities swirled in his mind like a maelstrom, making his anxiety spike.

Soniya, sensing his unease, placed a reassuring hand on his arm, her eyes locked on his, offering a silent message of encouragement. But even her calm demeanour couldn't dispel the sense of foreboding that hung over them like a dark cloud.

The silence between them was oppressive, punctuated only by the sound of Rajveer's ragged breathing and the distant hum of the city. It was as if time itself had slowed, stretching out the moments into an eternity of suspense.

As they stood there, frozen in anticipation, the door seemed to loom before them like a monolith, its surface etched with the promise of unknown consequences. Would they be welcomed, or would they be met with hostility? The uncertainty hung in the air, a challenge waiting to be met.

Without hesitation, Soniya pressed the doorbell for Rajveer.

The door swung to reveal Mr. Arash. He was a man in forties, his eyes sharp and unyielding. He was kind of a man who saw through people. He didnt notice before but Nava has his eyes. His gaze flickered over Rajveer before settling on Soniya.

Mr. Arash :(Gruffly) Yes? What do you want?

Soniya: (Stepped forward) We need to speak with Nava. It's important.

Mr. Arash :(Scoffed) She's not seeing anyone.

Rajveer: (Pleaded) Please, sir. I need to explain. I didn't mean to cause any trouble.

The man looked at Rajveer, his eyes narrowed. He hesitated before stepping aside.

Mr. Arash: (Warned)Don't make this any harder than it already is.

Rajveer and Soniya exchanged a hopeful glance and entered the house.

The living room was suffocating.

Rajveer, Nava, and Soniya sat uneasily as Nava's father stood before them. His presence menacing.

Mr. Arash: (Looked at Rajveer) You attacked Dhruv. There's no excuse for violence.

Rajveer: Sir, it wasn't like that. Dhruv started it. He attacked me first.

Nava's father scoffed.

Soniya: Sir, please listen to Rajveer. Dhruv was the one who hit him first. He was being so aggressive. I tried to stop him, but he pushed me too. Look at the stiches on my head! That's when Rajveer...

Mr. Arash: (Interrupted) Enough, Soniya. Stop taking his side.

Nava: (Frustrated) Dad, maybe Soniya is right. You're not even letting him explain.

Mr. Arash: (Sternly) Nava, you're grounded. No contact with Rajveer. I won't tolerate any kind of violence associated with my daughter.

Nava: (Angry) But Dad...

Mr. Arash: (Cutting her off) No buts! I will keep Dhruv away from you, but you are forbidden from seeing Rajveer.

Rajveer: (Calmly) Sir, I understand your concern. I don't want to cause any more trouble for Nava.

Soniya reached out and gave Rajveer's hand a reassuring squeeze.

Mr. Arash: (Spotted the gesture) Get out! Both of you!

Rajveer and Soniya exchanged a look. Her father was furious, there was nothing left to say without igniting his anger. They stood and walked towards the door. Soniya continued to hold Rajveer's hand as they left.

CHAPTER 9:
A CAGE OF SILENCE.

Rajveer sat by the window, watched the city lights blur into an indistinguishable haze. Each flicker of neon seemed to mock his own fading hope. Nava. The name echoed in the hollow chambers of his heart, a constant, agonizing refrain. Her father, a man of iron will and ancient prejudices, had erected an insurmountable wall between them.

The silence was deafening. No whispered messages on the wind, no furtive glances across crowded streets, no stolen moments of joy. Just the suffocating weight of forbidden love, a constant ache in his chest.

Soniya watched Rajveer from the doorway of his suite, his shoulders slumped, a desolate figure against the plush velvet sofa. She'd witnessed the cruel, shrewish behaviour of Mr. Arash, the man who had so callously shattered Rajveer's world. His pain was palpable, a raw, open wound.

Soniya knew, with a certainty that defied logic, that Rajveer needed her. He was irresistible, his raw vulnerability a potent aphrodisiac. Desire, fierce and untamed, ignited within her. She moved towards him, her fingers tracing the lines of his face, her touch featherlight. She trailed her hands down his broad chest, across his taut abdomen, feeling the ripple of muscles beneath.

Soniya wanted him, desperately. She pressed her body against his, feeling the heat radiating from him, the scent of his cologne intoxicating. But Rajveer remained motionless, a statue carved from grief. His heart, shattered and broken, was a million miles away, lost in the memory of Nava.

Soniya, despite her best efforts, couldn't penetrate the wall of despair that surrounded him. Her seductive advances were met with an icy indifference, her touch eliciting no response. Rajveer's body, though physically present, was utterly detached, a vessel adrift in a sea of sorrow.

After gaining consciousness of the reality, he pulled Soniya into a tight embrace, his arms wrapped around her waist, his fingers pressing against the back of her head, tucking into his shoulder. Tears streamed down his face, which he didn't want her to see. Soniya finally understood his body language, she was felt guilty for her sensual advances towards him, and hugged him back with sympathy. She wanted Rajveer to be okay, she was ready to offer her unconditional support to him. She wanted him, but all she could do right now was just to be with him. She knew Rajveer had a flight to catch tomorrow. She kissed his cheek, and grabbed his hand, directing him to the sofa. She coaxed his head on her thighs, played with his hair gently, and emotionally leaving him alone in his grief. Rajveer rested without saying a word.

Next day, Rajveer boarded his flight back home.

Days bled into weeks, weeks into months. Each passing moment was a cruel reminder of the life they could have had, the laughter they could have shared, the dreams they could have built together. He imagined her face, her smile, the way her eyes would light up when she saw him. Now, those images were poisoned by the bitter taste of despair. He tried to distract himself, to bury himself in work, in friends, in the gym, in boxing, and in the mundane routines of life. But the silence was relentless, a persistent whisper of what he had lost. Every joyous sound, every shared laughter, was a fresh wound, a stark reminder of the happiness stolen from him.

The thought of Nava, trapped and suffocated by her father's tyranny, gnawed at him. Was she happy? Was she even alright? Did she ever think of him? These questions, unanswered and unanswerable, tormented him.

He felt like a bird with clipped wings, yearning for flight, for freedom, for the sky. But the cage of his despair was too strong, its bars too unforgiving. He was trapped, a prisoner of his own longing, with no escape in sight.

This misery, this agonizing limbo, was a constant suffocating presence in his life. It threatened to consume him, to extinguish the flickering embers of his joy. And in the face of this unending torment, Rajveer felt utterly helpless, adrift in a sea of despair.

CHAPTER 10:
THE END OF AGONIZING UNCERTAINTY.

Six months later

The phone line crackled, a familiar static buzzed through the air, and then, her voice. It was softer than he remembered, laced with a tremor that mirrored the one in his own chest. "Rajveer?"

The name, spoken after so long, felt both foreign and achingly familiar. Six months. Six months of silence, of unanswered calls, of letters returned to sender. Six months of imagining her voice, the timbre, the inflections, the way she'd always pronounce his name with a hint of a smile.

"Nava," he breathed, the word catching in his throat. He wanted to rush into the silence, to fill it with the words he'd been hoarding, the questions he'd been dying to ask. But all that came out was a strangled whisper.

He heard a sniffle on the other end of the line. "I missed you," she said, the words barely audible.

And in that moment, all the pain, the longing, the agonizing uncertainty - it all washed away. There was only her voice, fragile and real, and the overwhelming joy of hearing it again. The world, with its cruelties and its distance, seemed to shrink away, leaving only the two of them, connected by this fragile thread of sound.

He wanted to tell her everything—about the sleepless nights, the phantom touches, the way her laughter still echoed in the empty rooms of his heart. But words seemed inadequate, clumsy attempts to capture the depth of his emotions.

"I missed you too," he finally managed, his voice thick with unshed tears. And in that shared silence, a thousand unspoken words passed between them. A silent apology, a whispered promise, a desperate plea to never let go again.

The line crackled again, a reminder of the distance that still separated them. But for that precious moment, it didn't matter. They were together, their souls entwined in the fragile magic of a phone call, healing the wounds of silence and rekindling the embers of a love that had never truly died.

Rajveer: (Voice trembled) Nava, how? How did your dad even let you call me?

Nava: (Voice cracked) I don't know, Rajveer. I've been trying so hard these past six months. I've been the good girl. I helped around the house, studied hard, never went out late... I just wanted to earn back their trust.

Rajveer: (Tears welled up) Nava, I missed you so much. Every day feels like an eternity.

Nava: (Sniffling) I know, Rajveer. I missed you too. More than words can say. But you have to understand. My family... they've never had to deal with the police. They don't believe in violence. You... your image in their eyes... it's not good, Rajveer. They see you as a troublemaker.

Rajveer: (Voice thick with emotion) I know, Nava. I know, I haven't been the best. But I'm willing to change. I'll do anything. I'll prove to them that I'm not the person they think I am. I'll prove to them that I can be a good man, a good son-in-law.

Nava: (Hopeful) Really, Rajveer? You'll do anything?

Rajveer: Anything. Show them I'm responsible, I'm mature. I'll show them I can take care of you.

Nava: (Tears streamed down her face) I know you will, Rajveer. I believe in you. But please, be patient. It's going to take time.

Rajveer: I'll wait, Nava. I'll wait as long as it takes. Just promise me you'll keep talking to me.

Nava: I promise. I love you, Rajveer.

Rajveer: I love you too, Nava. More than anything.

Rajveer sat slumped on his couch, the phone still clutched in his hand, the warmth of Nava's voice lingering like a phantom. Six months. Six agonizing months of silence, of unanswered calls, of unanswered texts. Six months of wondering, of doubting, of fearing he'd lost her forever. And now, finally, her voice, a melody that had been missing from his soul, had filled his ears, a symphony of joy and relief washing over him.

But the joy was bittersweet. He remembered the disappointment in Nava's voice when she spoke of her parents' disapproval, the hurt in her eyes when she confessed their doubts about him. He knew he had to do something, had to prove them wrong. He had to change their perception, to show them the man Nava saw, the man who loved her fiercely, who would cherish her forever.

A determined glint entered his eyes. He would work harder, he would build a better future, he would become the man they wanted him to be. He would show them he was worthy of their daughter's love, worthy of a place in their family. He would fight for Nava, for their love, with every fiber of his being.

He knew it wouldn't be easy. It would require sacrifices, it would demand patience, and it would test his resolve. But the thought of losing Nava again, of seeing that flicker of doubt in her eyes, was unbearable. He would do whatever it took. He would rise above their expectations, he would exceed their wildest dreams, and he would earn their respect, their acceptance, and their blessings.

He stood up, a newfound resolve surging through him. He wouldn't just win back Nava's love; he would win over her parents too. He would show them that love—true love—conquers all.

CHAPTER 11:
"THE PURSUIT OF APPROVAL"

Rajveer took the leap of faith and resigned from his comfortable position in Pune. He knew for sure, that if he had to win her parent's approval, he had to get out of his comfort zone. He tried to convince his own family about moving to Bhuvaneswar and getting a job there.

Initially, he faced resistance. They were concerned about his career and financial stability. However, he managed to convince them with his unwavering determination and passion for pursuing his love for Nava. His mother understood that gaining her parents approval won't be an easy task, but she knew how much he loved her. His mother gave him her blessings. His siblings helped him pack and spent some quality time with him, as they were not sure when would they meet their elder brother again.

He embarked on a new chapter by moving to Bhubaneswar—a city unknown to him. Rajveer gathered his courage and mental strength, knocked at Nava's door, ready to meet her father once again.

He came face-to-face with Mr. Arash. Who was surprised upon seeing Rajveer. Initially sceptical, he left the door open, gesturing him to come inside.

Mr. Arash: Rajveer, please sit down. I wasn't expecting you.

Rajveer clasped his hands tightly as he sat before her father.

Rajveer: Uncle, I know I hurt you and Nava deeply. I'm ashamed of my past actions.

Mr. Arash: You left a trail of broken trust and shattered peace in our lives. Do you think a few words can mend that?

Rajveer: I don't expect forgiveness easily, Uncle. But I've been working on myself these past months. I even sought professional help to address my anger issues and understand the impact of my violence.

Mr. Arash: (Scoffed) Therapy? You think a few sessions can erase destructive behaviour in the future completely?

Rajveer: It's not a quick fix, Uncle. It's a continuous journey. I'm learning to manage my emotions, communicate constructively, and respect boundaries. I've also found a stable job.

Mr. Arash: (Sighed) Rajveer, I've seen your aggression, the effects of it. After listening to Nava and Soniya... I understand it's not your fault.

Surprised, Rajveer looked up.

Nava tried her best to explain the story behind the incident. Dhruv, whom I used to trust was playing games between you two. Soniya visited me after you went back to Pune— she told me everything. Look Rajveer, I don't like violence. But I understand now— you weren't fighting for yourself. You fought for my daughter. I know you are a boxer. Nava told me. I can see, you came unscathed in the fight. Violence is not the solution for everything. One day, you might encounter people who are stronger than you, someone who won't stop until you're broken. I don't want that kind of life for my daughter. Nava deserves someone who can offer her stability, security, and peaceful life. Can you honestly say you're that person now?

Rajveer paused, then continues in assuring voice.

Rajveer: I can't undo the past, Uncle. But I can build a better future. I'm committed to being the man Nava deserves—the man I want to be. I'll spend the rest of my life working harder, by providing stability and security to her. I can assure you, uncle, I never used my boxing skills for my benefit outside the ring, not until that day. Before I fought Dhruv, I warned him. I even confronted him, telling him to stop playing games with Nava's life. But he got obsessed, even when Nava wasn't interest in him. It made him aggressive and then you know the rest.

Mr. Arash: (Looked at Rajveer intently) I know Nava still cares for you. Despite everything, she won't let go. I won't deny her that chance, but I won't turn a blind eye either. I'll be watching your every step, Rajveer. This is your last chance.

Rajveer exhaled, relief washing over him.

Rajveer: Thank you very much Sir!

Rajveer secures a modest yet comfortable living space near Navas society, a crucial step in his plan to be close to her.

He actively sought employment opportunities in Bhuvaneswar, facing challenges and setbacks along the way. He finally got a job as a software developer in a private company, though the salary was little less compared to what he earned in Pune. He joined a local boxing club, channelling his energy and frustrations into rigorous training. This not only helped him stay physically fit but also instills a sense of discipline and focus.

Rajveer enrolled in snger management classes and attended workshops to learn healthy coping mechanisms and demonstrate his willingness to change.

He consistently met Nava at the park, but she maintained a firm stance on their physical relationship until her parents' approval.

Rajveer continued his relentless pursuit for Mr. Arash's approval. He tried engaging in conversations, offered help, and demonstrateed his genuine concern for the well-being of the family. Despite her father's indifference, Nava is deeply impressed by Rajveer's dedication. She saw his relentless hard work in Bhuvaneswar, and his genuine efforts to improve their lives. Six months had passed since Rajveer's last conversation with Mr. Arash.

Though he outwardly ignored Rajveer, he subtly observed his actions, noticed his helpful nature and commitment to the cause, and his consistent presence in their lives.

One Year Later

After a year of dedicated effort, Rajveer has successfully established himself in Bhuvaneswar. While Mr. Arash's approval remains elusive, his unwavering commitment and genuine character have significantly impacted Nava and her family.

One evening, her father invited Rajveer over for lunch.

Mr. Arash entered the living room, a thoughtful expression on his face. Rajveer, seated on the sofa, looked a bit nervous.

Mr. Arash: Rajveer, I've been observing you for the past year. You're a hardworking young man, always willing to help others. You've shown tremendous character and responsibility.

Rajveer: (Smiled) Thank you, sir. It means a lot to me that you've noticed.

Mr. Arash: I've also noticed how much you mean to Nava. You've been a positive influence on her. That's why I was allowed her to meet you at the park every day. It's given her a sense of joy and purpose.

Nava: (Beamed) Papa!

Mr. Arash: (Smiled at Nava) I know, I know. I've seen the change in you.

(He pauses, then turns to Rajveer with a serious look.)

Mr. Arash: Rajveer, I want to be honest with you. I've been concerned about your relationship with Nava. But seeing you now, I understand that my concerns were unfounded.

Rajveer: (Relieved) Sir, I understand your concern. I value your trust and respect for Nava.

Mr. Arash: What are your intentions, Rajveer?

Rajveer: (Looked at Nava, then back at her father) Sir, I love Nava very much. She's the most important person in my life. I would be honoured to marry her, if you would give us your blessings.

Mr. Arash: (Smiled warmly) Rajveer, I can see the love you have for Nava. It's genuine and pure.

(He turned to Nava, who is overjoyed.)

Mr. Arash: Nava, you've found a good man. I'm happy for you both.

Nava: (Hugged her father tightly) Thank you, Papa! Thank you so much!

Mr. Arash: I am going for a business trip to Manali for two months. Once I am back, I would like to invite your family to Bhuvaneswar. Let's discuss the marriage. I want to see this union happen soon.

Rajveer: (Thrilled) Sir, that would be an honour. We would be delighted to come.

Nava: (Jumped up and down) Oh, Papa! This is amazing!

Rajveer and Nava embraced, their joy overflowing. Their happiness knows no bounds.

The next morning, Mr. Arash leaves for Manali. Before boarding, he requested Rajveer to take of his family in his absence. Rajveer said it would be an honour. He watched his future father-in-law disappear into the airport.

That evening, Rajveer and Nava went to Rajveer's house, which Nava had already transformed into a home with some cute decorations and paintings. They decide it's time to call his family to share the good news. He initiates the video call.

Rajveer: (Beamed) Guys, you won't believe this!

Nava: (Eyes wide) Spill the beans!

Rajveer: My father-in-law... I mean, Mr. Arash, he gave us his blessings.

Shubhangi: (Excited) Oh my God! Did he say yes?

Rajveer: Yes! He said he's so happy for us and he wants us to come to Bhuvaneswar in two months from now.

Anya: (Clapped) That's amazing!

Reyansh: Wow, this is happening!

Nava: (Blushed) I can't believe it!

Rajveer: He left for a business trip to Manali for a few weeks. So, we have plenty of time to plan everything.

Shubhangi: This is the best news ever! We're going to have the best wedding!

Anya: We need to start planning right away! Decorations, food, music...

Nava: (Laughed) We'll need a huge one!

Rajveer: I'm so happy, Nava. This is a dream come true.

Nava: Me too, Rajveer. I can't wait to spend the rest of my life with you.

Shubhangi: (Teased) You two are so cheesy!

Anya: But in a good way!

Reyansh: Let the wedding plan begin!

Rajveer: I can't wait to see you all in two months.

Nava: I can't wait either!

All: Cheers!

The video call ends.

The air crackled with unspoken words as Nava and Rajveer stood face to face. Their hands reaching out, fingers tracing the contours of each other's faces, memorizing every line, every scar, every freckle etched by time and hardship. Two years. Two years of longing, of whispered promises across states, of yearning for this touch, this embrace, and this release.

Rajveer cupped Nava's face, his thumb gently brushing away a stray tear that escaped her eyes. "My love," he breathed, his voice husky with emotion. "You are more beautiful than I ever imagined."

Nava smiled, a watery, shimmering thing, and leaned into his touch, burying her face in the crook of his neck, inhaling the scent of him—woodsmoke and something uniquely Rajveer, a blend of spice and sunshine. "You too," she murmured, "More than I ever dreamed."

He pulled her close, their bodies fitting together like pieces of a long-lost puzzle. The years of separation, the agonizing distance, the endless nights spent gazing at the moon, all melted away in this moment. There was only now, only them.

His lips met hers, a tentative touch at first, then a desperate claim, a hunger that had been building for years. Nava responded with equal fervour, her hands tangling in his hair, pulling him closer, deeper. They explored each other with a reverence born of longing, every touch a revelation, every kiss a promise.

They moved, their bodies a symphony of movement, a dance of passion and longing. The bed beneath them seemed to melt away, leaving them suspended in a world of sensation. Laughter mingled with sighs, whispers with moans, as they surrendered to the raw, primal joy of being together.

In those stolen moments, they found solace, found release, found a love that had endured the test of time and distance—a love that was now stronger, more profound, more beautiful than ever before.

CHAPTER 12:
A MONTH OF BLOSSOMING BONDS.

Rajveer's integration into the Navas household was seamless. He quickly became a fixture, his presence warmly welcomed by all except Mina—Nava's mother—who initially harboured reservations about an inter-caste marriage.

Daria, the elder sister, formed a strong bond with Rajveer, finding a confidante and a friend in him.

Rajveer, in turn, cherished his time with the family. He seamlessly blended into their daily lives, taking on household chores with ease – from maintaining the garden, watering the plants, and assisting with grocery shopping. He often treated them to dinners and breakfasts, creating cherished memories together.

Mr. Arash, who had entrusted Rajveer with the care of his family during his month-long absence, felt a profound sense of gratitude when he used to call. He had told by Daria how Rajveer had not only fulfilled his duties, but also brought joy and warmth to their lives.

While Mina's initial scepticism lingered, she couldn't deny the positive impact Rajveer had on her family. She watched as her daughter's happiness bloomed, and the warmth that radiated from Rajveer's presence slowly melting away her reservations.

The month passed in a whirlwind of happiness and contentment. Rajveer had found a home away from home in the Nava's household, and the Nava's family had found a cherished member in him. As the month drew to a close, the seeds of love had been sown, and the future promised a blossoming relationship for Rajveer and Nava.

CHAPTER 13:
THE BEGINNING OF THE END.

Mr. Arash, after a month-long trip to Manali, fell seriously ill. He was admitted to the Kullu Valley Hospital where he was initially diagnosed with liver cirrhosis. The disease took a significant toll on him, and after a month of battling the illness, his elder brother stepped forward as a living donor, and the liver transplant surgery was scheduled. The surgery was a challenging ordeal, both physically and emotionally.

The extended hospitalization period placed a tremendous strain on Arash's family. His wife, Mina, was emotionally and physically drained by the constant worry and the demands of caring for their two daughters, Daria and Nava. The financial burden of the medical expenses was immense, adding to the family's existing stress.

During this difficult time, Rajveer visited Arash in Manali to offer support. However, due to his professional commitments, he had to return to Bhuvaneswar, promising the family he would return as soon as possible. Tragically, shortly after Rajveer's departure, Arash slipped into a coma.

Nava calls Rajveer,

Nava (Cried): Rajveer... I... I don't know what to do... Papa... Papa is still unconscious...

Rajveer: Nava, what happened? What's wrong? Are you okay?

Nava (Sobbed): The operation... it didn't go as planned. He... he's in a coma, Rajveer. The doctors... they don't know when he'll wake up.

Rajveer: Oh no, Nava. I'm so sorry. I can't imagine how you must be feeling.

Nava: It's been two months, Rajveer. Two months in the hospital. And the bills... they're piling up. We need so much money... I don't know what to do.

Rajveer: Nava, listen to me. I'm coming back as soon as I can. I'll figure something out. I'll get you some money.

Nava: But Rajveer... what if... what if he doesn't wake up?

Rajveer: Nava, don't say that. Don't even think that. Your father is strong. He'll fight through this. You need to be strong too.

Nava: (sniffled) I'm scared, Rajveer. I'm so scared.

Rajveer: I know, I know. But you have to be strong for him. He needs your strength.

Nava: You'll come back soon, right?

Rajveer: I promise. I'll be there as soon as I can. I'll make sure everything will be alright.

Nava: You promise?

Rajveer: I promise, Nava. I promise you with all my heart that I'll do everything I can to make sure your father gets better.

Nava: You know we are staying at a small house in Manali near to the hospital rite.

Rajveer: Yes baby.

Nava: Thank you, Rajveer. Thank you for being there for me.

Rajveer: Always, Nava. Always.

After that call, Nava sat by the window. It was cold and chilly, but she barley nioticed. Its been months now, she, Daria and her mother were taking turns to be with her father in the hospital. They had drained all their savings and had to stop the school they ran in Bhuvaneswar, renting it out. They still needed around 30 lakhs to pay for the surgery and was uncertain is to when her father would gain conscious. While thinking about the situation, Nava got a call from her mother, asking her to come to hospital. She wore her leather jacket and started walking towards the hospital.

Inside the dimly lit room, Mina and Mrs. Amani— a wealthy Iranian women and a longtime friend of Nava's father— sat beside Arash's unconscious form.

Mrs. Amani: (Sympathetically) Mina, I know this is not the time for such things, but we came a long way, and I wanted to express our gratitude. We are so grateful for Arash, for his bravery. We want to help in any way we can.

Mina: (Hesitanted) Thank you, Mrs. Amani. It is very kind of you.

Mrs. Amani: Please, call me Amani, and don't worry about the expenses. Consider it settled. Thrity lakhs should be enough for now, but if more is needed, don't hesitate to ask.

Just then, Nava received a notification from bank. A deposit of ₹100,000 from Rajveer. Her breath hitched and a text message followed: "On the next flight. Can't wait to see you."

Nava smiled brightly.

Mina: (Looked at Amani) Amani, it's very generous of you, but...

Amani: (Insisted) Please, Mina. Consider it our way of showing our appreciation. Arash is family.

Mina, seeing no other option, finally nods in agreement.

Mina: (To Nava) Beta, go get us some coffee.

Nava: (Excitedly) Sure, Ma.

(Nava left the room. As soon as she's gone the atmosphere in the room shifted...)

Amani: Mina, I know this is not the right time, but I wanted to discuss something important.

Mina: (Nervously) Yes, Amani?

Amani: We would be honoured if you would consider our son, Ali, for Nava. He is a wonderful young man, kind, and successful. He would take good care of Nava. And in Iran, she would have the best life.

Mina: (Surprised) Amani, this is... unexpected.

Amani: I understand. But please consider it. Nava deserves happiness.

Mina: (Sighed) Amani, to be honest, Mr. Arash had already given his word to Rajveer, her boyfriend.

Amani: Rajveer?

Mina: Yes. He's a good boy, but... different background. I wasn't entirely comfortable with it. But they are in love, and Rajveer worked very hard to win her father's approval.

Amani: I see. But Arash needs your support now. And I know Ali would make Nava very happy.

Mina: (Looked down) I know. I will... I will talk to Nava. I give you, my word.

Outside the door, Nava stood frozen. Unable to hide her shock, the coffee tray slipped from her hands. Before she could process it, Daria enters the hallway and spotted her sister's ashen face.

Daria: What happened?

Without responding, Nava walked past her, numb, straight into the hospital room. Mrs. Amani walked outside, clutching her phone to her ear, already on call with her family.

Nava sat beside her father, the pain of her father being in coma, and the disbelief and shock her mother gave her, she was torn apart. She wished her father was well, holding his hands and rested her forehead against it. Mina tried to console Nava, but Nava pushes her away gently, ignoring her mother. Mina tells Daria everything. Daria swallowed hard. She liked Rajveer—respected him. He did everything for their family. Now Nava was expected to sacrifice him? She wanted to console her sister, fight for her love. But the financial situation they were in— she caved. Daria was unhappy that Nava had to sacrifice her love, she gave Nava her space. It was their mother's decision, everything would depend on Nava now.

It was Daria's turns to stay with her father. Mina and Nava walked towards the hospital exit in silence. Nava still ignoring her mother. When they arrived, Mina, collapsed onto the bed, exhausted. Guilt gnawed at her, their financial problem was solved, but at what cost? She prayed God for her happiness. Meanwhile, Nava lay awake in the dark, staring at the ceiling. Her body was exhausted, but she couldn't put her mind to rest. She turned sideways, trying to ease her ache in her heart. Tears welled uncontrobally, she tried to force them back. What would happen now?

CHAPTER 14:
THE LAST NAIL IN THE COFFIN

Next morning, Mina sat with Nava at the breakfast table. The aroma of food lingered in the air. Mina noticed Nava was troubled.

Mina: (Smiled) Come on, Nava, finish your breakfast. It's getting cold.

Nava: (Distracted) I'm not hungry, ma.

Mina: (Concerned) What's wrong, beta? You seem upset.

Nava: (Sighed) It's just... Ali Amani...

Mina: (Beamed) He's a wonderful boy, Nava. Rich, handsome, from a respectable family.

Nava: I know, Maman. But... I don't love him.

Mina: (Sighed) This is not about love, Nava. It's about your future. Ali can give you a life of comfort, security.

Nava: (Frustrated) But what about my happiness? I love Rajveer.

Mina: (Scoffed) Rajveer? What can he offer you?

Nava: (Pulled out her phone) He just transferred one lakh rupees to my account yesterday. See? He's trying, ma. He's working hard.

Mina: (Dismissed) One lakh rupee is not enough, Nava. This is not a game of petty cash.

Nava: We can sell the school in Bhubaneswar.

Mina: (Aghast) The school? That's our only stable income!

Nava: Then what? You want me to sacrifice my happiness for money?

Mina: (Voice rising) This is not about sacrificing anything! It's about securing your future, Nava! I have already given my consent to Ali.

Nava: (Furious) You're trading me like a commodity!

Mina: (Hurt) Don't talk to me like that, Nava.

Nava: You're being manipulative, maman. You're trying to force me into something I don't want. Why don't you offer Daria to Ali? She's single.

Mina: (Angrily) Don't you dare compare yourself to your sister!

Nava: (Tears welled up) I won't marry Ali! I will not sacrifice my love for Rajveer!

Mina: (Voice trembled) You have no other choice, Nava.

Nava: (Yelled) I will find a way! I will not let you ruin my life!

Mina: (Tears streamied down her face) I don't know what else to do, Nava.

Nava bursts into tears. Rajveer, who has been standing at the door, unnoticed, hears the entire conversation. He stands there, stunned and heartbroken.

Present

Rajveer had a whirlwind of emotions, a tempestuous sea of despair churning within him. He'd overheard the chilling truth: Nava, his love, was to be sacrificed on the altar for her family's financial ruin. Mina, her mother, had made a pact with a wealthy stranger, a gilded cage awaiting Nava in exchange for the lifeline her family desperately needed.

The news hit him like a physical blow. He stumbled, dazed and reeling, seeking solace in the nicotine haze of a nearby pan shop. The cigarettes, once a casual indulgence, became a lifeline, a desperate attempt to numb the searing pain in his chest. He smoked incessantly, the acrid smoke mirroring the turmoil within him.

Rajveer was determined to save Nava. He vowed to find a way, to somehow amass the astronomical sum demanded by the situation. He called his mother, his voice thick with desperation, pouring out the tragic tale. Shubhangi, his mother, offered what support she could, a generous sum of 5 lakhs, a testament to her love for her son.

Rajveer, however, needed a miracle. He contacted his friends, pleading for help, even offering to sell his beloved bike. He explored every avenue, exhausting his bank accounts, seeking loans, but the numbers were insurmountable. His salary, though decent, was a mere trickle compared to the ocean of debt drowning Nava's family.

Eleven lakhs. A paltry sum compared to the staggering amount needed. Despair threatened to engulf him. He felt utterly powerless, a helpless observer in the tragedy unfolding before him. God, he thought bitterly, was testing him, pushing him to his limits.

The weight of the situation was crushing. Nava's mother, Mina, was a woman trapped, her choices dictated by the cruel hand of circumstance. Her husband lay in a coma, a silent sentinel of their shattered lives. The uncertainty of his recovery hung heavy in the air, a constant reminder of the precariousness of their existence. Rajveer, who had always considered Mr. Arash a second father, felt a deep ache for the family, for the man who had always treated him like his own.

Rajveer was lost in a sea of grief and frustration, his love for Nava a beacon in the encroaching darkness, a flame flickering precariously against the gale of despair. Rajveer decides to go inside the house and speak with Nava and her mother.

Rajveer: Aunty, I've managed to arrange eleven lakhs.

Mina (Tears welled up): Beta, I really, really appreciate your efforts. But we can't take your money. It's been arranged already.

Rajveer: I heard how it's been arranged. You had to kill our love for it. I'm not ready to give up on my true love.

Nava (Joined them, voice trembling): I can try borrowing money from somewhere. Call and tell Mrs. Amani a big no.

Mina (Emotional turmoil): (Looked at Nava, then at Rajveer) I... I love my husband. I feel guilty already, forcing you to sacrifice your love for my family. (Mina breaks down, sobbing uncontrollably)

As Rajveer witnessed Nava's mother breaking down, her body shaking with uncontrollable sobs, he felt a searing pain in his chest. It was as if his heart was being torn apart, unable to bear the sight of this strong, resilient woman reduced to tears.

Rajveer's eyes welled up with empathy, his vision blurring as he struggled to maintain his composure. He felt a lump form in his throat, making it hard to swallow. His instincts screamed at him to comfort her, to wrap his arms around her and assure her that everything would be okay.

But he knew he couldn't. Not now, not when the wounds still lingered. Instead, he steeled himself, his jaw clenched in determination. He knew what he had to do, no matter how difficult it was.

With a heavy heart, Rajveer made the decision to convince Nava to listen to her mother. He knew it was the only solution to their financial problems, the only way to secure their future. He remembered the promise he had made to Mr. Arash—to take care of his family in his absence.

As he stood there, witnessing Mina's distress, Rajveer's resolve hardened. He would do whatever it took to protect this family, to ensure their well-being. Even if it meant sacrificing his own happiness and his love, his pure unconditional love.

Rajveer: Aunty, please don't cry. I'll talk to Nava. I'll convince her.

With a deep breath, Rajveer steeled himself for the challenge ahead. He would convince Nava to listen to her mother, no matter how difficult the conversation would be. He would put aside his own feelings, and do what was best for this family.

Rajveer's love for Nava was a flame that burned bright and true, a beacon of devotion that guided him through the darkest of times. It was a love that asked for nothing in return, a love that was willing to sacrifice everything for the happiness and well-being of the one he adored.

As he stood before Nava, his heart heavy with the weight of his decision, Rajveer's love shone like a ray of sunlight, illuminating the path he knew he had to take. He knew that convincing Nava to marry Ali would be a bitter pill to swallow, but he also knew that it was the only way to ensure Arash's health and well-being.

With a deep breath, Rajveer began to speak, his words pouring out like a river of sacrifice. He told Nava of Arash's frail health, of the worry that lined his face, of the fear that gripped his heart. He told her of the promise he had made to Arash, to take care of his family, to ensure their happiness and well-being.

As he spoke, Rajveer's eyes locked onto Nava's, his gaze burning with an intensity that seemed to pierce her very soul. He could see the tears welling up in her eyes, the pain and the sorrow that threatened to consume her. But he also saw the love, the love that they shared, the love that had brought them to this moment.

With a gentle touch, Rajveer reached out and took Nava's hand, his fingers intertwining with hers in a gesture of love and sacrifice. He knew that this was the hardest thing he would ever have to do, but he also knew that it was the only way to ensure the happiness and well-being of the people he loved.

As he spoke, Rajveer's heart broke, shattered into a million pieces by the weight of his sacrifice. But even in the midst of his pain, he knew that he was doing the right thing, that he was putting the needs of others before his own.

And in that moment, Rajveer's love for Nava became even more pure, even more unconditional. He loved her not just for himself, but for the happiness and well-being of those around her. He loved her with a love that was willing to sacrifice everything, a love that would endure even in the face of adversity.

Mina (Looked at Rajveer with disbelief): I wish for a son-in-law like you. But I'm helpless.

(Mina kissed Rajveer's forehead) God bless you, beta. You are one of a kind.

(Mina left the house, giving Rajveer and Nava some privacy)

Rajveer: (Voice trembled) Nava, I know this is hard. I know you love me, and I love you more than anything. But look at your Maman. See how much she's suffering? She's blaming herself, thinking she's cursed.

Nava: (Tears streamed down her face) I can't see her like this either, Rajveer. I can't bear the guilt of seeing her break down. But...

Rajveer: (Interrupted) There's no "but," Nava. Your father's health is more important. We can't even arrange half the amount they're demanding. I promised you I'd get him better, and I will. I won't let anything stop me.

Nava: (Sobbed) But what about us?

Rajveer: (Held her close) We'll find a way. Maybe not now, maybe not soon. But we'll be together someday. I promise.

Nava: (Buried her face in his chest) I don't know how I'll live without you.

Nava's emotions were a turbulent storm, a whirlpool of feelings that threatened to consume her. As Rajveer's words washed over her, she felt like she was drowning in a sea of despair. The thought of marrying Ali, of spending the rest of her life with someone she didn't love, was a suffocating weight that crushed her chest.

She felt like she was being torn apart, her heart ripped into two conflicting desires. On one hand, she wanted to be with Rajveer, to spend forever with the man she loved. On the other hand, she knew that she couldn't ignore her father's health, couldn't turn her back on the man who had offered her everything.

As she looked into Rajveer's eyes, she saw the depth of his sacrifice, the magnitude of his love. He was willing to give up his own happiness, his own love, for the sake of her father's health. And in that moment, Nava felt a surge of awe and admiration for Rajveer. She was humbled by his selflessness, his willingness to put others before himself.

But even as she felt this sense of wonder, Nava's heart was breaking. She didn't want to marry Ali, didn't want to spend her life with someone she didn't love. She wanted to be with Rajveer, to feel his arms around her, to taste his lips on hers.

As the reality of her situation sank in, Nava felt a wave of resignation wash over her. She knew that she had no choice, that she had to sacrifice her own love for the sake of her father's health. And so, with a heavy heart, she nodded her agreement. She would marry Ali, would do what was expected of her, even though it meant giving up on her own dreams, her own desires.

As she looked at Rajveer, Nava felt a sense of sorrow, a sense of loss. She knew that she would never forget him, never forget the way he made her feel. And she knew that she would always be grateful for his sacrifice, for his willingness to put others before himself.

Rajveer: (Kissed her forehead) I'll be there for you, always.

Nava: (Looked up at him with tear-filled eyes) You're the best man I know, Rajveer. You're sacrificing everything for my family.

Rajveer: (Smiling sadly) You know I would do anything for you, Nava.

They share a long, lingering kiss, a silent promise of their love amidst the pain.

The room is dimly lit, the only sound the soft rain against the window. Nava lay on the bed, her body trembling. Rajveer moved towards her, his eyes filled with a mixture of love and despair. He traced the contours of her face, his fingers lingering on her tears.

Rajveer: (Whispered) I love you, Nava.

Nava: (Sobbed) I love you too, Rajveer.

He pulled her close, his body fitting perfectly against hers. They begin to move slowly, passionately, a desperate attempt to capture every moment. Their bodies ache with a longing that transcends mere physicality.

Tears streamed down their faces as they make love, each touch a bittersweet reminder of what they are losing. They cry for the love they shared, for the future that might never be, for the sacrifices they are forced to make.

The room is filled with the sounds of their sobs and the rhythmic movements of their bodies. They hold each other tightly, their souls intertwined in a final, desperate embrace.

As the intensity subsides, they lie spent, their bodies intertwined. Rajveer holds Nava close, his heart heavy with the weight of their unspoken sorrow. They know this might be their last time together, a final farewell whispered through the language of their bodies.

Rajveer and Nava arrived at the hospital, Arash lay unconscious, his face pale, and his body weak. Rajveer gave an assuring look towards Mina. Mina smiles back with guilt and small relief. Mina, Rajveer and Nava prayed for his health. Then, the door opened. Mrs Amani entered, Ali by her side. His presence reminded him, this is it. Rajveer exhaled slowly. This was his cue. His time with this family ahs come to an end. He walked towards the exit. Behind him, footsteps hurried. Arms wrapped around him from behind. His chest ached, but he forced himself to be strong. He turned to look at her, memorising every detail— her tear-filled eyes, her quivering lips, and the way she clung to him.

Rajveer: I will send you another lakh when I reach home.

She shook her head, but Rajveer silenced her. Tears welled up in his eyes, but he forced it back.

Rajveer: I'll always check on your father. And you... take care of yourself.

He hugged her tightly, carrying a piece of their remaining time. With tears blurring his vision, he pulled away and walked towards the exit. He did not look back.

Rajveer walked aimlessly in the streets, his body drained, and was emotionally exhausted. he walked towards a wine shop, gets a bottle of whiskey. By the time he reached railway station, half bottle was gone. Once in Bhuvaneswar, he called his boss and quits his job. He buys another bottle of whiskey, another night drowning in the misery. He lay motionless on the bed, doesn't remember when he passed out. The next day, his decision was made. He packed. He booked a flight, after making all the arrangements, he left. After one and half years later, he was home. He was glad to see his family. He hugged his mother, sister and brother, they were aware of the tragic end to his love story, but they were proud of him. He kept his promise to Nava and tried his best, by sacrificing his love for Nava's family.

He went to his room and crashed on his bed. He drank and drank, trying to numb his pain before it could reach him. Next day, he sold his bike, and transferred ₹100000 to Nava. Moments later, she replied with thank you love. Her father was still unconscious.

Rajveer's heart was a desolate wasteland, a barren expanse where the vibrant hues of love had been replaced by the dull greys of despair. The loss of Nava, the love of his life, had shattered him, leaving him adrift in a sea of sorrow. Grief, a relentless tide, threatened to drown him, pulling him deeper into the abyss of despair.

He sought solace in the bottle, its contents a temporary balm to his aching soul. The burning sensation of alcohol provided a fleeting escape from the icy grip of despair, numbing the pain that gnawed at his heart. Cigarettes, his constant companions, offered a similar respite, their smoke curling like tendrils of smoke, obscuring the harsh reality of his life.

His once vibrant spirit was now a flicker, extinguished by the weight of his grief. The joy of life had faded, replaced by a monotonous routine of self-destruction.

Days bled into nights, each marked by the same ritual of despair: the clinking of glasses, the acrid smell of smoke, and the gnawing emptiness in his stomach.

Eight months had passed since Nava's departure, and Rajveer remained a prisoner in his own room, a hermit in his own world. The world outside, with its vibrant colours and bustling life, seemed a distant dream, a reality he could no longer connect with.

News of Nava's marriage to Ali reached him. Each word a fresh stab to his wounded heart. The news of her father's recovery, a flicker of hope in the midst of his despair, was quickly overshadowed by the crushing weight of her new life, a life that no longer included him.

Nava, in an unexpected gesture, returned the two lakh rupees he had once entrusted to her. The money, a symbol of their shared past, now lay dormant in his bank account, a constant reminder of their lost love. Rajveer, in a moment of clarity, transferred one lakh to his mother, a small act of kindness amidst his self-destruction.

The remaining sum, however, remained untouched, a burden he carried with him. In a desperate attempt to escape the suffocating grip of his grief, Rajveer decided to embark on a solo trip to Tarkarli— a coastal town known for its serene beauty. He hoped that the vastness of the sea, the gentle caress of the waves, and the solitude of the shore would offer him a semblance of peace, a chance to rediscover himself.

As he packed his bags, a flicker of hope, a faint glimmer of light, emerged from the depths of his despair. The journey ahead was uncertain, but Rajveer clung to the belief that somewhere, beyond the horizon, lay a path to healing, a chance to rebuild his shattered life.

CHAPTER 15:
CHEERS TO THE NEW BEGINNINGS!!

Rajveer drove to Tarkarli.

Tarkarli, a hidden gem on the Konkan coast of Maharashtra, boasts pristine white sand beaches that stretch for miles. It's a haven of tranquillity, where the sound of waves crashing against the shore is the only music you need. Rajveer, seeking solace and a fresh start, had chosen Tarkarli for his solo detox mission. He rented a charming villa which belonged to his friend Parag, at a nominal price, right on the beach.

Days were spent getting lost in the rhythmic sounds of the waves, with the pristine clear water inviting him for a swim. He rediscovered the joy of simple pleasures - long runs along the beach, intense boxing sessions in the sand, and healthy, nourishing meals. He practiced yoga and meditation for his mental health and stability. He bid farewell to alcohol and cigarettes, this rejuvenating routine continued for a month, transforming both his body and mind.

One day, the allure of Tarkarli's vibrant marine life drew Rajveer towards the water sports centre. After a brief training session, he embarked on a thrilling scuba diving adventure. Descending into the underwater world, he marvelled at the kaleidoscope of colours – vibrant corals, schools of colourful fish darting through the water, and the gentle swaying of sea anemones.

He noticed another diver exploring the underwater landscape alongside him. They spent the next half-hour, seemingly oblivious to each other, captivated by the underwater wonders. As Rajveer surfaced, removed his mask, and caught his breath, his eyes met the other diver—a breathtakingly beautiful girl. Mesmerized by her beauty and the way her swimsuit accentuated her figure, he instinctively swam towards her.

"Wow," he exclaimed, "You're incredible! I've never seen someone so graceful underwater."

The girl blushed, a shy smile gracing her lips. "Thank you," she replied.

And just like that, a chance encounter in the depths of the ocean sparked a connection that neither of them could have anticipated.

Rajveer and the girl climbed back on the boat, which would take them back to the seashore.

Rajveer: (Smiled brightly) "That was incredible, wasn't it? I've never seen so many vibrant colours underwater."

Stranger: (Laughed) "I know, right? It felt like we were in a completely different world. I'm Nehal Mehra, by the way."

Rajveer: "Rajveer. Rajveer Rana. And it was a pleasure exploring that world with you, Nehal."

Nehal: "The pleasure was all mine, Rajveer. I'm still a bit awestruck."

Rajveer: "Me too. But if I'm being honest, I was a bit distracted by the most beautiful mermaid I've ever seen."

Nehal: (Blushed) "Oh, stop it. You're making me blush."

Rajveer: "I'm just being honest. You're stunning, Nehal. Inside and out."

Nehal: (Smiled shyly) "Thank you, Rajveer. That's very sweet of you to say."

Rajveer: "It's the truth. And I hope this isn't the last time we explore new worlds together."

Nehal: "I'd like that very much, Rajveer."

Rajveer and Nehal reached the seashore.

Rajveer: (Smiled) This white sand... it's so soft, it feels like walking on clouds. Almost as soft as your hands, I bet.

Nehal: (Giggled) Oh, you're quite the charmer, aren't you? And you think my hands are soft? You should feel my feet then.

Rajveer: (Winked) I'm sure they're as soft as the rest of you. The sunset is absolutely breathtaking.

Nehal: It is, isn't it? The sky is on fire. It reminds me of... well, you know.

Rajveer: (Chuckled) Me? On fire? I'm flattered. But seriously, this place is magical. I was thinking... maybe we could continue this conversation later?

Nehal: (Playfully) Oh? And how do you propose we do that?

Rajveer: I was hoping you'd join me for dinner at my villa. I have a little garden overlooking the sea, and I was thinking... candlelight, red wine, maybe some fresh fish...

Nehal: (Eyes widened) That sounds... incredibly tempting.

Rajveer: I'd be honoured if you'd say yes.

Nehal: (Smiled mischievously) I'm not sure I can resist such an offer.

Rajveer: (Grinned) I knew you wouldn't.

Nehal: (Leaned closer) But I have one condition.

Rajveer: (Intrigued) And what might that be?

Nehal: You have to keep an unlimited stock of red wine.

Rajveer: (Laughed) Deal. See you at eight?

Nehal: (Winked) I'm looking forward to it.

Rajveer: (Thrilled) I am too.

Rajveer ran to his villa to make the necessary arrangements for the date tonight. After getting the place cleaned in and out, he went to the market, bought a case of red wine, many candles, crystal glasses, silverware, a bouquet. and fish on his way back to his villa. He told his chef to prepare starters and the main course. He then went outside to the garden, set the table, then placed a table cloth, scented candles, and some decorative lighting which he had bought. He placed the wine glasses before heading inside his bedroom upstairs and took a shower.

Rajveer stood in front of the mirror, adjusting his cufflinks for what felt like the hundredth time. He was determined to make a lasting impression on Nehal.

He had chosen a sleek, black dress shirt that accentuated his broad shoulders and chiselled features. The fabric was smooth and luxurious, catching the light in a way that made it look like an expensive one.

His trousers were a perfect match, fitted to perfection and breaking just so at the ankles. He had paired them with a slim, black tie that added a touch of sophistication to his overall look.

On his feet, he wore a pair of polished, black shoes that gleamed in the light. They were sleek and modern, with a subtle brogue detailing that added a touch of elegance.

As he finished getting dressed, Rajveer couldn't help but feel a sense of confidence and anticipation. He knew that he looked good, his intense workout sessions and detoxification for weeks was showing up on his face with a glow. He was eager to see the look on Nehal's face when she saw him.

He took a deep breath, smoothing out his shirt and tie one last time. He was ready for this, ready to make this night a memorable one.

With a final glance in the mirror, he looked at the clock, it was time. His eyes were fixed on the pathway waiting for a glimpse of her, then he saw a red figure approaching his gate. Rajveer rushed out of the door, his heart pounding with excitement. He knew that this was just the beginning of a night that would change everything.

CHAPTER 16:
"WHISPERS IN THE MOONLIGHT."

Rajveer's eyes locked onto Nehal, and he couldn't help but smile. She looked stunning, Nehal's outfit was nothing short of a showstopper, a red-hot, one-piece that hugged her curves in all the right places. The dress was a deep, bold red that seemed to ignite the air around her. It was a fitted bodycon design that showcased her toned physique, accentuating her waist and highlighting her assets.

The one-piece was made of a luxurious, silky fabric that seemed to shimmer and shine in the soft light of the candles. It had a subtle sheen to it, catching the light in a way that made Nehal's skin glow with a warm, golden undertone.

The neckline of the dress was high and rounded, framing Nehal's face and drawing attention to her striking features. Her skin looked radiant against the bold red of the dress, her eyes sparkling like diamonds in the soft light.

The sleeves of the dress were long and fitted, accentuating Nehal's toned arms and adding to the overall sense of sophistication and glamour. The dress was a masterclass in understated elegance, a perfect blend of style and sensuality.

As Nehal moved, the dress seemed to mold itself to her body, highlighting her every curve and contour. It was a truly

breathtaking sight, one that left Rajveer speechless and awestruck.

Nehal's hair was styled in loose, flowing waves, cascading down her back like a rich, dark waterfall. Her makeup was subtle yet effective, enhancing her natural beauty without overpowering it.

Rajveer's heart skipped a beat as he took in the sight of her, his confidence soaring. He knew that he had made the right decision in dressing up, in making an effort to impress her.

Rajveer had spared no detail in setting up a romantic candlelight dinner for Nehal. The setting was his beautiful garden, nestled in front of his luxurious villa. The garden was a tranquil oasis, filled with lush greenery and vibrant flowers that bloomed in every colour of the rainbow, casting a warm orange glow over the garden. Rajveer's staff lit hundreds of candles, placing them strategically around the dinner area. The soft, golden light of the candles danced across the garden, creating a magical ambiance that was both intimate and enchanting.

The table was adorned with fine China, crystal glasses, and elegant silverware. A crisp, white tablecloth covered the table, and a delicate lace runner added a touch of whimsy and romance.

In the centre of the table, a stunning floral arrangement took pride of place. The arrangement was a masterpiece of colourful blooms, carefully crafted to resemble a work of art. The flowers were arranged in a delicate, curved shape, creating a sense of movement and energy.

Rajveer had also set up a small, portable speaker system, which played soft, romantic music in the background. To complete the setting, Rajveer had arranged for a personalized, three-course menu to be prepared by his staff. The menu was an attempt to tailor to Nehal's tastes and preferences, and each dish was carefully crafted to delight her senses. The garden was transformed into a romantic paradise, a magical setting that would make Nehal feel like a queen.

Rajveer pulled backed a chair and requested Nehal to have a sit without taking his eyes off her. Rajveer took his seat infront on Nehal, eyes still locked into each other and time seemed to stand still.

As they looked at each other from top to bottom, they were both mesmerized. The air was electric with tension, and the flame of attraction between them was palpable.

Their eyes locked, and for a moment, they just stared at each other, the world around them melting away. Rajveer's eyes burned with intensity, his gaze drinking in every detail of Nehal's face. Nehal's eyes, too, shone with a soft, dreamy light, her pupils dilating as she took in the sight of Rajveer.

The silence between them was thick with anticipation, the only sound the soft flicker of the candles. Rajveer's heart pounded in his chest, and Nehal's pulse raced with excitement.

As they sat there, frozen in time, the attraction between them grew stronger, until it was almost tangible. They both knew, in that moment, that they were falling for each other, hard and fast.

And yet, they didn't need to say a word. They didn't need to touch. The connection between them was strong enough to transcend physical boundaries. They were two souls, drawn together by an invisible thread, their hearts beating as one.

As the moment stretched out, Rajveer finally broke the silence, his voice low and husky. "You look stunning," he whispered, his eyes never leaving Nehal's face.

Nehal's cheeks flushed, and she smiled, her eyes sparkling with delight. "Thank you," she replied, her voice barely above a whisper.

And with that, the spell was broken. They both smiled, and the tension between them dissipated, replaced by a sense of warmth and connection. They knew, in that moment, this is going somewhere they both eagerly anticipated.

"You look absolutely breathtaking," Rajveer murmured again, his voice husky with admiration.

Nehal blushed, her eyes sparkling. "Thank you, Rajveer. You clean up nicely yourself."

Rajveer poured wine from the bottle, filling up their individual glasses.

Nehal: Are you planning on getting me drunk?

Rajveer: (Laughed) You did ask for an unlimited supply remember?

Nehal: Yes, I do, you remember every detail! Colour me impressed.

Rajveer: (Blushed) Cheers to our first date and many more to come.

Nehal and Rajveer clinked their glasses.

Nehal: Cheers!!

Rajveer: (Gestured his staff to bring out the starters) I hope you can drink like a fish, because I am planning to get you drunk!

Nehal: (Laughed and looked away from Rajveer.)

Rajveer: Why aren't you looking at me?

Nehal: I am wondering when would the starters arrive, I am starving.

As if in cue, the staff appeared with two dishes of Surmai Rava fry for each. Nehal's face brightened up. The staff placed the silverware on their table and went back into the kitchen.

Rajveer: Wow!! The timing! Anyways it is not advised to drink on empty stomach.

Rajveer and Nehal savoured the dish and wine.

Staff kept bringing the starters, this time it was prawns.

Their conversation flowed effortlessly, punctuated by stolen glances and shy smiles. They shared stories about their lives, each revelation deepening their connection. Nehal said that she had been previously married but had to leave her husband due to his impotence. Rajveer, in turn, shared his own heartbreak—a love story cut short by her family's financial crisis. His ex-girlfriend, Nava, had been forced to marry another man to repay a debt that had crippled her family.

As the wine flowed, their conversation deepened, their laughter echoing through the night. They held each other's gaze, lost in the magic of the moment, unaware of the growing attraction between them. Their hands brushed against each other, a spark igniting between them. Nehal, with a mischievous glint in her eyes, leaned in and fed Rajveer a piece of fish, a gesture that sent a jolt of unexpected intimacy through him. Lost in the intoxicating blend of wine, moonlight, and each other's company, they drifted further and further into a blissful oblivion, their hearts pounding in unison.

Nehal: (Smiled gently, offering Rajveer a piece of prawn) "Try this."

Rajveer: (took a bite, eyes sparkling) "It's delicious. But I bet you're a better cook." (Winked)

Nehal: (Blushed) "Oh, you flatter me! I'm still learning."

Rajveer: (Took a sip of wine) "Well, that is for the future to unfold its surprises. As of now this dinner is incredible."

Nehal: (Leaned closer, their hands brushing) "Obviously it is"

Every five minutes, their chairs move closer together, the space between them shrinking.

Rajveer: (Gazed at her intently) "You're even more beautiful than I imagined."

Nehal: (Heart pounded) "And you... you're breathtaking."

Rajveer: (Held her hand, his voice husky) "I feel like I've known you forever."

Nehal: (Nodded, her eyes filled with warmth) "Me too. It feels like destiny."

Nehal, mesmeried by the moment, feeds Rajveer a piece of prawn. Their eyes remain locked.

Rajveer: (Leaned closer) "The secret ingredient is... you."

They both took a sip of wine, the atmosphere electric.

Nehal: (Her voice trembled slightly) "Rajveer..."

Rajveer: (His voice low and husky) "Nehal..."

(The space between them is gone, they're practically touching. An irresistible pull draws them closer.)

Nehal: (Looked into his eyes, her breath catching) "I... I think I'm falling for you."

Rajveer: (Cupped her face, his eyes filled with emotion) "I think I am too."

Their lips meet in a soft, passionate kiss, the candlelight casting a warm glow on their faces. The world ceased to exist.

After a romantic dinner, Rajveer walked Nehal back to her villa.

Rajveer and Nehal walked hand in hand along the beach, the moonlight painting a silver path on the water. A comfortable silence settled between them after their first kiss.

Nehal: (Smiled, a little breathless) That was... unexpected.

Rajveer: (Chuckled, his eyes still on hers) Unexpected, but... not unwelcome, I hope?

Nehal: (Looked down, playfully kicking at the sand) Definitely not unwelcome. It's just... everything feels so... fast.

Rajveer: I know. It's like... we've known each other just for a day, and yet, I feel like I have known you forever, it's a bit crazy, isn't it?

Nehal: Crazy good. But... (She hesitated) I should probably head back to my villa.

Rajveer: (His grip on her hand tightened slightly) I know you should. But... (He looked out at the ocean) It feels too soon.

Nehal: (Nodded in agreement) I know. But I'm here with two of my friends. They'd wonder where I've vanished. It wouldn't look right...

Rajveer: (Understood) Of course. You're right. I wouldn't want to cause any... villa gossip. (He grinned)

Nehal: (Laughed) Exactly! Besides... (She stepped closer to him) if I stayed... who knows what might happen? We might just skip straight to the happily ever after.

Rajveer: (Raised an eyebrow playfully) And would that be so bad?

Nehal: (Teasingly, tilted her head) Maybe. We need some time to... savor the anticipation. Build the excitement.

Rajveer: (His voice softened) You're right. Anticipation is a powerful thing. So, tomorrow then? Dolphin ride? Tsunami Island? Are you bringing your friends along?

Nehal: (Her eyes lit up) Absolutely! I'm already looking forward to it. Bright and early?

Rajveer: The earlier, the better. I can't wait to see you again.

Nehal: (Stood on her tiptoes and gave him a quick, chaste kiss on the cheek) Me neither. Goodnight, Rajveer.

Rajveer: Goodnight, Nehal. (He watched her as she walked towards her villa, a smile playing on his lips. He knows, deep down, that tomorrow can't come soon enough.)

Back in his villa, Rajveer stretched out on his bed, excited for tomorrow's adventures with Nehal and her friends. Suddenly the smile fades, and he gets lost in his own thoughts. Rajveer's heart was a battlefield, a confusing mess of conflicting emotions. Nava. Her name was etched into his soul, a love so deep it had weathered the harshest storms. He missed her, ached for her, even after all this time. He'd endured the torment of her being with another man, a sacrifice born of desperate circumstances, a past that clung to him like a shroud. He'd tolerated it, a hollow ache in his chest his constant companion.

Then there was Nehal. She was a breath of fresh air, a vibrant spark that reignited something within him he thought long extinguished. With Nehal, he felt alive, truly alive, in a way he hadn't in years. Her laughter was music, her presence a warmth that spread through his chilled bones. But was it love? Real love, like he felt for Nava? Or was it simply a refuge, a beautiful, intoxicating distraction from the pain that had become his constant companion? He was lost in the labyrinth of his own heart, unsure if he was falling in love or merely grasping at a lifeline in the turbulent sea of his emotions. The confusion gnawed at him, a constant question mark hanging over his every interaction with Nehal, a shadow lurking in the corners of his newfound joy.

The pull towards Nehal was irresistible, he was completely into her. When she was around, Rajveer thought she was his present, and hopefully, the future. He realised there is no point dwelling in the past, and then he was asleep and in his dreams.

CHAPTER 17:
DOLPHINS, FRIENDS AND A BOAT.

Early in the morning, Rajveer went for a run, it was both intoxicating and refreshing. He had some coffee and got ready, and went to meet Nehal and her friends around 6 am at their villa.

Nehal opened the door and impressed to see Rajveer being on time. She invited him inside, she said they are yet to have coffee, and leave once I'ts over. Rajveer agreed as he was always up for a coffee.

"Hey guys, this is Rajveer," Nehal said, beaming. "Rajveer, these are my friends, Advika and Aadita."

Rajveer smiled and extended his hand. "It's a pleasure to meet you both."

Advika, petite and energetic, shook his hand with a warm smile. "Likewise, Rajveer! Nehal's told us a lot about you."

Aadita, tall and graceful, with striking cheekbones, gave him a more lingering handshake. "The pleasure is all ours, Rajveer. Nehal keeps her best treasures well-hidden; it seems." She gave Nehal a playful wink.

Nehal rolled her eyes, but couldn't suppress a smile. "Oh, here she goes..."

They settled down on the couch. "So, Rajveer," Aadita began, leaning forward slightly, "what do you do besides dazzling Nehal?"

Rajveer chuckled. "I'm a software developer. And Nehal's pretty dazzling herself, so the competition is stiff."

Advika giggled. "Software developer, huh? So, you're good with computers? Maybe you can fix my perpetually crashing laptop."

"I can certainly try," Rajveer replied, smiling at Advika.

Aadita raised an eyebrow playfully. "Oh, I'm sure Rajveer can fix more than just laptops," she purred, glancing at Nehal.

Nehal playfully shoved Aadita's arm. "Stop it, Aadita! You're embarrassing me."

Aadita just laughed. "I'm just stating the obvious. A handsome, intelligent man like Rajveer doesn't come along every day."

Rajveer blushed slightly, flattered by the attention. "Thank you, Aadita. That's very kind of you to say."

"Kindness has nothing to do with it," Aadita said with a sly smile. "It's the truth."

They chatted for a while longer, the conversation flowing easily. Aadita's playful banter kept things light and fun, while Advika chimed in with her cheerful enthusiasm.

"We should head over to the dolphin ride," Nehal suggested, glancing at her watch. "They're starting soon."

"Great idea!" Advika exclaimed. "I've been wanting to go."

Aadita winked at Rajveer. "Dolphins are so graceful and intelligent. Just like someone else I know."

Rajveer laughed, enjoying the playful banter. "Lead the way," he said, gesturing towards the exit.

As they walked towards the dolphin encounter, Aadita fell into step beside Rajveer. "So, Rajveer," she murmured, "Tell me, what's your favourite way to unwind after a long day of fixing computers.and dazzling Nehal, of course?"

Nehal, walking ahead with Advika, shook her head and smiled. Aadita was incorrigible, but her teasing was all in good fun. It was clear that everyone was enjoying themselves, and the day was shaping up to be a memorable one.

The motorboat hummed steadily as it cut through the turquoise water. Rajveer, Nehal, Aadita, and Advika leaned against the railings, the spray misting their faces.

They'd been out for about half an hour, the coastline shrinking behind them.

Suddenly, the guide raised his hand, a hush falling over the small vessel. He pointed towards the vast expanse of the ocean and gestured for silence.

A few tense, anticipatory moments passed. Then, a collective gasp rippled through the group. A pod of dolphins, dozens strong, had surrounded them. They were everywhere – sleek, grey bodies arcing out of the water, playful squeaks echoing across the waves. Some swam alongside the boat, close enough to touch. Others leaped high, twisting and turning in the air before crashing back into the sea with a splash.

"Oh my god!" Aadita whispered, her eyes wide with wonder.

"This is incredible!" Advika breathed, fumbling for her camera.

Rajveer was mesmerized, a wide grin splitting his face. He turned to Nehal, who stood beside him, equally captivated. "Have you ever seen anything like this?"

Nehal shook her head, her own smile mirroring his. "It's magical," she replied, her voice soft.

Aadita, who had been subtly vying for Rajveer's attention since they boarded, noticed the easy camaraderie between them. A flicker of something that resembled annoyance crossed her face, quickly masked by a smile.

Rajveer pulled out his phone. "Selfie time!" he announced, grinning at Nehal. They posed together, the playful dolphins forming a spectacular backdrop. Nehal leaned slightly closer, a little thrill ran through her as she noticed Aadita's gaze.

"Hey, lovebirds!" Aadita called out, her tone laced with playful teasing, though a slight edge was detectable. "Don't forget about us!" She and Advika moved to join them, playfully shoving their way into the frame.

"Alright, group photo!" Advika declared, taking Rajveer's phone. They all squeezed together, laughing as the dolphins continued their exuberant display, creating a memory they wouldn't soon forget. Even Aadita's initial annoyance seemed to melt away as the shared experience of witnessing such natural beauty took over.

The group headed towards Tsunami Island, the island is located off the coast of Malvan. It is popular among tourist because of its sandy beaches, which gets partially submerged during high tides and a thrilling playground for water sports.

The motorboat lurched violently, throwing spray over the bow. Nehal, gripped Rajveer's left hand in a vise-like hold, shot a glare across him at Aadita, who was doing the same on his right. Aadita, seemingly oblivious, was chattering excitedly about the dolphins they'd seen earlier. Advika, meanwhile, clung to a handrail, her knuckles white, as the boat bucked and swayed. Each wave sent a fresh cascade of water over the deck.

"Ugh, this is terrifying!" Advika shrieked, as another wave crashed against the side.

"Just hold on tight!" Rajveer yelled over the roar of the engine, wincing as the boat dropped into a trough.

Finally, the boat scraped onto the sandy shore of Tsunami Island. It was small, but breathtakingly beautiful. A single, thatched-roof shack stood near the beach. The group disembarked, shaking off the sea spray and taking in the tranquil scene.

"Wow," Aadita breathed, "It's... so peaceful."

"And look! Breakfast!" Advika pointed towards the shack, where a small spread of food was laid out. Steaming plates of Ukdiche Modak and Ghavan filled the air with a delicious aroma. After a satisfying breakfast, they decided to explore the island by kayak. Nehal and Rajveer paired up, while Aadita and Advika took another kayak.

Out on the water, with some much-needed privacy, Nehal finally addressed the elephant in the room. "Rajveer," she began, "I'm sorry about Aadita...you know..."

Rajveer chuckled. "About her...attentiveness? Don't worry about it. A little attention from a hot women never hurt anyone," he teased.

Nehal's eyes narrowed. "Oh, really? You liked it, did you?"

Rajveer laughed. "Hey, I'm just saying... But seriously, Nehal, it's you, I'm interested in." He paused, then added with a mischievous grin, "Maybe we should ditch the others and grab dinner later? Just the two of us?"

Nehal's face softened, a smile playing on her lips. "I'd like that," she said.

"Great! We'll take Aadita along," Rajveer added, winking before bursting into laughter at Nehal's mock-exasperated expression.

As they paddled, Rajveer's kayak pulled ahead of Aadita and Advika's. Nehal, with a playful glint in her eye, splashed a handful of water at their friends. A full-on water fight erupted, with shrieks of laughter echoing across the calm water. Even Advika, her earlier fear forgotten, joined in the fun, soaking Aadita in return. The turbulent boat ride was a distant memory, replaced by the joy of the moment.

After kayaking, the group relaxed on the tsunami island.

The sun was beginning to dip below the horizon, painting the sky in hues of orange and pink. The group relaxed on the soft, white sand of Tsunami Island. The gentle lapping of the turquoise water against the shore provided a soothing soundtrack to their conversation.

Rajveer: (Stretched back on his towel) Ah, this is the life! Sun, sand, and good company. Tsunami Island really lives up to the hype.

Nehal: (Laughed) It does, doesn't it? I was a little worried after hearing the name, though. It sounds a bit... ominous.

Aadita: (Chuckled) I know, right? I was picturing giant waves crashing down on us! But it's absolutely beautiful.

So peaceful. Did you guys try the coconut water from that little stall near the pier? Best I've ever had.

Advika: (Nodded) Oh yeah! The guy there was so friendly too. He told me about this hidden waterfall on the other side of the island. Apparently, it's a bit of a trek, but totally worth it. We should go tomorrow!

Rajveer: (Raised an eyebrow) A trek? On my vacation? I'm not sure about that. I was planning on spending the entire day perfecting my tan.

Nehal: (Teased) Come on, Rajveer! Live a little! It's not like we're climbing Mount Everest. A little hike to a waterfall sounds amazing. Imagine the photos we could get!

Aadita: Advika, tell us more about this waterfall! Is it swimmable?

Advika: Apparently, yes! It's a natural pool at the bottom, surrounded by lush greenery. The guy at the stall said it's a great place to escape the crowd.

Rajveer: Okay, okay, you've convinced me. But if I get eaten by a jungle beast, I'm blaming all of you.

Nehal: (Grinned) Deal. But if you find any hidden treasure, you're sharing it with us!

Aadita: Speaking of sharing, did anyone grab any snacks? I'm suddenly starving.

Advika: I have some chips and some of those amazing pineapple candies we saw at the market. I'll go grab them from my bag.

Advika got up and rummaged through her bag. The others continued to chat, the sound of the waves a constant, calming presence.

Rajveer: You know, this trip has been exactly what I needed. Just a chance to relax and disconnect.

Nehal: Totally. It's so nice to just hang out with you guys without any distractions.

Aadita: I agree. Tsunami Island, you've been good to us.

The group decided to head back to the sea shore.

The small boat bucked and swayed, a toy in the grip of the turbulent sea. Rajveer, Nehal, Aadita, and Advika clung on to whatever they could find, the journey back from Tsunami Island a far cry from the calm they'd hoped for. The low and high tides battled for control, tossing the vessel about like a cork. Nehal, pale and shaken, gripped Rajveer's left arm for support. Aadita, seemingly oblivious to Nehal's discomfort, mirrored her action, also clutching Rajveer's left arm. The shared point of contact created a tense, unspoken triangle between the two girls and Rajveer. At one point, Advika yelped as her clothing snagged on something sharp jutting from the boat's weathered wood. Finally, blessedly, the boat scraped against the familiar sands of the seashore. Relief washed over them; despite the harrowing ride, they were all safe.

After they reached the sea shore, Rajveer escorted the girls back to their villa, the earlier tension still lingering in the salty air. They made plans for a waterfall trek the following day, a shared adventure to erase the memory of the turbulent sea. As Rajveer turned to leave for his own villa, Nehal, in a sudden impulsive move, grabbed his arm and pulled him into a passionate kiss. Her lips met his in a searing moment that left Aadita and Advika in stunned silence. Advika quickly turned away, a flicker of hurt or embarrassment crossing her face. Aadita, however, stared, her eyes burning with a mixture of surprise and raw jealousy. The desire for Rajveer, already simmering within her intensified, fuelled by the kiss she had just witnessed. Rajveer and Nehal, lost in their own world, made plans to meet later that evening at his villa, a clandestine date born from the day's shared experience. They finally broke apart, Nehal's hand lingering in Rajveer's as they disbursed to their separate villas, leaving Aadita alone with her simmering emotions.

Nehal joined Rajveer for their second date at the specified time.

Soft music played in the background, the scent of vanilla and sandalwood filled the air. Red wine glasses gleamed under the candlelight. A platter of delicately arranged fish starters sat on the table.

Nehal: (Smiled softly) This is... beautiful, Rajveer. Thank you.

Rajveer: (His gaze warm) I wanted tonight to be special, Nehal. You deserve it.

Nehal: (Took a sip of wine) So, tell me more about yourself. You mentioned you're a software developer? And a boxer? That's quite a combination.

Rajveer: (Chuckled) Yeah, well, I like to keep things interesting. Software by day, boxing gloves by night. It keeps me balanced. And I also try to do my bit for the community whenever I can.

Nehal: (Nodded, her smile fading slightly) I'm a computer engineer too. Masters, actually. But my life... it hasn't always been easy. My parents... they weren't really around. I felt... invisible.

Rajveer: (Reacheed across the table, gently took her hand) Nehal, I'm so sorry. No one deserves to feel like that. I'm lucky. I have a great family. Very close. My childhood was... well, it was filled with love.

Nehal: (Looked at him, her eyes searching his) Love... That's what I've always wanted, Rajveer. More than anything.

(A moment of silence hanged between them. Nehal took a deep breath.)

Nehal: Rajveer, there's something I need to tell you. Something personal. I... I'm still a virgin. I was married once, but... my ex-husband... he had erectile dysfunction. We never... you know.

(Rajveer's expression softened with understanding. He squeezed her hand gently.)

Nehal: (Her voice trembled slightly as she started sharing her past)

"Rajveer," Nehal began, her voice soft, "I want to be completely honest with you about my past, about my first marriage."

Rajveer reached for her hand, his eyes filled with understanding. "I'm listening, Nehal. Whatever you want to share, I'm here for you."

Nehal took a deep breath. "From the outside, it probably looked... happy. But it was hollow. Completely hollow inside."

"What do you mean?" Rajveer asked gently.

"My ex-mother-in-law... she was over bearing. Always taking her son's side, no matter what. It was... suffocating. Like I was always walking on eggshells."

Rajveer squeezed her hand. "That sounds incredibly difficult."

"It was," Nehal confirmed. "But... my ex-father-in-law, he was different. He was actually very supportive. He... he was aware of his son's... erectile dysfunction problems." She paused, the words still a little difficult to say. "And he... he went out of his way to make me feel comfortable. He pampered me, treated me like his own daughter. He was truly a good man."

Rajveer nodded slowly, processing what she was telling him. "So, it was a complicated situation."

"Yes," Nehal said. "My marriage... it looked fine on the surface. But the emotional connection, the intimacy... it just wasn't there. And my mother-in-law's constant interference made everything worse. It was a happy marriage from the outside, but inside... I felt so alone."

Nehal started sharing her daunting past experience, her voice trembling slightly, "There's something...something more I need to tell you about my first marriage." She took a shaky breath, her eyes searching his. "It was arranged. Completely. I barely knew him."

Rajveer reached for her hand; his touch gentle. "Nehal, you don't have to-"

"No, I do," she interrupted, her voice gaining strength, fuelled by the memory. "We went to Mauritius for our honeymoon. First night, big party. We drank; we laughed... everyone was so happy for us. Back in the hotel room..." Her voice dropped to a whisper. "I... I wanted him. I was... eager. I was young, naive. I thought... I thought that was what you were supposed to do on your honeymoon."

She looked away, a flush rising on her cheeks. "He was hesitant. I... I tried. I... I rubbed against him. I was drunk, maybe that was the problem, but I initiated. He... he didn't participate. At all. His... his temple didn't even rise." Nehal's voice cracked. "I kept trying for a while. I thought, maybe... maybe this is how it is. I had no experience, no knowledge. Finally, I just gave up. I was exhausted, confused, and I slept."

Rajveer squeezed her hand, his concern evident in his eyes.

"For two years, Rajveer," she continued, her voice filled with a mixture of anger and pain, "For two whole years, he made me believe that... that that was sex. That it was normal. That it was... enough. I thought something was wrong with me, that I was frigid, that I wasn't good enough, that I was a failure as a wife."

Tears welled up in her eyes. "Then, I talked to Aadita.

She... she told me the truth. She told me what real intimacy was. What real sex was. And I realised... he had been pretending. For two years, he'd been lying to me. Cheating me, in a way. Making me feel like I was the one who was wrong. Like I was broken."

She sobbed, her body shaking. "I felt so violated. So stupid. So... used. But what could I do? I couldn't tell my parents. The shame, the embarrassment... I couldn't bear to hurt them like that. Divorce? The thought was there, but I couldn't bring myself to do it. Not then. I was trapped."

Nehal wiped her eyes with the back of her hand. "It took two more years, Rajveer. Two more years of... of nothing. Of feeling like a shell. Finally, I confided in my mom. She was... heartbroken for me. She understood. She saw how miserable I was. And she... she convinced my father. She convinced him to let me go. She convinced him that

I deserved to be happy." A single tear rolled down her cheek. "And that's how I got divorced. I have everything now, Rajveer. A great job, a Thar, a couple of houses... I'm financially secure. But... all I crave is love. Real, genuine love. And... (Her gaze met his) I... I think I might be falling for you.

Rajveer was taken aback. He was moved by her vulnerability, by the raw honesty in her eyes. He knew he should tell her about his current job situation, but the words caught in his throat. He couldn't bring himself to shatter this moment of intimacy.

Rajveer: (His voice thick with emotion) Nehal... Hearing you say that... it means the world to me. You're... you're incredible. So beautiful, so strong... and so deserving of love.

Nehal: (Tears welled up in her eyes) Do you... do you think you could give me that, Rajveer? Could you love me?

Rajveer: (His heart ached for her. He knows he has to be honest with her soon, but for now, he needs to reassure her.) Nehal... I promise you. I will do my absolute best to love you. With everything I have.

Nehal: That's all I need, Rajveer.

Rajveer: Nehal, what was that back there? Kissing me in front of Aadita... why?

Nehal: (Smiled slightly) Did it bother you?

Rajveer: No, not exactly. I'm just... curious.

Nehal: I wanted her to know.

Rajveer: Know what?

Nehal: That she can't have everything she sets her eyes on. Aadita is... spoiled. A brat, really. She thinks she can just waltz in and take whatever she wants.

Rajveer: And you think she wanted... me?

Nehal: Initially, I thought she was just being playful. Flirting a little. But even after she saw I wasn't happy about it; she didn't back down. She kept pushing. So, I showed her. Some things are off-limits.

Rajveer: (Took her hand) And I'm one of those things?

Nehal: (Raised an eyebrow playfully) You're catching on.

Nehal leaned in and kissed Rajveer softly. As the kiss deepened, a spark ignited between them. Finally, they break the kiss, breathless.

Nehal: (Whispered) Come upstairs with me.

Rajveer nodded, his eyes locked onto hers.

They hurried up the stairs to his bedroom. Inside, the door clicked shut behind them.

Moments later, they lay entwined on the bed. Nehal kissed Rajveer passionately, her fingers tangling in his hair. He returned the kiss with equal fervour, his hands exploring the curves of her body. Their movements become more urgent, driven by a raw desire. The first time was a whirlwind of passion, a release of pent-up emotions. The second time was slower, more sensual, an exploration of each other's bodies. By the third time, a comfortable rhythm has settled between them, a dance of love and lust. They made love until 2 am, lost in each other's arms.

From a distance, on the shore, Aadita watched the scene unfold. Unbeknownst to Rajveer and Nehal, they've forgotten to draw the curtains. Aadita's eyes were glued to the window, a mixture of lust and jealousy burning within her. Seeing Rajveer's animalistic passion with Nehal ignited something within her. She clenched her fists, her desire for Rajveer intensified. She wanted him. She neede him now. Witnessing his raw masculinity has only fuelled her determination. She will have him, no matter the cost.

CHAPTER 18:
RAJVEER'S CONFLICTED HEART AND HIS DAMAGED SOUL.

Rajveer is a man caught in a storm of conflicting emotions. His recent intimacy with Nehal has triggered a deep internal struggle. He clearly feels something for her. His efforts to make her happy, and the fact that he's agonizing over his feelings suggest more than just fleeting physical attraction. He recognizes her innocence and the newness of love for her, which adds to his internal pressure.

However, Rajveer wrestles with the possibility that his feelings are rooted in something other than genuine love. He questions whether it's simply lust, or if his loneliness and past heartbreak with Nava are clouding his judgment? He's afraid that his past experiences have damaged him to the point where he's incapable of truly reciprocating Nehal's affection, even though he recognizes her as a "gem." His frantic drinking and intense workout session are physical manifestations of this inner turmoil. He's trying to fight through the confusion and pain, but he's clearly lost and unsure of what he truly feels.

Meanwhile, Nehal remains blissfully unaware of Rajveer's internal conflict. Her first experience of intense physical pleasure has cemented her feelings for him; she's fallen deeply in love.

As soon as Nehal felt asleep, Aadita sneaked out of the villa and hurried towards Rajveer's bedroom. Her heart thumbed frantically with the anticipation of being finally alone with Rajveer, after such a long tedious wait.

Late in the night, Rajveer stood tall, his eyes blazed with intensity as he faced the punching bag. His gloved fists clenched, ready to unleash a torrent of punches. With a deep breath, he began to circle the bag, his feet dancing in a fluid rhythm.

The first punch landed with a resounding thud, the bag swayed violently as Rajveer's fist connected with precision. He followed up with a flurry of jabs, each one landing with increasing ferocity. The bag creaked and groaned under the onslaught, its chains rattling ominously. Rajveer's passion and fury poured out with every punch. His face contorted in effort, sweat dripped from his brow as he poured all his energy into the bag. The air was filled with the sound of pounding leather, the bag shuddered and swayed like a dancer in the wind.

A particularly vicious combination sent the bag crashing to the floor, its chains snapping wildly. Rajveer stood over it, his chest heaving, his fists still clenched. For a moment, he froze, his eyes blazed with a fierce inner fire.

The door creaked open. Rajveer, still catching his breath, gripped a glass of whiskey tightly. His body was erratic from the workout, his heart pounding fastly. His eyes flicked to the door and he froze.

Aadita stood in the doorway, with seductive smile. She desired Rajveer, and her observation of his post-coital energy, sets up a fire in inside her. \

Aadita: (Softly) Rajveer... you seem to have an untamed animal inside you.

Rajveer: (Muttered) What...?

His eyes widen in shock as he recognised her.

Aadita: (Stepped closer) You know very well that how much I want you? The moment I saw you in the morning.

Rajveer: Nehal knows about it already, that's why she kissed me in front of you. I admire Nehal, you are aware about the situation of her first marriage. I would request you to go back.

Aadita: (Chuckled) I was the one who told her that whatever was happening between her and her ex-husband was not sex. That clueless Nehal, didn't realise that kiss actually ignited something within me. It was my want for you.

Rajveer: (Wiped the sweat from his forehead) I'm... I'm flattered, these words coming out from an erotic goddess like you. But I am sorry I can't betray Nehal; she will be shattered.

Aadita: (Sat beside him, her hand gently traced his arm) She doesn't need to know. Unlike her, I am not emotionally needy. But I just need you to bring out the animal inside you and use me as you want.

Rajveer: (Stared at her, bewildered)

Aadita leaned closer.

Rajveer looked at her, his eyes widening. Aadita slowly removed her sweatshirt, revealing a set of sultry red lingerie. Rajveer's breath caught in his throat. He's mesmerized, a battle raging within him.

Rajveer: (Stuttered) A-Aadita... you... you can't be serious.

Aadita: (A seductive smile played on her lips) Why not?

Rajveer struggled to resist, his body betraying him with involuntary shivers. Aadita noticed and leaned in closer, her lips brushing against his ear.)

Aadita: Don't fight it, Rajveer. Give in to the temptation.

Rajveer, overwhelmed by desire, finally succumbs. He grabs her, pulling her close in a fierce, passionate kiss.

The kiss exploded, a desperate hunger consuming them both. Aadita throws her head back, a low moan escaping her lips. Rajveer, driven by a primal urge, tore away the remaining fabric, his hands exploring her body with a newfound urgency. He buried his face in her neck, inhaling her intoxicating scent.

Aadita arched her back, meeting his every touch with a desperate eagerness. She ran her hands through his hair, tugging gently, urging him on. Their bodies grind together, a raw, animalistic energy igniting between them.

Rajveer threw caution to the wind, his movements becoming rougher, more demanding. He pinned her beneath him, his gaze burning into hers. Aadita, eyes wild with desire, reached for him, her fingers digging into his back.

Their movements were a whirlwind of passion, a symphony of moans and gasps. They lose themselves in the moment, their bodies entwined in a desperate, primal dance. Rajveer was slumbering and gasping for air, little did he know Aadita was hungry for more. After a while, they both enjoyed whiskey together. Aadita sat on Rajveer's lap, her intoxicating fragrance was irresistible to Rajveer. She rolled her hips against him in a slow motion. Rajveer felt excited as she turned around in the same intensity and kissed him passionately. She grabbed his hands in a split second on her stacked chest, the beast within Rajveer roused violently. Aadita sprung between his thighs and used her tongue like a magician, driving Rajveer wild. Rajveer pulled her up and once again they lose themselves in the wilderness they created.

Rajveer lay spent, his mind wandered in thoughts. He had promised Nehal all the love in the world. He made sensual love to her, vowed to be there for her. While he was addressing the demons inside of him, he was tangled in the remnants of the night he couldn't take back. Aadita. He realised she was still with him. He requested Aadita to go back to her villa as they needed the sleep to embark on a trek in few hours. Aadita hesitantly obliged and left his bedroom.

Rajveer's mind was a maelstrom of conflicting emotions, as if a stormy sea was raging within him. Guilt and shame wrestled with the primal satisfaction that still lingered, a haunting reminder of his transgression. The beast within him, once satiated, now seemed to be gloating, its presence a constant, unsettling whisper in the darkness.

The memories of the fateful night swirled, taunting him with the pleasure he had experienced with Aadita, and before that, with Nehal. The pain and loneliness of the past months seemed to have been momentarily forgotten in the heat of those encounters. Yet, now, the weight of his betrayal threatened to crush him.

Rajveer's heart yearned for Nehal, He longed to be with her, to feel her warmth and gentle touch. But the fear of what the beast within him might demand next, hung over him like a Specter— a constant reminder of the darkness that lurked beneath his surface.

Torn between his desire for redemption and the primal urge that seemed to drive him, Rajveer felt lost and alone. He was unsure of how to reconcile the warring factions within himself. The turmoil raged on, a ceaseless battle between his heart and the beast that seemed determined to claim him.

Next day, he stood in front of Nehal's place. The few hours of sleep he'd managed to snatch had done little to alleviate the turmoil brewing inside him. His thoughts were a tangled web of guilt, anxiety, and desire.

The memories of the previous night's passionate encounter with Nehal still lingered, leaving him feeling tender and vulnerable. Yet, the erotic adventure with Aadita had awakened a primal hunger within him, one that he couldn't shake off. The secrecy surrounding his tryst with Aadita only added to his unease, making him wonder how he would navigate this complex web of relationships.

Rajveer's heart began to race with anticipation and apprehension. He was unsure of how to face Nehal, or how to reconcile his feelings for her with the desire that still lingered for Aadita. The fear of being discovered, of hurting Nehal, or of losing control again, threatened to overwhelm him.

Rajveer took a deep breath, trying to calm his racing thoughts. He knew he had to be careful, to tread a delicate balance between his emotions and his desires. But as he raised his hand to knock on the door, he couldn't shake off the feeling that he was stepping into a minefield, one that could potentially destroy everything he held dear.

CHAPTER 19:
THE HIDDEN CASCADE

The group of four set out on their adventurous trek, eager to reach the breathtaking waterfall deep within the jungle. Advika, who had organized the trip, led the way, armed with directions from a local coconut vendor.

As they ventured deeper into the dense foliage, the sounds of civilization grew fainter, replaced by the cacophony of the jungle. Birds chirped, leaves rustled, and the distant roar of the waterfall beckoned.

Rajveer and Nehal walked hand in hand, their love for each other evident in the way they moved in tandem. However, the tension between Rajveer and Aadita was palpable, their casual encounter still a secret from Nehal.

Advika, sensing the unease, kept the conversation light, pointing out exotic plants and sharing stories of her own adventures. As they trekked, the group encountered obstacles: steep inclines, rickety bridges, and muddy paths. But they persevered, driven by their determination to reach the waterfall.

After hours of walking, the sound of rushing water grew louder, and the group caught glimpse of the waterfall through the trees. Finally, they emerged into a clearing, and the breathtaking sight took their breath away.

The waterfall cascaded down a rocky face, creating a misty veil that surrounded the pool of crystal-clear water. The group stood in awe, feeling as though they had stumbled upon a hidden paradise.

As they gazed out at the natural wonder, the complexities of their relationships seemed to fade into the background. For a moment, they were just four friends, united in their quest for adventure and beauty. They reached the pool in front of the waterfall, the source of the water falling from above still a mystery to them but the water fall was deafening. It was crystal clear and the water was cold, which ended up in a large pool surrounded by rocks, a perfect natural swimming pool for the group to enjoy.

The group splashed each other in the pool, laughing and having a great time. Rajveer and Nehal were swimming together, while Aadita and Advika were playing in the shallow water.

Aadita: (giggled) This is amazing! I've never felt so alive!

Advika: (splashed water on Aadita) I know, right? This waterfall is incredible!

Rajveer: (swam up to the group) Come on, guys! Let's go behind the waterfall!

Nehal: (excitedly) Yes! Let's do it!

The group swam towards the waterfall, laughing and screaming as they get pummelled by the force of the water. They emerged on the other side, grinning from ear to ear. They found themselves in hidden chamber veiled by the waterfall curtain.

Aadita: (shook her head) Wow, that was intense!

Advika: (took a photo) Say cheese, guys!

The group posed for a photo, laughing and smiling. Rajveer wrapped his arm around Nehal, while Aadita and Advika made silly faces in the background.

Rajveer: (smiled) This is going to be an unforgettable trip!

Nehal: (smiled back) Definitely!

Aadita: (teased) And who knows, maybe we'll even find some hidden treasure!

Advika: (laughed) Yeah, right! But wouldn't that be awesome?

The group continued to revel in the moment, taking photos and making memories that will last a lifetime.

Eventually, the time to get back loomed above them. They packed their bags and began the journey back to their villas. Advika and Aadita walked forward while

Rajveer and Nehal are at a close distance behind them. Their bittersweet departure lingered as Nehal and the group were leaving for Pune after lunch.

Seated outside their villa, Rajveer and Nehal enjoyed the serene surroundings. A gentle breeze carried the scent of saltwater and damp earth.

Nehal: (sighed) We're driving back to Pune today after lunch.

Rajveer: (nodded) I know. I'll miss you so much. Please message me once you reach home safely.

Nehal: (smiled) Obviously, I'll miss you too. So much has happened on this trip... I don't want it to end.

Rajveer: (reassured) Don't worry, I'll come back to Pune in a couple of days. We'll talk every day, and I'll meet you soon.

Nehal: (smiled) Promise?

Rajveer: (smiled back) Promise.

Suddenly, Aadita strolled over, her expression unreadable, and interrupted the couple. Without a word, she slipped her hand into Rajveer's pocket and took his phone. Rajveer stomach flipped.

Aadita: (dialled her number) Hey, I'll create a group for all of us, so we can stay in touch.

Nehal: (flashed an uneasy smile) That sounds like fun.

Aadita: (smiled) Great! I'll add everyone's numbers.

Rajveers swallowed, stealing a glance at Nehal. Her expression remained neutral, but something in her felt uncomfortable. Did she sense it?

The group enjoyed one last lunch together, chatting and laughing.

Nehal and her group packed up their belongings and prepared to leave.

Nehal: (hugged Rajveer) I'll talk to you soon. Take care.

Rajveer: (hugged her back) You too. Drive safely.

With that, Nehal and her group departed, leaving Rajveer behind.

CHAPTER 20:
RIPPLES OF THE HEART.

Rajveer had two days left for his stay in Tarkarli, and he was grateful to Parag for renting him his villa at a nominal price. Rajveer used this alone time to be true to his emotions. His workout routine, yoga, and meditation allowed him to clear his mind and gave him a clear picture of what he felt about Nehal. During dinner time, Rajveer received a text from Nehal stating she had reached Pune safely. The text brought a smile on his face. In some time, he received a text from an unknown number stating she reached Mumbai safely. Rajveer got confused and quickly replied questioning who was it—it was Aadita. He was glad that she didn't stay in the same city as him. Pushing aside, He called Nehal.

Rajveer: Nehal! Hi! How are you? Did you reach Pune safely?

Nehal: Yes, yes, I reached just fine. The journey was smooth. I'm already missing you like crazy!

Rajveer: I miss you too, Nehal. It feels so quiet here without you.

Nehal: (Softly) I love you.

Rajveer: I love you too, Nehal. So much. Listen, I have some good news. I'll be back in Pune on Saturday!

Nehal: (Excitedly) Really? Oh, Rajveer, that's wonderful! I can't wait!

Rajveer: Me neither! We can finally meet. I've been thinking about all the things we can do.

Nehal: Me too! We can go out clubbing, have romantic dinners, anything you want my love. Or we have just be inside your house the whole day, watch Netflix and cook food together. I forgot to ask, what are your work timings?

Rajveer: (Tensed and felt guilty) Auh, normal 9 to 5. But if you are coming on a weekday I can take a leave. So, you don't worry about it, I just want to be with you.

Nehal: Okay. that sounds great. I miss Tarkaril— walking hand in hand on the beach with you, the delicious seafood, and just being with you… it was perfect. I keep thinking about the garden in your villa.

Rajveer: Yeah… a friend of mine had rented it to me. Saturday, we can go for a long drive, maybe catch a movie…

Nehal: Or just stay in and cuddle and talk. I've missed our conversations.

Rajveer: I've missed everything about you. I'm counting down the hours until Saturday.

Nehal: Me too. Okay, I should let you go now. Just wanted to let you know I reached safely and that I'm missing you terribly.

Rajveer: Alright. Take care of yourself, Nehal. And I'll see you on Saturday. I love you.

Nehal: I love you too, Rajveer. Bye!

Rajveer: Bye!

Rajveer's emotional state was a complex mix of longing, guilt, and anxiety as he spent his last day in Tarkarli alone. The absence of Nehal had left a gaping void in his heart, making him restless and yearning for her presence. Every minute felt like an eternity as he counted down the hours until he could return home and be reunited with her.

However, amidst his longing, a heavy sense of guilt weighed on his conscience. He had decided to confess the truth about his job and the casual encounter with Aadita. A decision that filled him with trepidation. The thought of potentially losing Nehal's trust and love was unbearable, and Rajveer's heart felt heavy with the burden of his secrets.

As he reflected on his actions, Rajveer couldn't help but regret his stupid mistake with Aadita. He wished he could turn back time and erase the encounter, but the weight of his guilt remained, a constant reminder of his transgression.

Rajveer's mind was a jumble of emotions, torn between his love for Nehal and the fear of losing her. He was scared that Nehal might never forgive him, that his mistakes would irreparably damage their relationship. The uncertainty was suffocating, leaving Rajveer feeling anxious and on edge.

As the day drew to a close, Rajveer couldn't shake off the feeling of unease that had settled in his heart. He knew that the journey ahead would be challenging, but he was determined to face the consequences of his actions and fight for the love and forgiveness of the woman he cherished most.

Rajveer packed his stuff and started his drive back to Pune on friday afternoon. He reached Pune late at night. The next day, Rajveer spent time with his family, his mother, sister Anya and brother Reyansh were happy to see him. They were happy that he had overcome the heartbreak he had faced. It had been months since he felt this sense of warmth. Rajveer didn't inform his family about Nehal yet. They spent the entire day chit-chatting, laughing, eating, and having a good time together after months. In the evening, Rajveer called Nehal, she was ready to meet. Later, Rajveer picked Nehal up, and together they left for the cafe.

At café, Rajveer and Nehal both settled in their seats.

Rajveer: Nehal, it's so good to see you! How have you been?

Nehal: Rajveer! I'm great now that we're together. Life's been a bit of a roller coaster, you know? Work, family, the usual. But I'm so glad to be here with you.

Rajveer: Me too. It feels like ages. So, tell me everything. What's new?

Nehal: Well, remember Aadita? I was so worried she'd try to stir things up after what happened in Tarkarli. But thankfully, she hasn't created any drama. I'm so relieved.

Rajveer: (Nervously) Yeah, about Tarkarli... there's something I need to tell you.

Nehal: What is it?

Rajveer: After you left that night. I made a mistake. I... I had a casual encounter with Aadita.

A stunned silence settled between them.

Nehal: (Confused) What do you mean?

Rajveer: (Voice barely a whisper) It was nothing serious, just a moment of weakness. But I should have told you sooner.

Nehal hand trembled as she looked at Rajveer.

Nehal: (Hurt) Rajveer, why didn't you tell me before?

Rajveer: I was ashamed, Nehal. I felt terrible about it. And after Nava got married, I fell into a deep depression. I was so lonely, when you came in my life all of a sudden, I had mixed emotions inside me. Aadita, brought out the beast inside me and I caved in. I even quit my job, and I've been out of work for seven months.

Nehal: (Shocked) Seven months? Rajveer, why didn't you tell me?

Rajveer: I didn't want to burden you. I know you have your own life, your own problems. But now I realize I should have been honest with you from the start.

Nehal: (Tears welled up) Rajveer, I don't know what to say.

Rajveer: I know I've messed up, Nehal. But I promise I'll make things right. I'm going to rejoin a local boxing club and try to get my career back on track.

Nehal clenched her fists, her body trembling with pain and anger.

Rajveer: Nehal. I promise I'll never lie to you again.

Nehal: (Sniffled) I don't know, this was the reason I forbid myself from falling in love, because it hurts. You went behind my back on the same night I gave you my heart. That spoiled brat, Aadita, she always gets what she wants. But Rajveer, you have broken my trust and heart.

Tears streamed down her eyes. Rajveer tried to wipe them, but Nehal snapped at him to not touch her.

Nehal: And what a beautiful return gift you have given me?

Rajveer: Nehal. I promise I'll do everything to earn your trust and love back.

Nehal: I don't know, Rajveer. But I guess love isn't made for me, I can't trust you anymore, I am sorry. Nehal stood up abruptly, pushing her chair back.

Rajveer: Nehal... please don't go.

Nehal turned away, blinking away more tears.

Rajveer followed her, but she stopped him with a glare. A auto pulled up, before Rajveer could say anything, she was gone.

Nehal goes back to her room, slamming the door shut behind her. Nehal's heart shattered into a million pieces as Rajveer's words pierced her soul like a dagger. The revelation that he had cheated on her with Aadita on the same night they had made love—a night that held so much significance and intimacy for her— left her feeling utterly devastated.

For the first time in her life, Nehal had experienced the warmth of love, the thrill of physical ecstasy, and the joy of being desired. But in an instant, it all came crashing down.

Aadita. Her name alone was enough to fill her with fury.

Her presence in Rajveer's life had screwed up the one thing that had brought Nehal out of the darkness of her failed marriage.

As the reality of Rajveer's infidelity sunk in, Nehal felt herself being pulled back into the abyss of depression, that she had been struggling to escape. The emotional scars of her past, which had begun to heal, were now ripped open once again.

Nehal's mind was a mixture of emotions—shock, anger, hurt, and betrayal. She felt like she was drowning in a sea of despair, unable to find a lifeline to cling to. The physical ecstasy she had experienced with Rajveer now seemed tainted, a reminder of the pain and heartache that followed.

As she gazed at Rajveer's picture on her phone, Nehal saw a stranger standing before her, a person she no longer recognized. The man she loved, the man she thought she knew, had vanished, replaced by a deceitful and unfaithful individual.

Tears streamed down Nehal's face as she grappled with the ruins of their relationship. She felt lost, alone, and unsure of how to navigate this treacherous landscape.

The future, once bright and promising, now seemed uncertain and ominous.

In that moment, Nehal felt like she was staring into the abyss, with no safety net to catch her if she fell. The heartbreak and pain were suffocating, threatening to consume her entire being. As she stood there, shattered and heartbroken, Nehal wondered if she would ever be able to escape the darkness that had engulfed her once again.

The darkness within Nehal was a palpable, suffocating entity that threatened to consume her entire being. It was as if a black hole had formed inside her chest, sucking in all the light, hope, and joy she had once known.

The pain of Rajveer's betrayal cut deep, like a knife twisting in her heart. She had given him everything— her love, her trust, her vulnerability. And he had repaid her with deceit, lies, and infidelity. The thought of him with Aadita, her childhood friend, was a constant, gnawing ache that refused to subside.

Nehal felt like she was drowning in a sea of despair. Every breath she took felt like a struggle. Every heartbeat a reminder of the pain she was enduring. She was trapped in a living nightmare, with no escape in sight.

The darkness within her was a manifestation of her shattered dreams, her broken trust, and her lost innocence. It was a toxic, corrosive force that was eating away at her soul, leaving her feeling hollow, empty, and devoid of purpose.

As the days passed, Nehal found herself withdrawing from the world, unable to face the reality of her situation. She stopped taking care of herself, stopped socializing, and stopped living. The darkness within her had become a self-perpetuating cycle of pain, anger and sadness, and she didn't know how to break free.

Before meeting Rajveer, Nehal had gone through an emotional trauma. Nehal's sexless marriage had left her feeling unfulfilled, unwanted, and unloved. Which lead to feelings of low self-esteem, self-doubt, and inadequacy.

The absence of physical and emotional intimacy in her marriage had made her feel disconnected from her own desires and needs. Aadita's words opened Nehal's eyes to the reality of her situation, making her realize that she had been living in a state of emotional numbness. After meeting Rajveer, she thought she finally found love in her life, but little did she knew, even he was a victim of his past. He had sacrificed his love for his ex's father's health and had taken a toll on his mental health. The beast which came out within Rajveer was his coping mechanism, she knew Rajveer had a keen eye for beauty and glamour. But Nehal loved and trusted him, she couldn't notice, that he is a womanizer who just can't get enough, She was so sure if she probed him enough, she will find out that apart from Nava, there will be girls he was attached too in some or the other way.

Rajveer's cheating has shattered Nehal's trust and left her feeling betrayed, hurt, and vulnerable.

Aadita's actions were a stark contrast to the friendship they had shared for so many years. Nehal had confided in Aadita about the struggles she faced in her first marriage, including the lack of intimacy and emotional connection. Aadita had been a supportive and empathetic listener, offering words of encouragement and advice. Now Nehal thought, Aadita must had a satisfactory feeling inside her back then. Nehal always had achieved more than Aadita— academically at first, then financially.

Had Aadita found some twisted satisfaction in luring Rajveer away, by tauting Nehal's first love experience?

She was shocked to discover how dark Aadita's intensions were, she knows she is a sex addict. But now, she knew she will get whatever she wants, inconsiderate of anyone else's feelings.

But now, it seemed that Aadita's own desires had taken precedence over their friendship. Nehal couldn't understand why Aadita would choose to hook up with Rajveer, knowing how much he meant to Nehal. It was as if Aadita had discarded their years of friendship like a worn-out garment, without a second thought.

The pain of Aadita's betrayal was compounded by the fact that Nehal had considered her a true friend—someone who would stand by her through thick and thin. They had shared countless memories, travelled to many places together, and supported each other through life's ups and downs.

But now, Nehal felt like she was staring at a stranger, someone who had been hiding behind a mask of friendship all these years. Aadita's actions had exposed a side of her personality that Nehal had never seen before—a side that was selfish, manipulative, and willing to hurt others to satisfy her own desires.

As Nehal struggled to come to terms with Aadita's betrayal, she couldn't help but wonder if she had ever really known her friend at all. Had Aadita been hiding her true nature all along, even as they shared their deepest secrets and laughter?

Nehal's heart was heavy with grief, her mind reeling with questions and doubts. She felt like she was mourning the loss of a friendship that had meant the world to her. The pain of Aadita's betrayal would take a long time to heal, leaving scars that would remain forever.

With double blows to her heart Nehal was struggling with depression, feeling hopeless, and disconnected from the world around her. The trauma she has experienced lead to anxiety, making her feel on edge, and uncertain about her future. Nehal's self-esteem has taken a hit, making her doubt her worth, and her ability maintain healthy relationships.

Emotional trauma led to physical exhaustion, making Nehal feel drained, and lacking in energy. Nehal experienced insomnia, or difficulty in sleeping, due to the emotional turmoil she was experiencing.

Nehal started withdrawing from social interactions, feeling uncomfortable, or anxious around others. Kept herself within the confines of her room, working perpetually, her emotional pain made it challenging for her to focus, or concentrate on daily tasks. Her mother took care of her, unaware is to what exactly had happened to her. She tried asking Nehal a few times, but Nehal ignored the questions by burying herself in her work. Nehal's relationships with family, and friends become strained, as she struggled to cope with her emotions. Nehal always kept her phone away from her, as she was getting calls from Rajveer and a few calls and texts from Aadita, she ignored them both.

CHAPTER 21:
A MONTH OF ATONEMENT.

Rajveer was determined to win Nehal's trust and her love back. Willing to anything, to mend their shattered connection.

Next day, he called her, she ignored his calls. Desperate, he sent her an email.

My dearest Nehal,

I don't even know where to begin. I'm sitting here with a heavy heart, filled with regret and sorrow for what I've done. I'm ashamed to admit that I cheated on you, and even more ashamed that I lied to you about it.

I know that my actions have caused you immense pain, and for that, I am truly, deeply sorry. I can only imagine how you must feel—betrayed, hurt, and confused. I don't blame you one bit for feeling that way.

Nehal, I love you. I love you more than words can express. I was blind to my own feelings, and I realize now that I took you for granted. I thought I could get away with my infidelity, that I could keep it hidden and pretend that everything was fine. But the truth is, everything was not fine. I was living a lie, and I was hurting the one person I love most.

I miss you, Nehal. I miss your smile, your laughter, your kindness. I miss our late-night conversations, our silly jokes, and our deep, meaningful talks. I miss everything about you.

I know that forgiveness won't come easily, and I don't expect it to. But I hope that someday, you'll be able to find it in your heart to forgive me. I promise to spend the rest of my life making it up to you, proving to you that my love for you is true and unwavering.

If I could go back in time, I would do things differently. I would cherish and appreciate you more. I would communicate with you more openly and honestly, and I would never, ever betray your trust.

But I can't turn back time. All I can do is move forward, with the hope that you'll join me on this journey. I love you, Nehal, and I always will.

Yours always,

Rajveer.

After sending the mail—hoping that Nehal reads it—Rajveer decides to give her the space she needed. After ten days, he tried calling her. She still didn't answer his calls. He kept sending her a few text every day checking on her health and wellbeing.

He sends another text stating that he had blocked Aadita, he had never called her or messaged her after Tarkarli. In the future, he will never try to communicate with her. He tried calling her again but the efforts go in vain. After a couple of days, Rajveer sent her a gold-plated bracelet with her name engraved on it.

Next day, he sent her a personalized photo album, beautiful designed filled with pictures of their favourite memories.

The next day, Rajveer sent a monogrammed handbag with an apology letter inside. He still did not hear anything from Nehal, twenty five days since their last meet.

On the next day, Rajveer rented a billboard in front of Nehal's house with a message declaring his love and commitment to her.

Nehal texted Rajveer to stop all this nonsense and go find a job first.

Rajveer playfully jumped in the air with joy, as he got some response from her.

Next evening, Rajveer sent her a text.

"Nehal, at 8 pm, stand on your balcony. Look up."

She didn't reply. At 8pm, she stepped outside and she looked up.

The customized fireworks display was a breathtaking spectacle, meticulously designed to convey Rajveer's love and apology to Nehal. The night sky transformed into a canvas of vibrant colours, patterns, and shapes, weaving a narrative of devotion and regret.

The display began with a burst of golden sparks, forming the words "I Love You" in bold, cursive script, suspended in mid-air.

This was followed by a series of heart-shaped explosions, each one bursting into a kaleidoscope of colours, symbolizing the love that Rajveer and Nehal shared.

Next, a trail of silver sparks spelled out "I'm Sorry" in elegant, handwritten letters, conveying Rajveer's remorse for his past mistakes.

The display then transitioned to a mesmerizing pattern of interconnected hearts, pulsing with a soft, blue glow. This represented the unbreakable bond between Rajveer and Nehal.

The grand finale featured a majestic display of fireworks, culminating in a glittering, diamond-shaped explosion. Within the diamond, the words "Forever Yours" shone brightly, sealing Rajveer's promise of eternal love and commitment to Nehal.

The customized fireworks display was a poignant expression of Rajveer's love, regret, and devotion, leaving a lasting impression on Nehal's heart.

As Nehal gazed up at the night sky, witnessing the breathtaking customized fireworks display, a tumultuous storm of emotions swirled inside her. Her facial expressions reflected the intense turmoil, as if her heart was being rearranged by the sheer magnitude of Rajveer's gesture.

At first, Nehal's eyes widened in surprise, her eyebrows arching upwards as she took in the spectacle. Her lips parted slightly, a soft gasp escaping her throat as the golden sparks formed the words "I Love You" in the sky.

As the heart-shaped explosions burst forth, Nehal's expression softened, her defences slowly melting away. Her eyes glistened with unshed tears, her lower lip trembling ever so slightly as she struggled to contain her emotions.

When the silver sparks spelled out "I'm Sorry", Nehal's face contorted in a mix of sorrow and regret. Her eyes welled up with tears, a single drop rolling down her cheek as she felt the weight of Rajveer's remorse.

As the interconnected hearts pulsed with a soft, blue glow, Nehal's expression transformed, her eyes filling with a glimmer of hope and longing. Her lips curled into a faint, wistful smile, as if she was remembering the love they once shared.

The final message, "Forever Yours", ignited a firework of emotions within Nehal. Her face crumpled, tears streaming down her cheeks as she felt the full force of Rajveer's love and devotion. Her lips trembled, her body shaking with sobs, as she struggled to process the intensity of her emotions.

In that moment, Nehal's facial expressions revealed the depth of her feelings, a poignant reflection of the turmoil and transformation taking place within her heart. Wiping her tears of joy, she called Rajveer. Rajveer was watching her from a distance, he was smiling in anticipation that she might be calling him. His phone rang, the moment he was waiting for almost an entire month.

Rajveer: Hello!

Nehal: Let's meet, I want to talk to you.

Rajveer: When and where?

Nehal: Arthur's theme in an hour?

Rajveer: I can be there in ten minutes.

Nehal: What? Where are you?

Rajveer: Across the street in front of your house. If you want, I will wait for you here, and we can go together.

Nehal: Asshole!! Just wait there. I will be down in 20 minutes.

She disconnected the call.

Rajveer's happiness knew no bounds, a giddy, childlike joy flooded him. She appeared after thirty minutes, they got in the car and drove to Arthur's theme.

CHAPTER 22:
"NEHAL'S LEAP OF FAITH"

As they arrive, Rajveer pulled out a chair for Nehal before ordering two bottles of red wine, and some garlic bread and pasta.

Nehal: Rajveer, can we talk?

Rajveer: (Beamed) Of course, Nehal. Anything. I'm all ears. I've been waiting for this moment.

Nehal: I know. And I... I've been thinking. I read every email, every text. I accepted the gifts.

Rajveer: (Hopeful) And...?

Nehal: And... (She took a deep breath) Rajveer, the billboard... the fireworks... wow. They were... grand gestures. They touched me. They showed me how much you were trying.

Rajveer: I was, Nehal. I am. I messed up, I know. I just... I love you. I truly do.

Nehal: I know you do. And... I love you too, Rajveer. That's why this has been so hard.

Rajveer: (His face lit up) You mean...?

Nehal: (Nodded slowly) I forgive you, Rajveer. I'm giving you another chance. A last chance.

Rajveer: (Overwhelmed with joy) Nehal! I... I don't know what to say. I'm on top of the world! Thank you! Thank you for believing in me.

Nehal: (Smiled slightly) Don't thank me yet. There's something we need to talk about. Something important.

Rajveer: Anything. Name it.

Nehal: Your boxing... it's a great hobby. I admire your passion. But Rajveer, a hobby isn't a career. Not yet, anyway. And until it is, you need to start looking for a stable job.

Rajveer: (His smile faltered slightly) A job?

Nehal: Yes. My parents... they've given me a year. One year to sort things out and get married. They're... they're actively looking for a groom for me.

Rajveer: (His heart sinked) They are?

Nehal: They were. I've managed to convince them to hold off for now. I told them I love you. But Rajveer, they won't accept you if you don't have some stability. And honestly... I need that too. We need that.

Rajveer: (Understanding dawned on him) You're right. You're absolutely right. I understand. I'll start looking.

Passively at first, but seriously. I promise. I won't let you down. I won't let us down.

Nehal: (Reached out and took his hand) I know you won't. I believe in you.

Rajveer: (Brought her hand to his lips and kissed it softly) Thank you, Nehal. Thank you for everything. For the forgiveness, the trust, the love... for this chance.

Nehal: (Leaned in and kissed him softly) Don't mention it. Just... don't mess it up.

Rajveer: (Grinned) Never again.

Next evening, they went out for another date— this time at 1000 Oaks. They had a great time together, the warmth between was inevitable as they ended the night with sweet romantic kiss.

The day after, they meet at The One. The connection between them growing stronger, the past began blurring into the background.

Rajveer: Nehal, I know I messed up big time. But I promise you, I'll spend the rest of my life making it up to you. You're my soulmate, the one I'm meant to be with.

Nehal: I know, Rajveer. I feel it too. But what happened with Aadita... it hurt me so much.

Rajveer: I understand. I was an idiot. But I swear, nothing happened between us after Tarkarli. You're the only one for me, Nehal.

Nehal took Rajveer's phone from the table asking for the password. Rajveer told her confidently. Nehal checked his phone for a while, and kept it on the table, satisfied.

Nehal: I believe you, Rajveer. I do. But how can we move forward? I can't keep living like this, always wondering if you're being honest with me.

Rajveer: Then don't. Move in with me, Come live with me and my family.

Nehal: What! What will I tell my parents?

Rajveer: Tell them you had to shift. Let's build our future together, a future where we never have to be apart again.

Nehal: (Surprised) Rajveer... I don't know what to say.

Rajveer: Say yes. Convince your parents to that your company requires you to move to Delhi office.I promise, you won't regret it.

Nehal: (Smiled) Okay, Rajveer I will convince them, because I love you so much and can't live without you anymore. I'll move in with you. But on one condition: no more lies, no more secrets. We have to be completely honest with each other, always.

Rajveer: Deal. I promise, Nehal. I'll never lie to you again.

They kissed, sealing their promise with a deep, passionate one. As Rajveer drove Nehal home, they kissed each other at every red light, their love for each other growing stronger with each passing moment.

CHAPTER 23:
"LOVE'S NEW ADDRESS"

Rajveer had already convinced his family about Nehal. He spoke about her amazing qualities, his journey together with Nehal so far, and how she had forgiven him and given him a second chance. His family was happy that Rajveer was in love and jubilant again.

The next morning, Rajveer arrived at Nehal's house, his heart racing with excitement and nervousness. Nehal, looking radiant in a bright smile, bid farewell to her parents, telling them that Rajveer was kindly dropping her off at the airport. Her parents, none the wiser, agreed, and Nehal slipped into the car beside Rajveer.

As they drove to Rajveer's house, Nehal's anticipation grew. She had never imagined that she would be moving in with Rajveer, but now, she couldn't wait to start this new chapter.

Rajveer Rana's family flat was a stunning three-bedroom, 1500 square feet apartment that exuded luxury and sophistication. Located in a posh neighbourhood, the flat was a testament to Rajveer mother's refined taste and style.

Upon arrival, Rajveer's family welcomed Nehal with open arms. His mother, Shubhangi, enveloped her in a warm hug, while his sister, Anya, and brother showered her with affection. The atmosphere was filled with laughter and chatter, instantly making Nehal feel at home.

As she stepped inside, she were greeted by the opulent interiors, carefully crafted to create a warm and inviting atmosphere. The walls were painted a soothing cream colour, complemented by elegant flooring that added a touch of sophistication to the space. The flat was fully air-conditioned, with sleek AC units discreetly installed in each bedroom and the hall, ensuring a comfortable temperature throughout.

Rajveer's bedroom was a serene retreat that reflected his personality and style. The room was dominated by a stunning king-size bed, adorned with plush pillows and a comfortable mattress. The bed was positioned against a wall covered in a beautiful blue-themed wallpaper, which added a touch of elegance to the room. The wallpaper's subtle pattern and soothing colour created a calming ambiance, perfect for relaxation.

The room's interiors were carefully designed to create a sense of luxury and sophistication. A sleek, modern dresser and a comfortable armchair were positioned against adjacent walls, while a large window allowed natural light to flood the room. The window was dressed in elegant curtains that filtered the sunlight, adding a touch of warmth to the space. A flat-screen TV was mounted on the wall opposite the bed, providing entertainment options for Rajveer.

With Rajveer's assistance, Nehal began to unpack, and he helped her set up her workstation on his study table. Her massive Samsung screen fit perfectly, and Rajveer insisted she take his chair, making her feel like the queen of the castle.

As Nehal settled into her new surroundings, she felt an overwhelming sense of joy and gratitude. This house, filled with love, laughter, and warmth, was now her home. She knew that she had made the right decision in giving Rajveer a second chance, and she couldn't wait to start this new journey with him and his wonderful family.

Nehal's initial days at Rajveer's house were a whirlwind of emotions. She was excited to start this new chapter with the love of her life, but she was also nervous about adjusting to a new family dynamic.

Shubhangi, Rajveer's mother, immediately put Nehal at ease with her warm smile and open arms. "Beta, you're home now," she said, embracing Nehal tightly. Nehal felt a lump form in her throat as she hugged Shubhangi back, feeling a deep sense of gratitude and love.

As the days went by, Nehal found herself growing closer to Shubhangi. They would spend hours in the kitchen, cooking and chatting about everything from recipes to life stories. Nehal was amazed by Shubhangi's wisdom, kindness, and generosity. She felt like she had found a second mother in her.

Anya, Rajveer's sister, was another person Nehal bonded with instantly. They shared a love for fashion, music, and movies. They would often stay up late, gossiping and laughing together. Nehal confided in Anya about her fears, dreams, and aspirations, and Anya offered valuable advice and support.

Reyansh, Rajveer's brother, was a different story altogether. He was a mischievous and playful young boy who loved to tease Nehal mercilessly. Nehal would often find herself laughing and chasing after him, trying to get him to behave. Despite their playful banter, Nehal grew fond of Reyansh and enjoyed their silly antics together.

As Nehal settled into her new life, she felt a deep sense of belonging and happiness. She knew that she had found her place in the world, surrounded by people who loved and accepted her for who she was.

One day, as she was helping Shubhangi in the kitchen, Nehal turned to her and said, "Aunty, I'm so grateful to be a part of this family. I feel like I've found my home." Shubhangi smiled and hugged her tightly, saying, "Beta, you've always been a part of this family. We're just glad you're finally here with us."

Rajveer was over the moon when Nehal agreed to move in with him. He had dreamed of waking up every morning with her by his side. But, as the days went by, he began to feel a growing sense of frustration.

With Nehal's demanding work schedule and his own rigorous boxing practice, they hardly got any time together. Nehal would start working early in the morning (WFH) till the wee hours in the evening. Rajveer was busy with his training sessions. They would often go for days without having a proper conversation or spending quality time together.

Rajveer felt like he was losing the connection he had with Nehal. They would steal glances at each other during family dinners, but that was about it. He longed for the days when they could just sit together, hold hands, and talk about their dreams and aspirations.

To make matters worse, the house was always bustling with activity. Shubhangi would often invite friends and family over for dinner, and Anya and Reyansh would always be around, demanding attention. Rajveer loved his family, but he couldn't help feeling like they were intruding on his private time with Nehal.

As the days turned into weeks, Rajveer began to feel like he was losing his mind. He was happy to see Nehal happy, but he couldn't help feeling like he was sacrificing his own happiness in the process. He started to wonder if this was what married life was going to be like — a never-ending cycle of work, family, and responsibilities, with no time for romance or intimacy.

Rajveer knew he had to find a way to balance this life, to make time for Nehal and their relationship. But, for now, he felt stuck, trapped in a cycle of busy-ness, with no escape in sight.

The evening sun cast a warm glow over the living room as Shubhangi gathered the family together, a bright smile spreading across her face. "I have some wonderful news to share with all of you," she announced, her eyes twinkling with excitement.

Anya, who had been sitting quietly in the corner, suddenly found herself at the centre of attention. "Anya has got a job in a multinational bank, and she'll be relocating to Bangalore!" Shubhangi exclaimed.

The room erupted into cheers and applause as Nehal, Rajveer, and Reyansh rushed to congratulate Anya. They were all beaming with pride, thrilled for Anya's achievement. Rajveer ruffled Anya's hair, saying, "We always knew you were a rockstar, sis!"

As the celebration continued, Shubhangi dropped another bombshell. "I've decided to accompany Anya to Bangalore to help her settle in," she said, a sly grin spreading across her face. "And Reyansh will come with us too!"

Rajveer, ever the helpful brother, offered to join them on the trip, but Shubhangi teasingly waved him off. "No, no, beta. You stay here and enjoy some alone time with Nehal. You two deserve it!"

Rajveer's face turned bright red as Nehal's cheeks flushed pink. They exchanged a sheepish glance, both of them aware that they had been craving some quality time together. The rest of the family burst out laughing, happy to see the lovebirds get some time to themselves.

As the evening drew to a close, the family shared a warm, fuzzy feeling, knowing that Anya was embarking on an exciting new chapter, and Rajveer and Nehal would finally get some much-needed alone time.

Few days later, Rajveer went to drop his family at the airport. Rajveer hugged everyone as he knew he would miss them.

As Rajveer returned home, he couldn't shake off the feeling of anticipation that had been building inside him for weeks. A month and a half had passed since Nehal moved in, but their busy schedules and constant family presence had left them craving for some much-needed alone time.

As he entered the house, he was greeted by an eerie silence, a stark contrast to the usual chaos that filled the halls. He called out Nehal's name, his voice echoing through the empty rooms. Suddenly, he heard the soft rustling of fabric, and Nehal emerged from the bedroom, her eyes locked intensely on his. Rajveer's heart skipped a beat as he took in the sight of Nehal, her hair cascading down her back like a waterfall of silk, her skin glowing with a soft, ethereal light. She was dressed in a flowing white gown, her curves accentuated by the delicate fabric. Rajveer's breath caught in his throat as he felt his desire for her ignite like a wildfire.

Nehal's eyes never left Rajveer's as she glided towards him, her movements sensual and deliberate. Rajveer's pulse quickened, his body responding to her proximity. As she reached him, she wrapped her arms around his waist, pulling him close.

Their lips met in a fierce, passionate kiss; the pent-up desire of weeks finally unleashed. Rajveer's hands roamed Nehal's body, reacquainting himself with every curve and contour. Nehal's fingers dug into his hair, pulling him deeper into the kiss.

As they broke apart for air, Rajveer swept Nehal off her feet, carrying her to the bedroom. They made love with a ferocity that left them both breathless, their bodies entwined in a passionate dance.

Again and again, they lost themselves in each other's arms, their love burning brighter with every passing moment. The world outside melted away, leaving only the two of them, lost in a sea of desire and passion.

As the night wore on, Rajveer and Nehal's love became a raging fire, consuming everything in its path. They were two souls, united in their passion, their love for each other burning brighter than ever before.

(Next sunny morning, Rajveer is already up, making coffee. Nehal stumbled into the bathroom, still half-asleep.)

Nehal: (Yawned dramatically) Ugh, morning. My toothbrush feels so...naked.

Rajveer: (Chuckled) Naked? What does a toothbrush wear these days? Tiny little toothpaste pyjama's?

Nehal: (Pouted) No, silly. It needs toothpaste! And I'm too sleepy to do it myself. If it doesn't get toothpaste, it doesn't get used. Simple as that.

Rajveer: (Laughed) You're serious? You're going to hold your toothbrush hostage until I apply the toothpaste? That's a new level of negotiation.

Nehal: (Nodded firmly) Absolutely. My dental hygiene is non-negotiable. Plus, it's cute when you do it.

Rajveer: (Raised an eyebrow) Cute, huh? Alright, your tyranny has been noted. (He squeezed the toothpaste onto her brush) Here you go, Your Majesty. Now, will you grace us with your presence in the land of the living?

Nehal: (Beamed) Thank you, my loyal servant. You may now be excused. (She started brushing her teeth, humming happily.)

Later, they sat together at the breakfast table. Rajveer made pancakes.

Rajveer: These pancakes are calling your name, Nehal. Especially the one shaped like a slightly lopsided heart.

Nehal: (Grinned) They look delicious. But... (She batted her eyelashes) ...I'm feeling exceptionally weak this morning. Maybe... someone could feed me?

Rajveer: (Laughs, surprised) You're kidding, right? You're perfectly capable of feeding yourself.

Nehal: (Playfully) But where's the romance in that? Imagine, me, helpless and dependent on your tender care. It's like a scene from a movie!

Rajveer: (Shook his head, still chuckling) You're incorrigible. But... (He picked up a fork and cuts a piece of pancake) Fine. Open wide, my princess.

Nehal: (Giggled and opened her mouth) Mumm, delicious! You're a keeper, Rajveer.

Later, Nehal was trying to work on her laptop at the kitchen table. Rajveer was nearby, supposedly reading a book, but his eyes kept drifting towards her.

Nehal: (Concentrating) Okay, almost there... just need to finish this report...

Rajveer: (Suddenly tickled her side) Boo!

Nehal: (Squealed and jumped) Rajveer! I almost spilled my coffee! What was that for?

Rajveer: (Grinned mischievously) Just testing your reflexes. They're clearly not as sharp as mine.

Nehal: (Rolled her eyes) I'm trying to work!

Rajveer: (Leaned closer, his voice dropping to a husky whisper) Work? What's more important than spending time with your incredibly handsome and charming boyfriend?

Nehal: (Tried to suppress a smile) My job, actually.

Rajveer: (Gently took her hand and started tracing circles on her palm) But your job isn't here. It's... (He pulled her closer) ...here. With me.

Nehal: (Her breath catching) Rajveer... I really need to focus.

Rajveer: (Nuzzled her neck) I'm helping you focus. Focus on me. On how much I adore you.

Nehal: (Laughed softly) You're impossible.

Rajveer: (Kissed her cheek) And you love it. Now, where were we? Oh yes, the incredibly handsome and charming boyfriend... (He started tickling her again.)

Nehal: (Laughed uncontrollably) Stop! Okay, okay, you win. Five more minutes of cuddles, then I really have to work.

Rajveer: (Pulled her into a hug) Deal. But I'm holding you to that five minute. And after that... maybe a movie night? With popcorn? And more cuddles?

Nehal: (Smiled and snuggled into his arms) Sounds perfect.

At cozy dinner table where plates were almost empty.Rajveer dramatically sighed, holding his plate out to Nehal.

Rajveer: Nehal, darling, my hand... it suddenly seized up. I think it's the carpal tunnel from all that... you know... intense work I've been doing. Can't possibly feed myself.

Nehal: (Raised an eyebrow, picking up her own fork) Intense work? Last I saw, you were intensely battling a level-seven goblin on your game. That requires thumbs, not wrists.

Rajveer: (Winced) It's a sympathetic reaction. My whole body is connected, you see. One overworked thumb, the wrist goes. It's... quantum physics, probably.

Nehal: (Chuckled) Sure, babe. Here, have some palak paneer. Maybe the spinach will miraculously cure your... quantum carpal tunnel.

Nehal scooped a small portion onto his plate. Rajveer pouted.

Rajveer: Is that all? I'm wasting away! I need sustenance! Think of the starving children... who also probably have better motor skills than me right now.

Nehal: (Laughed) Fine, fine. Open wide, Mr. Starving Child with Quantum Carpal Tunnel. But just this once. Next time, you're feeding me with your perfectly functional hand.

Nehal fed him a few bites. Rajveer beamed, making exaggerated chewing noises.

Later, when the time for dessert arrived—a shared tub of Baskin Robbins Honey Nut Crunch.

Nehal: (Scooped a generous amount) Ah, the perfect ending to a perfect... slightly dramatic... dinner.

(Rajveer eyed the tub with predatory focus.)

Rajveer: Wait a second! That's... that's a disproportionate scoop! You're hogging all the honeycomb! The honeycomb is the soul of Honey Nut Crunch!

Nehal: (Defensive) I am not hogging! Besides, you had your "quantum carpal tunnel" excuse for dinner. My excuse is... I love honeycomb.

(They both dig in, the tub rapidly emptying.)

Rajveer: (Pointed with his spoon) Look! You're creating a honeycomb avalanche! It's all sliding to your side! This is an ice cream injustice!

Nehal: It's called gravity, Rajveer. And besides, I'm clearly the superior ice cream scooper. My technique is flawless.

(Rajveer tried to subtly nudge the tub closer to him with his elbow. Nehal caught him.)

Nehal Oh no you don't! That's a strategic nudge! I saw that! You're trying to claim more territory!

Rajveer: (Feigned innocence) I... I was just admiring the... the curvature of the tub. Very aesthetically pleasing.

(They both stared at the rapidly diminishing ice cream.)

Nehal: You know what? This is ridiculous.

Rajveer: I agree! We need a bigger tub! This is clearly not enough Honey Nut Crunch for two people as sophisticated as us.

Nehal: (Grinned) Or... we could just... (She lunged forward, scooping a massive chunk of ice cream) ...eat it really, really fast!

(Rajveer let out a war cry and dived in after her. They ended up laughing, covered in ice cream, the tub almost empty.)

Rajveer: (Wiped his mouth) You know, for someone with such a refined palate, you're a surprisingly messy eater.

Nehal: (Smiled) And you, Mr. Quantum Carpal Tunnel, are a surprisingly competitive ice cream fiend.

(They both looked at the empty tub.)

Rajveer & Nehal (in unison): Baskin Robbins, anyone?

Next morning, Nehal: (Stretched luxuriously) Mmm, good morning.

Rajveer: (Smiled) Morning, sleepyhead. Did you sleep well?

Nehal: Like a log. But... (She pouted cutely) something's missing.

Rajveer: What's that?

Nehal glided her hand inside the blanket and eventually his boxer shorts. She felt the warmth of his hard morning wood on her palm, Nehal started breathing heavily, aroused and possessed by her primal desires. She stroked the wood rhythmically, craved for it to be inside of her, in the same motion she leaned on top of Rajveer and gestured him to open his mouth. As soon as he obliged, she touched his mouth with her drooling tongue, and they kissed each other passionately, their tongues dancing against each other. Then with the growing impatience and urgency with Nehal, she removed his boxer and threw them off. She positioned herself between his thighs, awakening the beast inside Rajveer. Rajveer lost in pleasure couldnt hold it anymore, the beast inside of him takes over and grabed Nehal's ass. He entered inside of her like a ferocious animal, **his movements becoming rougher, more demanding.** A desperate hunger consumed them both, as they drew closer, their lips met in a tender, exploratory kiss. The world around them melted away, leaving only the two of them, suspended in a sea of passion. Rajveer switched their positions taking over the control, Rajveer's hands roamed around Nehal's body, worshipping every curve and contour. His fingers danced across her skin, leaving trails of fire in their wake. Nehal's breath caught in her throat as Rajveer's touch ignited a deep, primal desire within her. Their kisses grew more urgent, more passionate, as they surrendered to the all-consuming flame of their love. Nehal's hands tangled in Rajveer's hair, pulling him deeper into their kiss. Rajveer's arms wrapped around her, holding her close as they devoured each other. In that moment, Nehal and Rajveer were one, their love a burning, all-consuming force that threatened to consume them whole. And yet, they wouldn't have had it any other way, for in each other's arms, they had found their true home.

Later, when Nehal stretched lazily, she blinked at Rajveer, a mischevious smile played on her lips.

Nehal: Your face. It needs... attention. (She gestured vaguely) You know... the fuzzy stuff.

Rajveer: You mean my magnificent beard? My rugged handsomeness? You want me to... shave it? (He feigned horror) Nehal, how could you?

Nehal: (Laughed) Don't be dramatic. It's just... a little trim. A little shaping. Please? (She gave him her best puppy-dog eyes)

Rajveer: (Sighed dramatically) Okay, okay. You've twisted my arm. But you're doing it.

Nehal: Me? I don't know how!

Rajveer: Exactly! A perfect opportunity for you to learn. Come on. (He got up and led her to the mirror, handing her the shaving cream and razor)

Nehal: (Hesitantly started applying the shaving cream) Okay... like this?

Rajveer: (Nodded) Yeah, just like that. Nice and foamy. (He watched her closely)

Nehal: (Concentrating hard) Is this enough?

Rajveer: Perfect. Now, the razor... gently...

Just as Nehal was about to start, Rajveer suddenly grabbed the can of shaving cream and playfully squirted a large dollop of foam onto Nehal's face.

Nehal: (Gasped, laughed as she tried to wipe the foam off her nose) Rajveer! What did you do?!

Rajveer: (Laughed hysterically) Consider it... a pre-shave facial! Besides, you were concentrating too hard. Needed to lighten the mood.

Nehal: (Spluttered with laughter) You... you... I'm going to get you back for this!

Rajveer: (Grinned) Can't wait. But first... (He gently wiped some foam off her cheek) You look absolutely adorable.

Nehal rolled her eyes and playfully flicked some shaving cream at him in retaliation.

Nehal is seated at desk, typing furiously on her laptop. She occasionally glanced at Rajveer, who was pretending to discreetly check his watch.)

Nehal: Rajveer?

Rajveer: (Tried to sound casual) Hmm?

Nehal: You're not looking at me.

Rajveer: I... I was just admiring the... uh... intricate design of the ceiling tiles. Very... inspiring.

Nehal: (Raised an eyebrow) Really? Because I distinctly remember you looking at your watch a second ago. I need you to look at me while I work. It helps me concentrate.

Rajveer: (Chuckled) You're kidding, right?

Nehal: Absolutely not. Eyes on me, Rajveer. Consider it... moral support.

(Rajveer sighed dramatically, but turns his gaze towards Nehal. He watched as she types, occasionally pushes her hair back, and bites her lip in concentration. After a few minutes...)

Rajveer: (Shifted in his seat) So... you sure you don't need anything? Water? A motivational speech? Perhaps a rendition of "Eye of the Tiger" to really get you in the zone?

Nehal: (Without looking up) Just your eyes on me. That's all the motivation I need.

(Rajveer watched for another few minutes, then stretched his arms. He glanced at his watch again, more openly this time.)

Rajveer: Nehal, my boxing practice...

Nehal: (Still typing) Is it more important than... my... concentration?

Rajveer: (Defeated) No, no, of course not. Your concentration is paramount. The fate of the world probably rests on it.

(He continued to watch her, but now a mischievous glint sparked in his eyes. He leaned back in his chair, adopting a more relaxed posture. He started humming softly, a low, seductive tune.)

Nehal: (Frowned slightly) Rajveer, what are you doing?

Rajveer: (Looked directly at her, his voice dropping to a husky whisper) Just... appreciating the... dedication. The focus. The... intense concentration. It's... captivating.

(He let his gaze travel slowly down her face, lingering on her lips.)

Nehal: (Stumbled slightly in her typing) Rajveer... I...

Rajveer: (Leaned forward slightly) You know, I've always admired your... work ethic. The way your brow furrows when you're deep in thought. It's... incredibly... distracting.

(He reached out and gently brushed a stray strand of hair from her face.)

Nehal: (Her breath hitches) Rajveer... I... I think I'm losing my... concentration.

Rajveer: (Smiled) Is that my fault?

(He moved closer, his eyes locked on hers.)

Nehal: (Drops her hands from the keyboard) Maybe... maybe.

(Rajveer leaned in and whispers in her ear.)

Rajveer: Perhaps... we should take a break? A very... concentrated break?

(Nehal's lips curve into a playful smile. She pushed her laptop aside.)

Nehal: I think... I think you've just given me a brilliant idea.

(Rajveer grinned as their eyes meet. The "work" is definitely forgotten.)

It was Friday evening, after Nehal finished her work with lots of difficulty and distractions, they decide to have a house party. Rajveer headed out to buy himself whiskey, Redwine for Nehal with apple flavoured hukkah, chicken starters, and chicken Biryani. (Upbeat Bollywood music blasted from the home theatre. Rajveer and Nehal were a whirlwind of limbs, laughing and twirling, drinks sloshing precariously in their hands.)

Rajveer: (Singing off-key) "Ooh, Munni Badnaam! My jam!"

Nehal: (Equally off-key, but with more enthusiasm) "Rajveer, you're going to pull a muscle! And spill my wine!"

(She narrowly avoided a red wine catastrophe.)

Rajveer: Worth it! (He dipped her dramatically, nearly sending her sprawling.) Whoa! Graceful as ever, my love.

Nehal: (Giggled) You call that graceful? I'm surprised the neighbours haven't called the cops yet. They probably think we're having a wrestling match.

Rajveer: Let them think what they want! It's Friday night! We're celebrating... surviving another week with our sanity intact.

Nehal: Speak for yourself. Mine's hanging by a thread. (She stumbled slightly.) Okay, new song! My choice!

(She grabbed the remote and switched to Elvis Presley's "Can't Help Falling in Love.")

Rajveer: Elvis? Seriously? Going all romantic on me now?

Nehal: (Smiled mischievously) Maybe. Come on, slow dance with me, Mr. Munni Badnaam.

The soft, sultry strains of the song filled the room, casting a romantic spell over Rajveer and Nehal. They stood facing each other, their eyes locked in a loving gaze, as they swayed to the music.

Rajveer's hands reached out, and he gently grasped Nehal's waist, pulling her close. Nehal's arms wrapped around his neck, her fingers tangling in his hair as they began to move in perfect harmony.

Their bodies swayed to the rhythm, their hips swishing in time, as they lost themselves in the music and each other's eyes. The world around them melted away, leaving only the two of them, suspended in a sea of love and desire.

As they danced, Rajveer's lips brushed against Nehal's ear, sending shivers down her spine. Nehal's eyes fluttered closed, and she let out a soft sigh.

Their dance was a sensual, intimate expression of their love, a celebration of the passion and desire that burned between them. As they twirled and swayed, their love seemed to grow, expanding to fill every corner of the room.

The music built to a crescendo, and Rajveer's hands tightened around Nehal's waist, pulling her closer. Nehal's eyes snapped open, and she gazed up at Rajveer, her eyes shining with love and adoration.

As the final notes of the song faded away, Rajveer's lips met Nehal's in a soft, gentle kiss. They stood there, wrapped in each other's arms, their hearts beating as one. The music lingered on, a reminder of the love that filled their souls.

Rajveer: You know, for someone who nearly knocked me over five times in the last ten minutes, you're surprisingly graceful when you want to be.

Nehal: (Leaned her head on his chest) Just depends on the music. And the dance partner.

(The song ended. Nehal finished her glass of red wine in one gulp, then eyed Rajveer's whiskey.)

Nehal: Mmm, Rajveer, please never change anything about you, under any circumstances. I just love they way you are. That looks good.

Rajveer: Hey! That's my...

(Before he can finish, she snatched his glass and downs his whiskey in one go.)

Nehal: (Smacked her lips) Delicious! Thanks!

Rajveer: (Stared at his empty glass) You... you drank my whiskey!

Nehal: (Grinning) You weren't using it. Besides, I'm feeling... adventurous.

(She threw her arms up in the air, swaying erratically.)

Rajveer: Adventurous is one word for it. Crazy is another.

Nehal: Maybe a little. But hey, it's Friday, right? (She grabbed his hand.) Come on, let's dance! (She started doing some wild, freestyle moves.)

Rajveer: (Laughed and shook his head) You're a menace. A beautiful, whiskey-stealing menace.

(He joined her, and soon they're dancing like mad people again, the Elvis romance forgotten in a haze of Bollywood beats and happy chaos.)

As they were exhausted from dancing for hours, the couple in high spirits finally settled down for dinner together.

Rajveer and Nehal sat at the table laden with chicken lollipop and biryani. Rajveer was trying to spear a particularly saucy lollipop.

Rajveer: (Slurringly) Nehal, my love... my Jaan... you must try this... this... phoenix eather of chicken. It's... (Struggled to get it on his fork) it's... defying gravity! Like my love for you!

Nehal: (Giggled uncontrollably, eyes sparkling) Rajveer, you're such a... a poet! But... (Pointing at the biryani) the real magic... is here. This biryani... it whispers secrets of... of... deliciousness!

(She scooped up a huge spoonful of biryani, nearly dropping half of it.)

Rajveer: (Eyes widening) Whoa! Careful there, Nehal! That's... that's enough biryani to feed a... a small army.

Nehal: (Shoved spoonful towards Rajveer's face) Open wide, my... my valiant knight! For I... I have brought you... the... the... holy grail of rice!

(Rajveer tried to open his mouth wide, but ends up getting biryani all over his cheek.)

Rajveer: (Laughed) Whoa! I think... I think the grail... just attacked me!

Nehal: (Wiped his cheek with the back of her hand, smearing biryani further) Nonsense! It... it was a love attack! A biryani... kiss!

(She giggled and tried to feed him again, this time managing to get some in his mouth.)

Rajveer: (Chewed enthusiastically) Mmm... you're right! It is... magical! It tastes like... like... sunshine and... and... victory!

Nehal: (Clapped her hands) Victory! Yes! We have conquered... the... the chicken kingdom!

(Rajveer grabbed a lollipop and tried to feed Nehal, but it slipped and fell on the table.)

Rajveer: (Stared at the fallen lollipop) Oh, no! The... the phoenix... has... has fallen!

Nehal: (Picked up the lollipop and popped it into her mouth) Don't worry, my love. It... it has merely... reincarnated! As... as a delicious... snack!

(They both burst into laughter, grabbing more food and continuing their chaotic, hilarious dinner.)

Rajveer: You know, Nehal... I think... I think I'm in love with you... and this... this... stupendous chicken!

Nehal: (Grinned) I think... I think I'm in love with you too, Rajveer... and... and this... insane amount of biryani!

(They clinked their glasses, spilling some whiskey in the process, and continued their merry, drunken feast.)

Next morning, they both woke with humongous hangover.

Rajveer: (Groaned) Ugh... my head feels like a construction site. Nehal, are you alive?

Nehal: (Barely audible) I think so... barely. My brain feels like it's trying to escape through my ears.

Rajveer: Tell me about it. I feel like I wrestled a bear last night... and the bear won. Miserably.

Nehal: We need help. Like, serious help. Lemon juice, ORS, or some food.

Rajveer: I agree. But who's going? I'm pretty sure I'm physically incapable of moving more than an inch.

Nehal: Not it! I think my soul left my body last night. It's probably at Irani Cafe right now, ordering Keema pav.

Rajveer: (Eyes widened slightly) Irani Cafe... Keema pav... Oh, that sounds heavenly. But still, who's going?

Nehal: (Dramatically) No! My hangover is clearly worse! I'm practically a vegetable!

Rajveer: So am I! I think I saw stars when I tried to sit up. Besides, you have two legs. I only have one and a half right now.

Nehal: (Suddenly) Wait a minute... why are we even debating this?

Rajveer: What do you mean?

Nehal: We have phones, right? And food delivery apps?

Rajveer: (Stared blankly) ...Oh. My god. You're a genius!

Nehal: I know, right? Even hungover, I'm brilliant. Now, let's see... Irani Cafe... Keema pav...cutlet, Samosa and maybe some of those delicious biscuits...

Nehal scrolled through the app and placed a massive order. Rajveer dialed the number of the medical shop nearby and placed an order for lots of Ors, lemon juice, and a few energy drinks.)

Rajveer: You know, for someone who's practically a vegetable, you're pretty efficient.

Nehal: Hey, even vegetables get hungry. And they definitely deserve keema pav after a night like that.

They settle back into their pillows, waiting for the delivery, their hangovers slightly forgotten in the anticipation of delicious food and refreshments.

After struggling for some time, the couple get out of the bed.(The black Hole they used to call it, as it was always difficult for them to get out of it). They took a shower together to save water, time, and energy. They had some Brunch and lots of fluids, and crashed on the bed for an afternoon nap.

They felt energetic in the evening, both exploring options to party today. Nehal suggested they go to" The Waters," Rajveer thinks it's a great idea and loads of fun.

Rajveer: (Tapped his foot impatiently, admiring himself in the mirror) Wow, I have to say, this three-piece suit is killing it. I look like I should be on the cover of "GQ: Gentlemen's Quarterly... Waiting Impatiently for His Girlfriend to Finish Getting Ready."

Nehal: (Struggled with a particularly stubborn curl) Almost... almost... just this one little piece of rebellion...

Rajveer: Rebellion? Darling, the only rebellion happening here is your hair against the natural laws of straightness. I swear, if we don't leave soon, the bouncers at The Waters will think I've been stood up and give my table to some other impeccably dressed, but sadly, single gentleman.

Nehal: (Scoffed) As if! You know no one can resist my charm.

Rajveer: Oh, I know someone who's resisting something... (He winked) It's a certain silver dress that's currently hiding behind a very stubborn head of hair. Care to reveal it? I've been waiting with bated breath, and my breath is starting to smell suspiciously like expensive cologne and mild desperation.

Nehal: (Turned, finally revealing the stunning silver dress, striking a pose) Ta-da! What do you think? Worth the wait?

Rajveer: (Jaw dropped) Worth the wait? Nehal, you look... you look like you're about to set the dance floor on fire. And possibly a few hearts as well. Mine included.

Nehal: (Grinned) Mission accomplished. Now, are you going to stand there admiring me all night, or are we going to go set this town on fire? Because this dress wasn't designed for a quiet night in.

Rajveer: (Extended his arm) My dear, with you in that dress, even a quiet night in would be an inferno. Let's go, before I spontaneously combust from sheer appreciation. Just promise me one thing.

Nehal: What?

Rajveer: That you'll save a dance for the guy who spent the last half hour waiting for you.

Nehal: (Laughed and took his arm) Deal. But be warned, my dance moves are as fiery as this dress.

Rajveer: (Smiled) That's exactly what I'm hoping for.

The nightclub, "The Waters", was a marvel of modern design, with its sleek, aquatic-themed decor and pulsating lights that seemed to dance across the walls. As Rajveer and Nehal stepped onto the crowded floor, they were immediately swept up in the infectious energy of the party.

The air was electric, charged with the collective excitement of the revellers. The sound system pulsed with a driving beat, a fusion of Hollywood and Bollywood dance numbers that had the crowd moving in perfect sync. Fireworks exploded in bursts of colourful light, casting a kaleidoscope of hues across the dance floor.Rajveer and Nehal lost themselves in the music, their bodies swaying to the rhythm as they laughed and spun to the beat. They sipped on Long Island Iced Teas, the sweet, tangy flavour fuelling their revelry as they danced the night away.

As the hours wore on, the crowd grew more frenzied, the energy building to a fever pitch. Rajveer and Nehal were caught up in the whirlwind, their senses overwhelmed by the sights, sounds, and sensations that surrounded them.

The aquariums that lined the walls of the club added an otherworldly touch to the proceedings, the glowing fish and sea creatures casting an ethereal glow over the dance floor. It was as if Rajveer and Nehal had stumbled into an underwater wonderland, where the rules of reality no longer applied.

And yet, even as they lost themselves in the anonymity of the crowd, they remained acutely aware of each other's presence, their connection a steady, pulsing heartbeat that underlay the wild, swirling energy of the party.

Loud music throbbed, the strobe lights flashed. Rajveer and Nehal danced in sync, a few feet apart.

(A girl in revealing clothes slided upto Rajveer, trying to get his attention.)

Girl: (Shouted over the music, bumping into Rajveer) Omg, this song is insane, right?!

Rajveer: (Nodded slowly and looked around vaguely) Uh, yeah. Good...beats.

Girl: (Moved closer, her voice barely audible) I love this place! You come here often?

Rajveer: (Shrugs, distracted) Sometimes.

(Nehal watched from a few feet away, a smirk playing on her lips.)

Girl: (Leaned in further) You look...familiar. Do I know you from somewhere?

Rajveer: (Squinted) Hmm...maybe? I have one of those faces.

(The girl pulled out a cigarette. Rajveer, ever the gentleman, automatically pulled out his lighter. He lit her cigarette.)

Girl: (Smiled brightly) Thanks! You're a lifesaver. I'm...

(Before she can finish, Rajveer, as if suddenly remembering something crucial, turned and walked towards Nehal, leaving the girl mid-sentence.)

(Rajveer reached Nehal and she playfully whacked him on the back of the head.)

Nehal: (Feigned annoyance) Rajveer, behave yourself! I thought you came here to dance with me, not light cigarettes for strangers.

Rajveer: (Rubbed his head, grinning sheepishly) What? Me? Never! She was just...asking a lighter. You know, which way is the...uh...fire exit. Important safety information.

Nehal: (Raised an eyebrow) Right. And the cigarette? Was that part of the fire safety demonstration?

Rajveer: (Chuckled nervously) Look, she seemed...lost. A damsel in distress. A knight in shining...sequins...had to help.

Nehal: (Laughed) You're incorrigible. Come on, let's actually dance before you get recruited as a designated lighter-wielder for the entire club.

(Nehal pulled Rajveer back towards the dance floor. As they danced, Nehal whispered in his ear.)

Nehal: Though, I have to admit, your "I have one of those faces" line was pretty smooth.

Rajveer: (Grinned) See? I'm a man of many talents. Including...avoiding awkward conversations.

(They both laughed and continued to dance.)

Rajveer and Nehal sank into the backseat of a cab, their bodies clearly exhausted, their mind still buzzing.

Rajveer: That was a blast, wasn't it? This night couldn't get any better.

Nehal: It sure was. I needed this after the week I've had.

Rajveer: Hey, speaking of the week, I've got a friendly boxing match tomorrow afternoon. I'd love for you to come and watch me in action.

Nehal: I'm not sure, Rajveer. I'm not really into violent sports.

Rajveer: Come on, it'll be fun! And it's not really violent, it's more like a dance with gloves.

Nehal: (Laughed) If you say so. But I'll only come if you join me for a swim later that evening.

Rajveer: That's a deal! I've always wanted to see you in your element.

Nehal: It's a date then. I'll see you at the ring tomorrow.

Rajveer: Awesome! I promise you won't regret it.

Nehal: I hope not. But if I do, you're buying me ice cream.

Rajveer: Deal. But I'm warning you, I'm a tough opponent.

Nehal: We'll see about that. I've got a few moves of my own.

Sunday afternoon, Rajveer and Nehal arrived at the boxing club. Nehal wished Rajveer good luck for his match, with a kiss on his cheek. The people around them watched with jealousy, and others with some awkwardness.

The air was electric as Rajveer and Aarav faced off in the ring, their eyes locked in a fierce stare. The crowd was on the edge of their seats, sensing that this was going to be a battle for the ages.

The bell rang, and the two fighters exploded into action, their fists flying in a flurry of punches. Rajveer and Aarav were evenly matched, each landing solid blows that sent the other stumbling back.

But Rajveer was determined to win, and he dug deep, finding a reservoir of strength and determination that he didn't know he possessed. He pushed himself to his limits, refusing to back down even when Aarav landed a series of brutal punches that sent him crashing to the canvas.

Rajveer struggled to his feet, his eyes blazing with a fierce determination. He knew that he had to give it everything he had if he was going to win. Aarav, sensing victory, came at him with a flurry of punches, but Rajveer was ready.

With a fierce cry, he launched himself at Aarav, landing a series of devastating punches that sent his opponent stumbling back. The crowd was on its feet, cheering and chanting Rajveer's name as he battled his way back into the fight.

Nehal watched in awe, her heart pounding with excitement and worry. She had never seen Rajveer fight before, and she was amazed by his skill, stamina, and determination. But she was also terrified for his safety, wincing every time Aarav landed a solid punch.

The fight raged on; each round more intense than the last. Rajveer and Aarav were evenly matched, each refusing to give an inch. But Rajveer's determination and persistence eventually began to pay off.

In the sixth round, he landed a devastating combination of punches that sent Aarav crashing to the canvas. The crowd erupted into cheers as Rajveer stood over his opponent, his arms raised in triumph.

Nehal was on her feet, screaming with excitement and relief. She rushed to Rajveer's side, throwing her arms around him and holding him tightly. Rajveer was bruised and battered, but he was grinning from ear to ear.

"I did it," he whispered, his voice hoarse from exhaustion. "I showed him what I'm made of."

Nehal looked up at him, her eyes shining with pride and admiration. "You were amazing," she whispered. "I'm so proud of you."

Rajveer smiled, his eyes locked on hers. "I couldn't have done it without you," he said.

"You're my everything, Nehal. My rock, my motivation, my reason for fighting."

Later, as they sat in the locker room, Nehal was tending to Rajveer's bruises.

"Ouch, careful!" Rajveer winced as Nehal dabbed at the cut above his eyebrow.

Nehal's hand trembled slightly. She was trying to be careful, but the sight of Rajveer's bruised face, especially the angry purple and black bloom around his eye, churned her stomach. "Rajveer, honestly..." she began, her voice a mix of worry and exasperation. "Do you really want this? This... this sport... as your career?"

He chuckled, a low, throaty sound. "Come on, Nehal. It's not that bad."

"Not that bad?" She gestured to his face with the cotton swab, careful not to touch the swollen areas. "You look like you went ten rounds with a grizzly bear! I know you're good, Rajveer. I saw you out there today. You were like... like an injured lion, the way you came back. It was incredible. But... what if next time you don't come back? What if you get hurt... badly?" Her voice trailed off, the unspoken fear hanging heavy in the air. She knew how dangerous his chosen sport was, and seeing him like this made her blood run cold.

Rajveer sighed, a flicker of something—annoyance—crossed his face before he masked it with a smile. "Nehal, you worry too much. It's part of the game. Besides," he added, trying to lighten the mood, "Someone has to win, right?"

Nehal pressed her lips together, unconvinced. "You could be doing something... safer. You were so good at software development. A stable job, good pay..." Rajveer reached out and took her hand, his touch surprisingly gentle. "I know, I know. You're right. It's just..." He trailed off, his gaze drifting to the window. "It's not just a sport, Nehal. It's... something more. I can't explain it." He squeezed her hand gently. "But hey, enough about me getting beat up. I'm more worried about you. You're going down next time we hit the pool. I've been practicing my butterfly stroke." He grinned, the black eye crinkling at the corner.

Nehal looked at him, her worry still etched on her face. She wanted to argue more, to make him see sense. But she knew Rajveer. Once he'd made up his mind, there was no changing it. She forced a small smile. "Oh, is that so? We'll see about that," she replied, trying to match his light tone. Inside, though, her fear for him lingered, a knot of anxiety tightening in her stomach.

As they left the club, they both stopped for refreshments, grabbed some energy drinks on the way.

The pool at the club sparkled like a diamond-studded oasis, inviting Rajveer and Nehal to dive into a friendly swimming competition. The air was alive with the sound of laughter and splashing water, as the two lovers faced off at the starting block.

Rajveer, still nursing bruises from his intense boxing match earlier that afternoon, grinned determinedly at Nehal. "I'm going to beat you, Nehal!" he declared, his eyes twinkling with mischief.

Nehal, a seasoned swimmer with years of experience, smiled sweetly at Rajveer. "Oh, I don't think so, Raj," she teased, her voice dripping with confidence.

The two competitors plunged into the water, their strokes powerful and swift.

Rajveer gave it his all, his muscles burning as he fought to keep up with Nehal's lightning-fast pace.

But despite his best efforts, Rajveer couldn't shake off the lingering effects of his boxing match. His bruises ached with every stroke, making it difficult for him to swim as freely as he would have liked.

Nehal, on the other hand, glided through the water with ease, her powerful strokes devouring the distance. She was a fish in water, her movements fluid and effortless.

As they approached the final lap, Nehal pulled ahead, her lead increasing with every stroke. Rajveer gritted his teeth, refusing to give up, but it was clear that Nehal was the superior swimmer.

With a triumphant cry, Nehal touched the wall, her arms raised in victory. Rajveer followed close behind, his chest heaving with exhaustion.

As they climbed out of the pool, Nehal turned to Rajveer, her eyes sparkling with amusement. "You're pretty fast for a boxer," she teased, "but I think I've got this whole swimming thing down pat!"

Rajveer grinned, his eyes admiring Nehal's sleek, athletic physique. "Yeah, I think you win this round, Nehal," he conceded, wrapping his arms around her waist. "But I'll be back, and next time, I won't be holding back!"

Nehal laughed, her eyes shining with excitement. "I'm looking forward to it, Raj," she whispered, her lips brushing against his ear.

After swimming, they made a quick stop to the doctor's clinic to check on Rajveer's bruises. The doctor exmined him with practiced eye, prescribing painkillers and soothing balm.

Back in the house, Rajveer ordered some dal khichadi and boiled eggs for dinner.

Rajveer winced slightly as he shifted on the sofa. "Ugh, every muscle in my body feels like it's been stretched to its limit."

Nehal, perched beside him, smiled gently. "I told you not to overdo it at the club today. Now, open up. One more bite of this khichdi. Doctor's orders, remember?" She held out the spoon, laden with fragrant dal khichdi.

Rajveer looked at her, his eyes filled with warmth. "You're the best doctor I could ask for, Nehal. Seriously, I don't know what I'd do without you fussing over me like this." He took the bite, savouring the taste and, more importantly, Nehal's care.

"This is... this is amazing." Nehal blushed, stirring the khichdi in the bowl.

She then picked up a boiled egg, peeling it carefully. "And here's your protein boost. Gotta gets you back to fighting fit."

Rajveer watched her, his heart swelling with affection. He reached out and gently took the egg from her hand. "Nehal," he began, his voice a little husky, "you're... you're incredible. The way you take care of me, the way you... everything about you. I'm completely, utterly, madly in love with you."

Nehal's eyes met his, her own brimming with emotion. She placed her hand over his. Rajveer brought the egg to her lips, offering her a bite. Nehal took it, her gaze never leaving his. "It's delicious," she whispered.

After a moment of comfortable silence, Rajveer took another spoonful of khichdi, then, with a slightly mischievous glint in his eyes, he held out the spoon to

Nehal. "Your turn. You deserve some of this love-filled khichdi too."

Nehal laughed, taking a small bite from the spoon. As she did, her expression turned a little more serious. "Rajveer," she started, her voice soft but firm, "This is wonderful, you're wonderful, and... and I love you too. But... you know we've talked about the future, about... us."

Rajveer nodded, his heart beating a little faster.

Nehal continued, "And... well, a stable job is important for that future, isn't it? So, we can, you know... get married, start our life together... soon?" She looked at him, her eyes searching his.

Rajveer smiled, understanding dawning in his eyes. He took her hand in his, squeezing it gently. "You're right, Nehal. Absolutely right. I've been looking, I promise. And I have a couple of promising leads. I want that future with you too, more than anything. I'll make it happen, I promise. Soon." He looked at her, his eyes filled with love and determination. "Very soon."

The three months that Rajveer and Nehal spent together at his place were nothing short of magical. With Rajveer's family away in Bangalore, the couple had the freedom to create their own little world—filled with love, laughter, and madness.

Every day was a new adventure, a new opportunity to explore each other's quirks and passions. They would spend hours cooking together, trying out new recipes and flavors. They would laugh together, watching old movies and TV shows, sharing inside jokes and silly memes.

But most of all, they would love each other, with every fiber of their being. They would cuddle up on the couch, holding hands and talking about their dreams and aspirations. They would gaze into each other's eyes, feeling the depth of their connection.

As the days turned into weeks, and the weeks turned into months, their love only grew stronger. They were falling for each other more and more with every passing second.

But as the three months drew to a close, Rajveer's family returned to Pune, bringing with them stories of their adventures in Bangalore. Shubhangi and Reyansh regaled Rajveer and Nehal with tales of the city's vibrant culture and delicious food.

Rajveer and Nehal, in turn, shared stories of their own adventures, of the laughter and love they had shared during their time alone together. They video-called Anya, who was thriving in her new job and new city.

As they sat down to lunch together, the atmosphere was filled with warmth and laughter. It was clear that the time apart had only strengthened their bond, and that they were all happy to be together again.

But as the days went by, Rajveer began to feel the pressure of finding a job. The market was down, and rejection after rejection chipped away his confidence. He was tense and worried, fearing that he would lose Nehal if he couldn't provide for her.

Nehal, sensing his distress, was emphatic in her encouragement. She told him to keep searching, to never give up on his dreams. She reminded him that she lovedhim for who he was, not for his job or his salary.

Rajveer felt a surge of gratitude towards Nehal, knowing that she was his rock, his support system. He vowed to keep fighting, to keep pushing forward, no matter what challenges lay ahead.

CHAPTER 24:
"SUNKISSED SERENITY"

(A sleeper bus rattled along the highway to Goa. Nehal struggled to get comfortable in her upper berth. Rajveer is in the lower berth, directly below her.)

Nehal: (Struggling) Ugh, this is like trying to fold myself into a samosa. Are you sure this thing is designed for humans and not, like, extremely flexible garden gnomes?

Rajveer: (From below) Tell me about it. I feel like I'm in a coffin designed for a very short, slightly chubby Dracula.

Nehal: (Lost her grip, nearly falling) Whoa! Did you just feel that? I think my hip tried to escape.

Rajveer: (Deadpaned) I felt something. I assumed it was your existential dread seeping through the mattress.

Nehal: (Finally settled, but precariously) Very funny. Just wait till you have to climb up here. You'll be singing a different tune when your knees are trying to have a conversation with your elbows.

Rajveer: Oh, I'm sure. I've been practicing my "old man getting out of a La-Z-Boy" routine for years. It's practically an Olympic sport.

Nehal: You know, for a "Dracula in a coffin," you're remarkably chatty.

Rajveer: Hey, even vampires need to socialize. Besides, what else am I going to do? Stare at the bottom of your mattress and contemplate the mysteries of lint?

Nehal: Good point. Although, there is a fascinating collection of crumbs down there. Looks like someone had a party with a bag of chips.

Rajveer: (Wrinkled his nose) Please don't point that out. I'm trying to maintain the illusion that I'm sleeping in a clean, hygienic environment. Let me live in my denial.

Nehal: Alright, alright. Just promise me you won't snore. I've heard sleeper buses are breeding grounds for nocturnal symphonies of epic proportions.

Rajveer: I can't make any promises. My nose has a mind of its own. Sometimes, it likes to perform an interpretive dance of a chainsaw.

Nehal: (Groaned) This is going to be a long trip.

Rajveer: Yep. But hey, at least we'll have some good stories to tell... if we survive.

Nehal: Don't jinx it! Now, if you'll excuse me, I'm going to attempt to sleep. Wish me luck.

Rajveer: May the odds be ever in your favor. And may your hip stay attached.

After a Humpty dumpty ride, they finally reached Goa. A half-hour ride later, they arrived at Agoda wellness.

They were greeted with a warm welcome by the manager.

Manager: Welcome to the Agoda Wellness Retreat in Goa, a serene haven designed to rejuvenate your mind, body, and soul.

Nestled amidst the picturesque landscape of Goa, this luxurious retreat offers a perfect blend of relaxation, wellness, and adventure. The retreat features elegantly designed villas, each equipped with modern amenities and breathtaking views of the surrounding landscape.

Every activity here indulged in a range of wellness, including yoga and meditation sessions, guided by expert instructors. Revitalizing your senses with rejuvenating spa treatments, or taking a leisurely stroll along the beach and feeling the warm sand between your toes.

The retreat's culinary team crafts delicious, healthy meals using locally sourced ingredients, ensuring a truly immersive experience. As the sun sets, gather around the bonfire, sharing stories and laughter with fellow travellers.

For Rajveer and Nehal, this retreat is the perfect opportunity to escape the chaos of their daily lives and reconnect with each other, surrounded by the serene beauty of Goa.

Once they got settled in their villa, the couple headed down to the beach. They go for a swim, then they ordered some refreshments and relaxed on the shack. Due to the traveling fatigue, they decided to spend the day relaxing.

Next morning, Rajveer suggested to visit a casino— Casino royale. They travelled by road to Panjim and with the help of a boat they reached Casino Royale.

(Rajveer and Nehal stood at the roulette table. Rajveer placed a chip on red.)

Rajveer: Red it is! Let's see if luck is on my side.

(The croupier spinned the wheel. The ball landed on red. Rajveer won a small amount.)

Rajveer: (Grinned) Told you!

Nehal: (Placed a chip on black) Alright, let's see if I can break this streak.

(The ball landed on red again. Nehal loses.)

Nehal: Ugh, not again!

Rajveer: Don't worry, it's just a game. Let's try again.

(Rajveer continued to win small amount on red, while Nehal experienced a losing streak.)

Nehal: Let's try our luck at blackjack. Maybe a change of game will bring us better fortune.

(They sat at a blackjack table. Both started with small bets and lost their initial hands.)

Nehal: This isn't looking good.

Rajveer: Keep calm. Tables may turn.

(They continued to play, gradually increasing their bets. Slowly, their luck began to turn. They start winning small hands, getting closer to 21.)

Rajveer: (Excited) I think we're on a roll!

Nehal: (Smiled) I think you're right!

(They continued to win, their winnings steadily increased. After a few more successful hands, they have accumulated enough to cover their Goa trip expenses and even afford a few expensive bottles of scotch to enjoy at home.)

Nehal: Wow, we actually did it!

Rajveer: I told you we'd turn things around.

(They spend the rest of the evening enjoying their winning streak at the blackjack table, savouring the excitement and the thrill of the game. They left the casino late at night, feeling exhilarated and content, with their winnings safely tucked away.)

Rajveer: What a night! I think we deserve a proper celebration.

Nehal: I couldn't agree more. Let's go to the villa and open one of those bottles of scotch we can purchase now.

(They headed home, reminiscing about their successful night at Casino Royale, eager to plan their upcoming Goa trip and enjoy the fruits of their winnings.)

CHAPTER 25:
"MARGARITA NIGHTS AND VILLA DELIGHTS"

Next day, the couple lounged on the shack. They ordered Kokam margaritas to give it a try on the bartender's request, they absolutely loved it.

The Kokam Margarita is a perfect blend of tangy, sweet, and citrusy flavors, with the kokum syrup adding a unique and refreshing twist. Cheers!

They asked the bartender, how did he make it? He said the magician never reveals his secrets! Nehal liked it so much that she ordered two more.

Nehal: "Ugh, I'm in the mood for margaritas today. Seriously, the best kind."

Rajveer: "Margaritas, huh? I'm in. Let's find the best spot in town."

Nehal: "Alright, let's see what the internet says."

Nehal: (Already on scrolling on the phone)"Hmm, this place looks promising... 'El Toro Blanco'... they claim to have the most authentic margaritas."

Rajveer: "El Toro Blanco? Sounds fancy. What about reviews?"

Nehal: "Reviews are mixed. Some people rave, others say it's overrated."

Rajveer: "Let's keep looking. There's got to be a margarita haven out there."

(More scrolling and reading)

Nehal: "Bingo! Miss Margarita! Look at these pictures! They look amazing!"

Rajveer: "Miss Margarita? That sounds fun. What do their reviews say?"

Nehal: "Mostly 5-star reviews! People are going crazy over their margaritas. They even have a whole menu dedicated to them!"

Rajveer: "Sold! Miss Margarita it is. Let's make a reservation."

Nehal: "Yes! Perfect. I'm already craving one."

Rajveer: "Me too. I can't wait to try those margaritas."

Miss Margarita, a vibrant and eclectic restaurant nestled in the heart of Goa, is a sensory delight that embodies the spirit of this tropical paradise. As they stepped through the doors, they were transported to a world of colourful charm and warmth.

The exterior, adorned with vibrant hues and whimsical decorations, hinted at the playful atmosphere. Inside, the restaurant unfolded like a treasure trove, with eclectic artifacts, vintage trinkets, and lively artwork adorning the walls.

The ambiance was lively and laid-back, with comfortable seating areas that invite you to linger over delicious meals and refreshing cocktails. The sound of upbeat music and the hum of conversation filled the air, creating a contagious energy that made you want to join in on the fun.

The pièce de résistance, however, is the stunning bar, which took the center stage in the restaurant. With its sleek, modern design and extensive selection of tequilas and mezcals, the bar was a haven for cocktail enthusiasts. The expert mixologists were always happy to craft a bespoke drink or guide you through their innovative menu.

When it came to the cuisine, Miss Margarita's chefs have crafted a menu that celebrates the bold flavours and vibrant spirit of Mexico, with a hint of Goan flair. From classic tacos and burritos to innovative fusion dishes, every bite was a testament to the restaurant's passion for creative, delicious food. Rajveer ordered a 1000 ml Bulldog Margarita, a feisty twist on the classic margarita. Made with tequila, lime juice, triple sec, and a splash of energizing Red Bull, this drink is not for the faint of heart. The combination of the crisp, citrus flavour of the lime and tequila, the sweetness of the triple sec, and the bold, slightly bitter taste of the Red Bull creates a truly unique and invigorating drinking experience. The Bulldog Margarita is perfect for those who want a drink that will keep them energized and ready to take on the night.

Nehal ordered Mango Chilli Margarita which is a sweet and spicy twist on the classic margarita. Made with tequila, mango puree, lime juice, triple sec, and a dash of chili flakes, this drink is a true flavour bomb. The sweetness of the mango puree pairs perfectly with the spiciness of the chili flakes, creating a delightful harmony of flavours. The tequila and lime juice added a crisp, citrusy note to the drink, while the triple sec provided a subtle sweetness. The Mango Chilli Margarita was perfect for those who want a drink that is both refreshing and adventurous.

Rajveer: (Slurped his Bulldog Margarita) Another one of these, and I'll be seeing double... or maybe just you, twice.

Nehal: (Giggled) You're already seeing double, Rajveer. My reflection in your eyes looks like a whole other person.

Rajveer: (Leaned closer, eyes twinkling) And a very beautiful person at that.

Nehal: (Took a sip of her Mango Chilli Margarita) You're handsome and charming, you know. Though the Margarita might be getting the best of you.

Rajveer: (Waved a dismissive hand) Margarita? Nah, it's just... this place, this music, you... it all adds up to something special.

Nehal: (Swirled the ice in her glass) I know what you mean. It feels like the whole world disappeared.

Nehal: (Intensely) Rajveer, there's something I need to tell you... something I've been wanting to say for a while now.

Rajveer: I...am all ears!

Nehal's eyes widened. She wanted to say it, to confess the secret that had been burning inside her. But the words caught in her throat. The tequila, the dim lighting, the sudden intensity of the moment, it all felt too much.

Nehal: (Stammered) I... I don't know what to say.

Rajveer: (Smiled gently) You don't have to say anything. If you are not comfortable.

He leaned in closer, their breaths mingling. Nehal closed her eyes, the taste of the Mango Chilli Margarita suddenly irrelevant.

This was bigger, more potent than any cocktail. This was a moment suspended in time, a shared secret hanging heavy in the air.

Rajveer: (Whispered) You're beautiful, Nehal. Absolutely breathtaking.

Nehal finally met his gaze, her eyes shimmering with unshed tears. She wanted to tell him everything, but the moment slipped away, replaced by a nervous laugh.

Rajveer raised his glass in a silent toast. Nehal clinked her glass against his, an awkward silence hanging between them. The secret remained unspoken, but the connection was undeniable. As they continued to sip their margaritas and savour the Mexican feast, Nehal knew in her mind that she will try to express again.

CHAPTER 26:
"UNRAVELLING THE PAST"

The next day, Rajveer and Nehal realized that they needed to detox, the fit couple went for a run on the beach. They pushed through, followed by an intense session of swimming in the ocean and in the pool, having healthy protein rich breakfast. They were supposed to go to Arambol beach in the evening experiencing the Russian flea market and enjoying Russian salsa. Nehal gets an important call from work, which couldn't wait.

Rajveer looked out of the window, two bottles of Chivas Regal on the table between them. Nehal is on the phone, looking stressed.

Rajveer: (Sighed) Still on the phone? It's been hours.

Nehal: (In the phone) Yes, I understand the urgency. I'll get on it immediately. (Hung up) I'm so sorry, Rajveer. This is a major client, and this project is critical.

Rajveer: (Frustrated) Critical? More critical than our vacation? We've been planning this for months!

Nehal: I know, and I feel terrible about it. But this simply can't wait.

Rajveer: (Scoffed) "Can't wait." Sounds like you're enjoying this. Working late, probably impressing your boss.

Nehal: (Irritated) Don't be ridiculous. This is my job. I have responsibilities.

Rajveer: Responsibilities? What about our plans? What about me?

Nehal: (Voice rising) What about you? You're on vacation! You're free to do whatever you want.

Rajveer: (Angry) Easy for you to say. You're always working. You never have any time for anything else.

Nehal: (Sarcastically) Oh, I'm so sorry I have a career. What would you know about work ethic, anyway? You're the expert at "relaxing."

(Rajveer slammed his fist on the table, making Nehal flinch. He grabbed the bottle of Chivas and poured himself a large drink.)

Rajveer: Don't you dare talk to me like that! I may not be working right now, but I have my own goals, my own dreams.

Nehal: (Scoffed) Dreams? All you do is travel and party.

Rajveer: (Voice thick with alcohol) At least I'm enjoying my life. You're just a workaholic, chasing some imaginary success.

Nehal: (Eyes narrowed) You know what? This is ridiculous. I'm going to get some work done.

Rajveer: (Grabbed her arm) No, you're not. You're staying here.

Nehal: (Pulled her arm away) Let go of me! I have to work.

Rajveer: (Stumbled to his feet) You're not going anywhere. You're going to spend some time with me.

(Nehal sighs, defeated. She knows this argument is going nowhere. Nehal poured herself another drink, her anger escalating.)

Nehal: (Quietly) Fine. But I'm bringing my laptop. I'll work from here.

Rajveer: (Scoffed) You're unbelievable.

(He gulped the rest of the drink and poured another. The argument continued, their voices rising and falling as the alcohol took its toll. The sound of the ocean waves seemed to mock their escalating conflict.)

The luxurious villa bathed in dimly lit with candles. Two empty bottles of Chivas Regal lie on the table. Rajveer watched Nehal intently as she furiously types on her laptop, completely engrossed in work. He sighed dramatically.)

Rajveer: (Slurred slightly) You know, it's a shame. Such a beautiful night, and you're buried in that... that...

Nehal: (Without looking up) "That" is a deadline, Rajveer. A very important one.

Rajveer: (Scoffed) Deadlines? What about me? Don't I deserve some of your attention?

Nehal: (Frustrated) Of course you do, but this is crucial.

Rajveer: (Voice rising) Crucial? More crucial than me?

Nehal: (Slammed her laptop shut) Okay, okay. I'm sorry. I'm just stressed.

Rajveer: (Still angry) Stressed? You've been stressed for weeks. All you ever do is work.

Nehal: (Stood up) Look, I'm sorry. I'll put it away.

(Nehal placed her laptop away and sat beside Rajveer on the couch, gently stroking his face.)

Nehal: I'm really sorry, baby. I didn't mean to ignore you.

Rajveer: (Softened) I know, love. I'm just... I feel a little neglected.

Nehal: (Smiled) I know. I'm a terrible girlfriend sometimes.

Rajveer: (Pulled her close) No, you're not. You're amazing.

(They share a passionate, drunken kiss.. They cuddle on the couch, laughter erupting and the tension dissipiated)

Nehal: (Giggled) I think we might have had a little too much.

Rajveer: (Grinned) A little? Maybe. But it was worth it.

(They moved to the bedroom and continued to cuddle. Nehal, drowsy, started to confess something.)

Nehal: (Muttered) There's something... something I need to tell you.

Rajveer: (Held her close) What is it, love?

Nehal: (Voice barely audible) Something bad happened to me baby.

Rajveer: (Confused) What do you mean?

Nehal: (Eyes fluttered) Something... terrible.

Rajveer: (Concerned) Tell me, Nehal.

Nehal: (Slurred) Someone hurt me.

Rajveer: (Shocked) Someone hurt you? Who?

Nehal: (Whispered) I... I don't think I will ever be able to forget that disgust. My fatherrr, that assholeeee, he touched me inappropriately in my teens.

(Rajveer's blood ran cold. He pulled away slightly, his eyes wide with disbelief. He tried to process what she's saying.)

Rajveer: (Voice trembled) What did he do Nehal?

Nehal: I tried avoiding, ignoring him, that monsterr, but he kept pursing it for months, After I turned 18, he eventually managed to do that he wanted for months and I couldn't stop him, couldn't share this with anyone but you babeaaa.

(Nehal's eyes flutter shut. She's asleep. Rajveer stared at her, his mind reeling. Tears welled up in his eyes. His body was filled with a mixture of shock, anger, and disbelief. He gently placed her on the pillow, his gaze fixed on her sleeping face, a storm brewing within him.)

Next day, they both headed to Arambol beach.

A simple, rustic shack illuminated in soft morning light. The salty breeze filtered through the gaps in the bamboo walls. Nehal stirred in her sleep, while Rajveer sat on the edge of the bed, lost in thought.

Rajveer: (Softly) Nehal... are you awake?

Nehal: (Groaned) Five more minutes...

Rajveer: (Hesitated) I... I couldn't sleep much.

Nehal: (Sat up) Oh, nightmares again?

Rajveer: (Stared at the floor) No, not nightmares.

Nehal: (Looked at him curiously) Then what?

Rajveer: (Cleared throat) I... I was just thinking about... what you told me.

Nehal: (Confused) What did I tell you? We talked about so many things last night.

Rajveer: (Avoided her gaze) About... you know... that thing.

Nehal: (Tilted her head) That thing? What thing? Did I tell you about that time I stole your whiskey after I drank my Wine and regretted it for three days?

Rajveer: (Frustrated) No, Nehal! The other thing. The... the horrible thing.

Nehal: (Her eyes widenied) Oh. That. Right. Did I tell you? I can't remember. I think I might have. Or maybe I was just thinking about it out loud.

Rajveer: (Stood up abruptly) I... I need some air.

Nehal: (Concerned) Rajveer, wait! Are you okay?

Rajveer: (Turned away) Yeah, fine. Just need to... clear my head.

Nehal: (Watched him go, a flicker of worry in her eyes) I hope I didn't say something which I wasn't supposed too ever!!

(Rajveer walked out of the shack, the sound of the waves crashing against the shore a distant comfort. He clenched his fists, the memory of Nehal's words, the pain in her voice, flooded back. He wanted to scream, to rage, to make things right. But he knows he can't. Not yet. Not without knowing for sure if she truly wanted him to know.

Nehal had work and sensed something burning inside Rajveer, he was not able to enjoy the trip anymore. The couple booked the first flight out of Goa, back to Pune.)

CHAPTER 27:
"TURBULENT EMOTIONS"

Rajveer's eyes burned with a fire that couldn't be extinguished, his mind a maelstrom of rage and fury. The dark secret Nehal had revealed to him had unleashed a torrent of emotions, each one more turbulent than the last. He felt like a stormy sea, waves crashing against the shores of his soul.

Despite living together, Rajveer found himself withdrawing from Nehal, unable to confront the emotions that threatened to consume him. He threw himself into his training, spending hours at the gym and boxing club, trying to vent out his frustration. The physical exertion was a temporary reprieve, but it did little to calm the tempest raging within.

Nehal, sensing the emotional chasm between them, buried herself in work, using her busy schedule as a shield against the awkwardness. She urged Rajveer to find a job, her parents' pressure to get married mounting by the day. Rajveer tried, giving a few interviews, but his heart wasn't in it. His mind was preoccupied with visions of revenge, his love for Nehal fuelling a burning desire for retribution.

As the days turned into weeks, weeks into months Rajveer felt like he was drowning in his rage. He loved Nehal more than anything in his life, but the pain and anger he felt on her behalf threatened to destroy him.

Rajveer's eyes locked onto Nehal's, his gaze burning with an intensity that made her heart skip a beat. The air was thick with tension as he rose from the couch, his movements deliberate and calculated. Nehal's instincts screamed at her to retreat, but her legs felt rooted to the spot.

"We need to talk," Rajveer's voice was low and husky, the words dripping with a quiet menace. Nehal's eyes widened as he took a step closer, his fists clenched at his sides.

Rajveer's face was a map of conflicting emotions, the rage and fury that had been simmering beneath the surface finally boiling over. Nehal could see the battle he was waging within himself, the struggle to contain the beast that had been unleashed by her secret.

"I've been trying to ignore it, to push it away," Rajveer's voice cracked with emotion. "But I can't. I won't. We need to confront this, Nehal. We need to face the elephant in the room."

Nehal's heart was racing as Rajveer took another step closer, his eyes blazing with a fierce determination. She knew that she couldn't avoid this conversation any longer, that Rajveer's rage and hurt needed to be addressed.

"Let's do this," Nehal's voice was barely above a whisper, but Rajveer's eyes flashed with a fierce approval.

The room seemed to shrink, the walls closing in as Rajveer's eyes bore into Nehal's soul. The air was electric with tension, the silence between them heavy with unspoken words.

Rajveer: Nehal, I need to tell you something. Something you said in Goa... you were drunk, I know, but you... you blurted out a dark secret.

Nehal: (Confused) What are you talking about, Rajveer? I don't remember anything.

Rajveer: You talked about your father. About how... how he hurt you. I couldn't believe it then, but now... now I see it. The fear in your eyes.

Nehal: (Panicked) No, Rajveer, you're wrong. You're imagining things.

Rajveer: I'm not imagining anything, Nehal. I saw it. I saw the pain in your eyes. And I can't... I can't stand seeing you hurt.

Nehal: (Tears welled up) Please, Rajveer, don't. Don't go there. He'll never believe me. He'll just... he'll just ignore it. He'll say I'm lying, that I'm making things up.

Rajveer: We can't let him get away with it. We need to file a police complaint.

Nehal: (Shook her head) No, no, no. Please, don't. It won't do any good. It'll just ruin everything.

Rajveer: (Frustrated) What about you, Nehal? What about your happiness? Your peace of mind?

Nehal: (Voice trembled) I don't want to cause any more trouble. Please, just... just focus on finding a job. We need to get married soon.

Rajveer: (Sighed) You think that's going to make it easier?

Nehal: (Desperate) Please, Rajveer. I beg you.

Rajveer: (Determined) No, Nehal. I won't let you go back to that house. I won't let him hurt you anymore.

Nehal: (Sobbed) But what about us? What about our future? I can't... I can't lose you too.

Rajveer: I'm not going anywhere. I'll find a job. Eventually. But right now, I need to make sure you're safe.

Nehal: (Looked at him, tears streaming down her face) You've failed three interviews. You're stressed; you're not eating properly.

Rajveer: (Took her hands in his) Because I can't stop thinking about you. Because I can't stand the thought of you going back to that house. I love you, Nehal. More than anything in the world. I can't bear to see you hurt.

Nehal sobbed uncontrollably

Rajveer pulled her into a tight embrace, holding her close as she cried. He ran his hands through her hair, whispering words of comfort. They remain locked in the embrace for a long time, the silence broken only by Nehal's sobs.

Nehal: Rajveer, listen to me. I know this is hard, I know you've been through hell. But holding onto this anger, this need for revenge... it's consuming you. It's keeping you from living.

Rajveer: (Voice rough) How can I forget? What your father did... to you...

Nehal: (Grabbed his hands) I know, I know. But unfortunately, he is my father. I can't stand him being hurt, it will ruin my family. I have to let it go and keep it shut.

Rajveer: (Looked at her, his eyes filled with pain) But he took everything from you. Your childhood, your innocence... and you...

Nehal: (Tears welled up) I'm here now, Rajveer. I'm with you. I love you more than anything. And I want to spend my life with you. But you have to let go of the past.

Rajveer: (Voice softened) I can't promise to forget, Nehal. But I promise I won't let it control me anymore. I promise to try for you.

Nehal: (Hugged him tightly) That's all I ask. Let's build a future together. A normal life. Get a job, we'll find a nice apartment, maybe even start a family someday.

Rajveer: (Smiled faintly) I want that too, Nehal. More than anything.

Nehal: (Looked at him with determination) Then prove it to me. Go to those interviews. Go to the gym, take those boxing classes. Went out your frustration in a healthy way.

Rajveer: (Nodded) I will. For you.

Nehal: (Kissed him) I know you can do this, Rajveer. I believe in you.

As the months drifted by, Rajveer and Nehal's lives became a serene and idyllic oasis. The past, with all its turmoil and heartache, was relegated to a distant memory, a reminder of the storms they had weathered together. The elephant in the room, once a looming presence, had been gently ushered out, replaced by a warm and comforting sense of normalcy.

Their days were filled with laughter and joy, as Rajveer poured his heart and soul into making Nehal happy. He treated her like a princess, pampering her with thoughtful gestures and sweet surprises. Every morning, he would wake her up with a gentle kiss and a steaming cup of coffee, just the way she liked it. He'd take her on romantic dinners, surprise her with her favourite flowers, and listen to her with a devotion that made her feel seen and heard.

Nehal, basking in the warmth of Rajveer's love, felt like the luckiest person alive. She'd gaze into his eyes, and her heart would skip a beat. She'd snuggle into his arms, and feel a sense of safety and security that she'd never known before. They'd talk for hours, sharing their dreams and desires, their fears and insecurities. And with each passing day, their love would grow stronger, a flame that burned brighter with every passing moment.

As they drifted off to sleep, wrapped in each other's arms, they'd both know that they couldn't imagine a life without each other. The thought of being apart was unbearable, a prospect that filled them with a sense of dread and desperation. They were two souls, entwined in a dance of love, their hearts beating as one. In this warm and golden light, the past receded, a distant memory that no longer had the power to hurt them. Rajveer and Nehal had created a new reality, one that was filled with laughter, joy, and an endless, abiding love for each other.

CHAPTER 28:
"INFINITE LOVE"

A soft melody drifted through the cozy apartment. Rajveer and Nehal danced slowly to "Falling in Love with You", their movements slow and delicate.

Rajveer: (Held Nehal close, his voice a low rumble) You know, I used to think finding someone like you was a fairytale.

Nehal: (Smiled, her head resting on his chest) And I used to think fairytales were just stories.

Rajveer: (Kissed her forehead) But here we are, dancing to this song, feeling like we're the only two people in the world.

Nehal: (Looked up at him, her eyes sparkling) I know, right? It's like the world fades away when I'm with you.

Rajveer: (Tilted her chin up) I'm so confident, Nehal. I'm going to ace those interviews. I'll land that job. We'll finally have our own place, a little nest of our own.

Nehal: (Smiled) I know you will, Rajveer. You're the most brilliant person I know.

Rajveer: (Cupped her face) And you're the most beautiful soul I've ever encountered. I can't wait to spend the rest of my life with you.

Nehal: (Tears welled up in her eyes) Me neither.

Nehal: (Hesitantly) Rajveer, my family... they miss me so much. My mom keeps calling, they want me to accompany them to Kashmir.

Rajveer: (His smile faltered slightly) I know,

Nehal. It's been a while.

Nehal: I was wondering... if... if I could go visit them? For a couple of weeks?

Rajveer: (A flicker of apprehension in his eyes) Kashmir?

Nehal: Yes. I miss them terribly. I promise I'll be careful. I'll come back to you as soon as possible.

Rajveer: (Looked at her, his heart aching) I... I don't want you to go.

Nehal: (Hugged him tightly) I know, baby. But I need to see them. And I promise, I'll come back to you.

Rajveer: (Sighed) Alright. Go. Spend time with your family. I'll be here, waiting for you.

Nehal: (Beamed) Really?

Rajveer: (Noded) Yes. I'll use this time to really focus on my job search.

Nehal: (Tears of joy streamed down her face) You mean it?

Rajveer: (Wiped her tears) I've never meant anything more in my life.

Nehal: (Threw her arms around him, burying her face in his neck) I love you, Rajveer. More than words can say.

Rajveer: (Held her close) I love you too, Nehal. More than anything.

A few days passed, and Nehal finally returned home to her family, excited to join them on a trip to the breathtakingly beautiful Kashmir. As they travelled through the picturesque landscapes, Nehal made sure to keep Rajveer updated on her status, wellbeing, and safety. She sent him messages and made brief calls, just to reassure him that she was thinking of him.

Meanwhile, back in Pune, Rajveer had been busy giving interviews, determined to land a job that would secure their future together. And then, it happened—he received the news that he'd been selected by a reputable software development company! Elated, Rajveer couldn't wait to share the news with Nehal. However, he decided to withhold the information over the phone, wanting to see the excitement and joy on her face when he told her in person.

A few days later, Nehal called Rajveer asking about the job. Rajveer, trying to contain his excitement, told her that he was still looking. Nehal, sensing his hesitation, teased him about lying. But Rajveer just chuckled, knowing that he'd soon be able to surprise her with the good news.

Nehal expressed her concerns about the pressure from her family, urging Rajveer to find a job as soon as possible. Rajveer reassured her, telling her to relax, that he'd take care of everything. And, true to his word, he began completing the documentation formalities with the company, eager to start his new role.

As the days passed, Nehal's trip to Kashmir came to an end, and she began her return journey to Pune. Rajveer, counting down the hours until they'd be reunited, couldn't help but feel a sense of excitement and anticipation. He knew that he had a surprise waiting for her, one that would change their lives forever.

As Nehal returned to Pune, she was greeted by a wave of exhaustion and illness. The stress of her work and the fatigue of her trip had finally caught up with her, leaving her feeling drained and weak. Her mom, sensing her condition, took charge, nursing her back to health with tender care.

Rajveer, concerned about Nehal's well-being, kept reaching out to her, checking on her health and offering his help. But Nehal, not wanting to burden him, reassured him that her mom was taking good care of her. She promised to return to his place as soon as her workload reduced and she felt better.

Meanwhile, Rajveer received some exciting news— a tentative joining date of 15th July for his new job! He was still waiting for his offer letter. He was ecstatic, but he wanted to share the news with Nehal in person. He waited patiently, counting down the days until they could meet again.

Twenty-two days passed, and finally, Nehal felt well enough to venture out. She made her way to Rajveer's place, eager to see him and catch up on lost time. As she arrived, Rajveer's face lit up with a warm smile, and he enveloped her in a gentle hug. Nehal felt a sense of comfort and peace wash over her, knowing that she was back in Rajveer's loving arms.

The stage was set for a joyful reunion, and Rajveer couldn't wait to share his exciting news with Nehal. On 9th July, they were finally together.

Nehal: (Smiled) You look... different. Happier.

Rajveer: (Smiled back) I am. I finally got the job!

Nehal: (Gasped) Oh my God, Rajveer! That's incredible! I knew you'd get it. You worked so hard.

Rajveer: (Pulled her close) I missed you so much these past days. Every day felt like an eternity.

Nehal: (Eyes glistened) I missed you too, more than words can say.

Rajveer: (Cupped her face) You have no idea how much I longed for this moment, to hold you like this.

Nehal: (Wrapped her arms around his neck) Me too. These past few weeks have been torture.

Rajveer: (His voice husky) Come here.

He pulled her closer, their lips meeting in a passionate kiss. His hands roamed over her back, tracing the curve of her spine. She sighed contentedly, melting into him.

Nehal: (Panted softly) Rajveer...

Rajveer: (Kissed her neck) I've been dreaming of this, of you. Every night.

He gently pushed her onto the couch, hovering above her. Their eyes met, filled with desire.

Nehal: (Whispered) I love you.

Rajveer: (His voice rough) I love you more than anything.

He leaned down, his lips trailing a path down her neck, eliciting a soft moan from her. His hands explored every inch of her body, sending shivers down her spine.

Nehal: (Gasped) Rajveer...

He continued his descent, his touch becoming more intimate, more urgent. She reached for him, pulling him closer, her fingers digging into his back.

Rajveer: (Whispered against her skin) You feel so good.

He enters her slowly, tenderly, and she arched into him, a soft moan escaping her lips. They move together in perfect rhythm, their bodies intertwined, their souls connected.

Nehal: (Panted) Oh, Rajveer...

Rajveer: (Kissed her deeply) That's it, baby. That's it.

They reach their peak together, a wave of ecstasy washing over them. They lie entwined, breathless and content, the sounds of their own hearts beating a slow and steady rhythm.

Nehal: (Smiled dreamily) I love you so much.

Rajveer: (Kissed her forehead) I love you too, more than words can say.

They hold each other close, savouring the afterglow, the intimacy, the love that bound them together.

As the hours passed, their love-making became more intense, more primal. They surrendered to their desires, their bodies speaking a language that only they could understand.

The room was filled with the sounds of their passion, the whispers, the moans, the sighs. Time lost all meaning, as they became one, their love a flame that burned brighter with every passing moment.

The sun dipped below the horizon, casting the room in a warm, golden light. Rajveer and Nehal finally lay still, their bodies sated, their hearts full. They knew that this day would be etched in their memories forever, a testament to the all-

consuming power of their love.

Nehal: (Nudged him playfully) Couldn't rest much, thinking about... you know.

Rajveer: (Leaned in, whispers) Thinking about me too?

Nehal: (Giggled) Of course! And about... us.

Rajveer: (Cupped her face) What about us?

Nehal: About our future.

Rajveer: (Eyes twinkled) Our future? You mean... forever?

Nehal: (Blushed) Maybe.

Rajveer: (Raised an eyebrow) Maybe?

Nehal: (Nervously) Well, you know... I've been thinking... with you finally getting that job...

Rajveer: (Excited) I know! I can finally take care of you.

Nehal: (Smiled) That's not all. I was thinking... maybe... we could... get married?

Rajveer: (Gasped dramatically) Marry? You're serious?

Nehal: (Noded shyly) I am.

Rajveer: (Pulled her close) Oh, Nehal... I... I don't know what to say.

Nehal: (Looked at him, eyes shining) Say yes.

Rajveer: (Buried his face in her neck) Yes, yes, a thousand times yes!

Nehal: (Threw her arms around him) Oh, Rajveer!

Rajveer: (Started peppering her with kisses) When? When can we do this?

Nehal: (Smiled) I'll go home today. Talk to my parents.

Rajveer: (Worried) What if they say no?

Nehal: (Confidently) They'll say yes. I will convince them.

Rajveer: (Grinned) I love you. More than words can say.

Nehal: (Tried to get out of bed) I should probably get going.

Rajveer: (Held her back) Don't go. Stay a little longer.

Nehal: (Teasingly) I have to go, Rajveer. My parents will be worried.

Rajveer: (Grabbed her hand) Just one more kiss.

Nehal: (Laughed) You're impossible!

Rajveer: (Kissed her deeply) I know.

Nehal: (Pulled away breathlessly) I have to go now.

Rajveer: (Sad) Okay. But promise me you'll come back soon.

Nehal: (Smiled) I promise. We'll get married soon, Rajveer.

Rajveer: (Released her) Go. But don't take too long.

Nehal: (Turned to leave, then turned back) I love you.

Rajveer: (Waved) I love you too. Go.

Nehal: (Blew him a kiss and finally left the room, her heart pounding with excitement.)

For four days, Rajveer tried to reach out to Nehal, eager to hear her voice and reconnect with her. But every time he called, she'd only respond with brief texts, citing her busy schedule as the reason for her absence.

"Hey, I'm at my cousin's engagement," she'd message. "Lots of work to catch up on. Will talk to you soon."

Or, "Still trying to convince my parents. Will keep you updated. Love you."

Rajveer's excitement about his new job couldn't be shared with the person he wanted to share it with the most. But he decided to send her his offer letter anyway, hoping it would bring a smile to her face.

As soon as Nehal received the letter, she messaged him, her words filled with joy and pride. "I'm so thrilled for you! Congratulations, my love!"

But even as she celebrated his success, Nehal's messages remained brief and cryptic. She'd reiterated her love for him, told him how much she missed him, but offered little in terms of concrete plans or reassurances.

Rajveer's patience was wearing thin. He longed to hear her voice, to see her smile, to hold her in his arms. But for now, he was left with only her texts, a reminder that she was still out there, fighting for their future together. He decided that they should meet and sort the issue. Rajveer tried calling Nehal, texted her, she was not responding. He then emailed her, requesting her to spare fifteen minutes. He wanted to see her before starting his new job. Rajveer emailed her once he left from his house, his emotions were a complex mix of frustration, anxiety, and desperation. He had been trying to reach Nehal for what felt like an eternity, but she ignored his messages, calls, and emails. The only response he got was through emails, but even those were brief and uninformative.

As he held his offer letter in his hands, Rajveer felt a sense of excitement and pride, but it was overshadowed by his concern for Nehal.

Rajveer's decision to meet Nehal at their usual spot was driven by a sense of urgency. He knew that from tomorrow, he would be fully immersed in his new job, and he wouldn't have the time or energy to pursue her. He needed to see her, to talk to her, to understand what was going on.

As he stood at the familiar location, surrounded by the shops, garden, and main road, Rajveer felt a pang of nostalgia. This was where they had shared so many laughter-filled moments, where they had whispered sweet nothings to each other. But now, the place felt empty and hollow, a reminder of Nehal's absence.

Rajveer's frustration grew with each passing minute. He called, texted, and emailed Nehal, but there was only silence. He felt like he was screaming into a void, with no response, no acknowledgement.

When he approached the tea stall worker, Rajveer's desperation was palpable. He needed to make that urgent call, to try and reach Nehal one last time. But when the worker declined his request, citing a lack of balance, Rajveer felt like he had hit a brick wall.

He stood there, frozen in frustration, his mind racing with thoughts of Nehal, his heart heavy with worry. Why was she ignoring him? What was going on? The not knowing was eating away at him, leaving him feeling helpless and lost.

Rajveer pushed open the door to the medical store, a sense of desperation washing over him. He approached the counter, where the shop owner was busy on his phone and computer.

"Excuse me," Rajveer said, trying to sound calm. "I'm having some issues with my phone. Could I request you to dial a number for me?"

The shop owner looked up, slightly annoyed. "I'm afraid I'm quite busy right now. I need my phone for work. It'll take me at least half an hour to finish what I'm doing."

Rajveer's frustration grew. "I'll wait," he said, trying to reason with the shop owner.

But the shop owner shook his head. "I'm afraid it's not advisable. I have a lot of work to do, and I don't have the time to spare."

Rajveer felt a surge of anger, but he bit it back. He couldn't afford to alienate anyone who might be able to help him.

He left the medical store, feeling more frustrated and clueless than ever. Why was it so difficult for Nehal to meet him for just fifteen minutes, or even call him back? Had something happened to her? Was she in trouble?

Rajveer's mind was racing with questions and fears. He pulled out his phone and dialled his mother's number, hoping she might be able to help.

"Mom, I need your help," he said, trying to keep his voice steady. "Can you please call Nehal? I've been trying to reach her all day, but she's not answering my calls or messages."

His mother agreed to help, but when she

called Nehal, she didn't answer. Rajveer tried calling his friends, persuading them to call Nehal, but she wasn't picking up anyone's calls.

Rajveer felt like he was going crazy. What was going on? Why was Nehal ignoring him? He was starting to feel like he was losing his mind.

Rajveer's emotional turmoil was a deep-seated mix of frustration, anxiety, and despair. He had been waiting for Nehal for over two hours, and her complete silence was eating away at him. He felt like he was losing his grip on reality, his mind consumed by thoughts of Nehal and why she was ignoring him.

As he sat on the steps of one of the shops, staring blankly at the ground, he felt a sense of exhaustion wash over him. His eyes felt heavy, his body weary, and his mind numb. He had tried every possible way to contact Nehal, but she seemed to have vanished into thin air.

In a last-ditch effort, Rajveer decided to text his sister Anya, hoping she might be able to help him get in touch with Nehal. But Anya's response was curt and dismissive. "I won't get involved in this, Rajveer," she texted back. "Leave me out of it."

Rajveer's heart sank. He felt like he was running out of options, like he was being slowly suffocated by Nehal's silence. He slumped back against the wall, feeling defeated and helpless.

Just as he was starting to lose hope, a stranger sat down beside him. The man was on his phone, talking to someone in a low, measured tone. Rajveer didn't pay much attention to him, too caught up in his own misery.

But when the stranger finished his call, Rajveer turned to him with a glimmer of hope. "Excuse me," he said, his voice shaking slightly. "I'm so sorry to bother you, but I'm having some trouble with my phone. Would you be able to make a call for me?"

The stranger looked at him with a kind expression, and Rajveer's heart skipped a beat. "Of course," the stranger said. "Who do you need to call?"

Rajveer's eyes welled up with tears as he gave the stranger Nehal's number. He watched, his heart in his throat, as the stranger dialled the number.

But when the stranger told him that Nehal's phone was switched off, Rajveer felt like he had been punched in the gut. He slumped back against the wall, feeling like he was at rock bottom.

Even when the stranger offered to try again after half an hour, Rajveer's hopes were dashed once more. This time, the phone rang, but there was no response from the other end.

Rajveer felt like he was trapped in a never-ending nightmare, with no escape from the pain and frustration that was consuming him.

Rajveer's emotional dilemma was a tangled web of confusion, frustration, and despair. He couldn't understand why Nehal was ignoring him, switching off her phone to avoid picking up his calls. The silence was deafening, and Rajveer's mind was racing with worst-case scenarios.

In a last-ditch effort, he called Parag, his friend and confidant, hoping he might offer some guidance or support. Rajveer poured out his heart, sharing every detail of his ordeal, from Nehal's initial silence to her eventual phone switch-off.

Parag listened attentively, but his response was not what Rajveer had expected. Instead of offering words of encouragement or advice, Parag told Rajveer to leave Nehal alone. "She's clearly not interested in meeting you or talking to you," Parag said bluntly. "You're only embarrassing yourself by persisting. Go home, Rajveer. Forget about her."

Rajveer was taken aback by Parag's words. He couldn't believe his friend was advising him to give up on Nehal. Rajveer's instincts screamed at him to keep trying, to get to the bottom of the problem and sort it out once and for all.

But Parag's words had planted a seed of doubt in Rajveer's mind. Was he indeed being foolish to persist? Was Nehal truly not interested in him? The questions swirled in his head, leaving him feeling confused and uncertain.

As he stood there, weighing his options, Rajveer's eyes wandered to Nehal's house, just a few minutes away. He was torn. Part of him wanted to march up to her door, demand answers, and clear the air once and for all. But another part of him hesitated, fearing he might cause trouble for Nehal by meeting her family behind her back.

Nehal's last email had mentioned trying to convince her parents, but Rajveer had waited for four hours, and there was only silence. The not knowing was killing him, and Rajveer's emotions were stretched to the breaking point.

What should he do? Should he take Parag's advice and walk away, or should he follow his heart and try to confront Nehal once and for all? The decision hung precariously in the balance, as Rajveer stood there, lost and uncertain.

Rajveer's emotional state was a complex

mix of denial, desperation, and determination. He was not ready to accept that Nehal was no longer interested in him, especially after their recent intimate encounter. He was convinced that Nehal loved him, and that this sudden silence was just a temporary misunderstanding.

As he struggled to come to terms with the situation, Rajveer's mind was filled with memories of their time together. He remembered the way Nehal smiled at him, the way she laughed at his jokes, and the way she loved him with all her heart. He couldn't shake off the feeling that this was all just a terrible mistake, and that Nehal would eventually come around and explain everything.

Feeling lost and uncertain, Rajveer turned to the one person he knew would always be there for him—his mother, Shubhangi. He called her again, hoping she might offer some guidance or reassurance.

"Mom, what should I do?" Rajveer asked, his voice shaking with emotion. "I want you to come with me to Nehal's house. I need your help to figure out what's going on."

Shubhangi, sensing her son's distress, agreed to accompany him. However, she was currently in her office, far away from the location. Rajveer asked if he should go on his own, and Shubhangi, aware of the reality of the situation, hesitated. She didn't want to hurt Rajveer, but she knew that confronting Nehal's parents might be the only way to get to the bottom of this.

"Go meet her parents, beta," Shubhangi advised, "Talk to them, and see if you can understand what's going on. But be prepared for anything, okay?"

Rajveer took a deep breath, steeling himself for what lay ahead. He decided to pay Nehal's house a visit, determined to get answers and clear up the misunderstanding once and for all. With a sense of trepidation and resolve, he set off towards Nehal's house, ready to face whatever lay ahead.

Rajveer stood outside Nehal's gate, his heart racing with anticipation. He had been waiting for four days, trying to reach out to her, but her brief texts had left him feeling frustrated and uncertain. With his new job, he knew he couldn't wait any longer to sort things out with Nehal.

He took a deep breath, clutching the offer letter in his hand, and saw Suresh Mehra and Sunita Mehra driving back to their bungalow. The sound of the car echoed through the silence, and Rajveer's nerves began to jangle.

Rajveer stood nervously outside the Mehra bungalow, the manicured lawn doing little to soothe his anxiety.

Suresh Mehra emerged, his face a carefully constructed mask of polite inquiry.

Rajveer frustration rose. This was the man who had misbehaved with Nehal. A man he had every reason to despise. But this wasn't the time or place to talk about the past, it was about Nehal. It was time to think about their future together. What if something had happened to her?

Taking a deep breath, Rajveer forced himself to remain calm.

"Mr. Mehra," Rajveer began, his voice a little rough, "I'm Rajveer, Nehal's boyfriend. I've been trying to reach Nehal but she is not responding. She told me she will try and convince you about our marriage. Please, whats going on? Is she okay?

Mr. Mehra's eyebrows lifted slightly. "Your marriage?"

"Yes," Rajveer pressed, taking a step closer. "We both thought... we both hoped..." He trailed off, the unspoken words hanging in the air. "Nehal told me she's been trying to talk to you. About our marriage."

A flicker of something—was it sadness?—crossed Mr. Mehra's face before he schooled his features into an expression of calm neutrality. He looked at Rajveer, his gaze steady.

"Rajveer," he said, his voice measured, "Please, come inside. Let's talk." He gestured towards the open door.

Mr. Mehra's bungalow was a grand, sprawling structure that exuded warmth and elegance. The interior was tastefully decorated, with plush furnishings and intricate artwork adorning the walls. The hall where Rajveer and Mr. Mehra sat was spacious, with high ceilings that seemed to stretch up to the sky.

As they sat facing each other on the sofa, Rajveer couldn't help but notice the familiar surroundings. On the left side of the hall, a large TV screen dominated the wall, and a corridor led off to the kitchen, where Rajveer had shared laughter and moments with Nehal on previous visits. He remembered the time he had come to pick Nehal up, and she had invited him inside, teasing him as they rummaged through the kitchen together.

On the right side of the hall, a elegant staircase curved upward, leading to the bedrooms above. Rajveer's gaze drifted up the stairs, his mind wandering to the memories he had made with Nehal in her bedroom

As Rajveer's thoughts drifted, Mr. Mehra's voice brought him back to the present. "Sunita, please get Rajveer a glass of water," he requested, his voice firm but polite. Sunita Mehra, Nehal's mother, nodded graciously and headed off to the kitchen, leaving Rajveer and Mr.

Mehra alone in the hall, the tension between them palpable.

Sunita Mehra entered the living room with a quiet elegance, a glass of water delicately balanced on a silver tray in her hand. Her eyes, warm and gentle, met Rajveer's as she approached him, a soft smile playing on her lips. She moved with a quiet confidence, her sari rustling softly as she walked.

As she handed the glass of water to Rajveer, her hands brushed against his, and for a moment, their eyes locked in a silent understanding. Rajveer took the glass from her, his fingers wrapping around it gratefully, and nodded his thanks.

Sunita Mehra's gaze lingered on Rajveer's face for a moment, her expression a mixture of kindness and concern. She seemed to sense the tension in the air, the unspoken words that hung between Rajveer and Mr. Mehra like a challenge.

Just as Sunita Mehra was about to turn away, Mr. Mehra cleared his throat, his eyes narrowing slightly as he began to speak. "Rajveer, I think it's time we had a talk," he said, his voice low and measured.

Rajveer's eyes flicked to Mr. Mehra's face, his heart sinking slightly as he sensed the weight of the conversation that was about to unfold. Sunita Mehra, sensing the tension, hesitated for a moment before quietly withdrawing from the room, leaving Rajveer and Mr. Mehra alone to navigate the difficult conversation that lay ahead.

Mr Mehra stared at Rajveer, his expression hardening. A flicker of something unreadable in his eyes. He let out a long, weary sigh. "Rajveer," he said, his voice low and grave, "I appreciate your... feelings. But what you're saying... it's simply not possible."

Rajveer frowned. "Not possible? Uncle, with all due respect, why not?"

Suresh's gaze intensified. "Because," he stated flatly, "Nehal is already married."

A stunned silence hung in the air. Rajveer's emotional state was one of utter shock and devastation as he heard the words that would shatter his world. "Nehal is already married," Mr. Mehra's words hung in the air like a toxic cloud, poisoning every happy memory Rajveer had of Nehal.

As the truth sank in, Rajveer's body began to react as if it had been physically punched. His eyes widened in horror, his face pale and drained of all colour. His lips parted in a silent gasp, as if he was struggling to breathe.

The glass of water in his right hand began to shiver rapidly, as if it was being manipulated by an invisible force. The water inside the glass sloshed violently, spilling drops onto Rajveer's jeans and the sofa. The sound of the water splashing was like a cruel mockery, a reminder that Rajveer's world was crashing down around him.

Rajveer's hand trembled uncontrollably, as if it was being shaken by a powerful earthquake. The glass of water seemed to be slipping from his grasp, but he couldn't seem to let go. It was as if he was frozen in time, unable to move or speak.

His mind was reeling with questions, each one more painful than the last. How could Nehal do this to him? Why had she lied to him? What had he done to deserve this kind of betrayal?

As the shock began to wear off, Rajveer felt a wave of intense pain wash over him. It was as if his heart was being ripped apart, torn into a million pieces by the brutal truth. He felt like he was drowning in a sea of despair, unable to find a lifeline to cling to.

The room around him began to spin, and Rajveer felt like he was going to collapse. He was vaguely aware of Mr. Mehra's voice, speaking words of apology and regret, but they were distant and meaningless.

All Rajveer could think about was Nehal, and the fact that she was gone, lost to him forever. The pain was overwhelming, a crushing weight that threatened to consume him whole.

Rajveer blinked, then let out a small, incredulous laugh. "Married? Uncle, what are you talking about? Nehal and I have been together..."

"She got married on 12th of July," Mr Mehra interrupted, his voice firm.

Rajveer's smile didn't falter. He knew Nehal. He knew her heart. This was some kind of misunderstanding, or perhaps a test. He played along, a playful glint in his eyes. "Oh, really? Married on the 12th of July? That's... quite specific. I'd love to see some pictures of this grand affair. Maybe even a video?"

Nehal's father's face flushed slightly. He seemed taken aback by Rajveer's reaction. "You... you think I'm lying?"

"Not at all, Uncle," Rajveer said smoothly. "Just curious. A marriage is a big event. Surely you have some mementos to share? Photos of the ceremony, the reception... the happy couple?"

Mr Mehra looked increasingly uncomfortable. He hesitated, then, with a visible effort, pulled out his phone. He scrolled through his gallery, his fingers shaking slightly. "Here," he said, thrusting the phone at Rajveer. "Here's your proof."

Rajveer took the phone, his heart beginning to pound in his chest. The first picture showed Nehal, radiant in a bridal lehenga, standing next to a man he'd never seen before. His stomach clenched. He swiped to the next image—the wedding ceremony, Nehal exchanging garlands with the stranger. Then came the invitation card, with Nehal's name and the stranger's printed on it, dated 12th July. And then, pictures of her engagement ceremony on 7th July.

Rajveer's eyes widened in horror as Mr. Mehra handed him his phone, displaying the devastating evidence of Nehal's marriage and engagement. The images on the screen were like a punch to the gut, leaving Rajveer breathless and reeling.

At first, Rajveer's mind refused to accept the truth. He thought it was some kind of cruel joke, a mistake, or a misunderstanding. But as he scrolled through the photos, his heart sank deeper into his chest. There was Nehal, smiling and radiant, standing beside a man Rajveer had never seen before. The man's arm was wrapped around Nehal's waist, pulling her close as they gazed into each other's eyes.

Rajveer's eyes scanned the photos, searching for any sign of deception or manipulation. But there was none. Nehal's smile was genuine, her eyes shining with happiness as she posed with her new husband. As the reality of the situation sunk in, Rajveer's body began to shut down. His vision blurred, and his hearing became muffled. He felt like he was drowning in a sea of despair, unable to find a lifeline to cling to.

Mr. Mehra's phone slipped from Rajveer's fingers, falling to the floor with a soft thud. Rajveer's eyes rolled back in his head, and his body swayed precariously before collapsing onto the sofa.

Rajveer's world went dark as he fainted, his mind overwhelmed by the shock and pain of Nehal's betrayal. The last thing he remembered was the sound of Mr. Mehra's voice, calling out to him in concern, before everything went black.

(Rajveer's eyes blazed with fury as he gazed at Suresh Mehra, his mind flooded with memories of the older man's heinous actions. He remembered the day Nehal had confided in him, her voice trembling as she revealed the shocking truth - her father had forced himself on her when she was just 18 years old. And with the news that Nehal was already married.

The rage that had been simmering within Rajveer for so long finally boiled over, and he lunged at him with a ferocity that couldn't be contained. His fists flew, boxing the old man with a series of swift and merciless blows.

Nehal's father stumbled backward, his eyes wide with shock and fear, but Rajveer showed no mercy. He was driven by a singular desire - to make the older man pay for his unspeakable crimes.

The sound of flesh hitting flesh echoed through the air, accompanied by the sickening crunch of bones. Mr

Mehra crumpled to the ground, his body battered and broken, as Rajveer continued to rain down blows upon him.

Finally, after what seemed like an eternity, Nehal's father lay motionless, knocked down unconscious within a pool of his own blood. Rajveer stood over him, his chest heaving with exertion, his eyes still blazing with fury.

For a moment, he just stood there, his mind reeling with the consequences of his actions. But as he gazed down at Nehal's father, he felt no remorse, no regret. All he felt was a deep-seated satisfaction, knowing that the man who had destroyed Nehal's innocence had finally been brought to justice.)

Rajveer slowly gained consciousness, his mind foggy and his body tense. As he opened his eyes, he saw Mr Mehra standing over him, a look of concern etched on his face. Rajveer's instincts took over, and he sprang up from the couch, his fists clenched and his eyes blazing with fury.

In a swift and deadly motion, he raised his hand, ready to land a crushing punch on his face. But just as his fist was about to connect, Rajveer's memory kicked in, and he remembered the promise he had made to Nehal. He had sworn to control his temper, sworn not to avenge Nehal and not hurt him.

With a Herculean effort, Rajveer stopped himself mid-action, his fist hovering mere inches from Mr Mehra face. He took a deep breath, and his rage slowly began to dissipate. He folded his hands in a namaste.

"Thank you for the information, sir," Rajveer said, his voice shaking with restraint. He was shivering from head to toe, his body trembling with the effort of controlling his temper.

Without another word, Rajveer turned and ran out of his house, afraid that if he stayed any longer, he might change his mind and give in to his rage. He didn't stop running until he was blocks away, his heart still racing with adrenaline and shattered into a million pieces.

As Rajveer slowly came to terms with the devastating truth about Nehal's marriage, he felt like his heart had been shattered into a million pieces. The pain was excruciating, a constant reminder of the love he had given so freely, only to be betrayed and rejected.

But despite the overwhelming grief that threatened to consume him, Rajveer knew he couldn't let his heartbreak define him. He had already faced the pain of rejection once before, and he had emerged stronger, wiser, and more resilient.

With a newfound determination, Rajveer steeled himself to face the challenges ahead. He knew it wouldn't be easy, that the road to healing would be long and arduous. But he was ready to take the first step, to begin the journey of rebuilding his shattered heart and rediscovering his sense of purpose.

As he looked to the future, Rajveer knew that his story was far from over. Despite the heartbreak, despite the pain, he was still standing, still breathing, and still alive. And with that realization came a sense of hope, a sense that perhaps, just perhaps, there was still a chance for him to find happiness, to find love, and to find himself.

The story of Rajveer would continue, a testament to the human spirit's capacity for resilience, for hope, and for redemption. Though his heart may have been broken twice, Rajveer's determination to rise above the pain, to learn from his experiences, and to keep moving forward would ultimately define him. The question was, what would the next chapter of his life hold?

A woman with an unaddressed father wound may unconsciously seek to fill the emotional void left by her father's absence, neglect, or abuse. This can lead her to form unhealthy relationships with men, often demanding the impossible from them.

The woman may subconsciously seek a man who can provide the emotional validation, love, and acceptance she never received from her father. She may expect her partner to be flawless, always knowing what to say and do to make her feel loved and secure.

She may assume her partner should intuitively know her needs, desires, and emotions, without her having to communicate them clearly.

She may demand that her partner be always present, attentive, and responsive to her needs, leaving no space for his own life, interests, or emotions.

She may expect her partner to heal her deep-seated emotional wounds, which can be an impossible task, even for the most loving and supportive partner.

This dynamic often attracts a man who feels unworthy, insecure, or inadequate.

He may doubt his ability to meet the woman's demands, leading to feelings of inadequacy and low self-esteem.

He may try to meet the woman's impossible demands, sacrificing his own needs, desires, and boundaries in the process.

He may live in constant fear of being rejected or abandoned by the woman, leading to anxiety, stress, and a desperate need for reassurance.

This can lead her to form unhealthy relationships with men, often demanding the impossible from them.

Break the Silence, Shatter the Shame.

To all the daughters who have been wounded by their fathers' actions, we see you. We hear you. We believe you.

For too long, the weight of family reputation and societal expectations has silenced your voices and hidden your pain. But no more!

We urge you to come forward, to share your stories, and to demand justice. Lodge a police complaint, seek support from trusted friends, family, or authorities.

Remember, your father's actions are not your shame to carry. You are not responsible for his crimes. He should be held accountable, not you.

A Message to Fathers

To all the fathers who have committed heinous crimes against their daughters, we have a message for you:

Think thousands of times before laying a hand on your daughter or inflicting emotional trauma. Consider the lifelong impact of your actions on her mental health, self-worth, and relationships.

You have a responsibility to protect, nurture, and respect your daughter. Failing to do so is a betrayal of the highest order.

Let us create a society where daughters feel safe, supported, and empowered to speak out against injustice. Where fathers are held accountable for their actions, and where family reputation is not prioritized over a daughter's well-being.

Join us in this fight against patriarchal silence and shame. Let us break the cycle of abuse and create a brighter future for all daughters.

*Resources: *

- National Domestic Violence Hotline (1-800-799-7233)

- National Child Abuse Hotline (1-800-422-4453)

- Contact Local authorities and support groups

*Remember: *

You are not alone. Your voice matters. Your story deserves to be heard.

www.ingramcontent.com/pod-product-compliance
Lightning Source LLC
LaVergne TN
LVHW091619070526
838199LV00044B/862